Dead Trouble

Dead Trouble

MARGARET DUFFY

This edition published in Great Britain in 2004 by
Allison & Busby Limited
Bon Marche Centre
241-251 Ferndale Road
Brixton, London SW9 8BJ
http://www.allisonandbusby.com

A catalogue record for this book is available from the British Library

ISBN 0 7490 0623 4

Printed and bound by
Creative Print + Design, Ebbw Vale

MARGARET DUFFY was born in Woodford, Essex and has worked for the Inland Revenue and the Ministry of Defence. She now lives in Devon in a one-time crossing-keeper's cottage with her husband and three cats and divides her time between writing and garden design. *Dead Trouble* is the eighth novel to feature Patrick Gillard and Ingrid Langley.

1

The body had been disinterred overnight by a specialist exhumation company and now lay on a mortuary table in the light, bright room. This illumination was entirely artificial, emanating from the kind of lights used in operating theatres, and quite merciless, hiding no detail of disintegrated skin, protruding bone, the remnants of straight dark hair.

One quick glance had told me these things and then I had put distance between myself and the object on the table, walking over to where the deceased's dental and medical records had been put in readiness for the pathologist to refer to on a stainless steel trolley. If there had been a window I would have gazed out: even the prospect of a blank wall would have been preferable to what was within the room. But there were no windows: this mortuary at the Royal United Hospital in Bath was underground and fans whirred to provide most welcome ventilation.

I was beginning to regret my wish for authenticity. My conscience was giving me hell too. Was it right and proper that a writer should capitalise on a post-mortem carried out on the body of a woman merely to furnish her latest book with grisly details in order to titillate her readers? Or was I being a little harsh with myself? However, it was too late to change my mind now as one of the most eminent pathologists in the country had agreed to be interviewed and was allowing me to watch him at work.

He had agreed readily enough and making the arrangements had been simplicity itself. I had come up from Devon on an early train and Patrick, my husband, had taken the day off and was driving down from Camberley, Surrey, where he works all week. We were staying with his parents for the weekend at the village of Hinton Littlemoor, some three miles from Bath, where Patrick's father, John, is rector.

The door opened and two men entered, mortuary attendants, attired as I was in protective clothing and wearing latex gloves, and busied themselves preparing instruments,I had absolutely no intention of touching anything needless to say: the necessity was to protect us from germs and prevent any contamination of evidence. For if this woman had not died from a heart attack, as the death certificate had stated, or from other closely allied natural causes, a murder investigation might well be instigated.

I supposed I should have counted myself lucky – a crime writer hitting quite accidentally upon a subject-related case – but right now I was not feeling at all fortunate, mostly for the already stated reasons and also, despite the efforts of the extractor-fans, because of the gut-wrenching smell of putrefaction.

And where the hell was the great man? my jangling nerves demanded to know.

Again the door opened and another man entered. I had been told that the police officer who would be in charge of the case, should the matter arise, would also be present but had not expected it to be someone I knew.

'James! I thought you were in Scotland.'

James Carrick – whom I had recognised by his blue eyes and a wisp of fair hair that had escaped from the confines of his plastic head-covering, spoke through his surgical mask to say, 'We came back three days early. It was raining so hard I couldn't see the front end of the car bonnet. Strictly speaking I'm still on leave but Professor Norton asked me if I'd like to be present.'

'How's Joanna getting on with her degree course?'

'Thanking her lucky stars she decided to go for an Open University course and study mostly at home.'

'Why?'

'She's pregnant.'

'Oh, congratulations!'

'She's two and a half months now. Sorry I didn't tell you before.'

Nothing further could be said on that matter just then as another door opened and in walked Professor John Norton. He was a big man in every sense of the word, making even James Carrick's slightly over six feet in height and broad shoulders appear modest. Although he greeted James and me in friendly fashion I stayed right where I was, feeling increasingly uncomfortable and superfluous.

'She's been dead for the best part of two years,' Norton boomed and then, as if realising that he was not giving a lecture this time, lowered his voice to say, 'As you know, Chief Inspector, her husband when she was alive is still a GP in Bristol. He got a crony to write out the death certificate, a crony whom I discovered only this lunchtime has subsequently been struck off for an unrelated misdemeanour and taken himself off to Africa.'

'Zambia,' Carrick volunteered.

'You're right up to date on this, are you?' Norton asked him, sounding surprised.

Carrick said that he was, succeeding in conveying in subtle fashion and despite the mask that he himself was surprised at the query.

'Hand me the info, would you?' Norton requested, looking at me with his slightly unsettling dark eyes.

I passed over the folders.

'Nadine Bates,' he said, not having to remind himself from the files. 'For your benefit, Miss Langley, I'll add that she was Bates's first wife and was forty-three years old when she died. His second has just had a nasty accident and is in intensive care here. She might die too. She was mumbling when they brought her in that she thought Bates was responsible.

According to her he got drunk a few years ago and told her he'd killed Nadine one weekend.'

I asked, 'What sort of accident has the second Mrs Bates had?'

'A car crash. She thinks he mucked about with the brakes and steering of her Rover.'

'There's a recently taken out and hefty life insurance policy on Mrs Bates,' Carrick explained. 'As there was on the first.'

'Stinks, doesn't it?' said Norton, not referring to what was in front of him. 'I realise I'm not really supposed to comment on cases that might involve a criminal act but this time it's right in my own back yard, so to speak. Let's get on with it, shall we? I shall fully explore all possibilities.'

I had already decided that the second Mrs Bates could not be very bright in sticking around after her husband's confession and despite the present circumstances found myself wondering what my reaction would be if Patrick – after consuming a drop too much single malt one evening – confessed to doing away with a past girlfriend. Run, screaming? Possibly.

Mostly addressing me Norton said, 'We might have to rely on bone for toxilogical tests as the thoracic and abdominal organs have probably gone after all this time. I'm hopeful though as much of the soft tissue appears to have been reduced to adipocere, a waxy substance that forms when the body fats undergo a change due to the presence of moisture and certain bacteria. It can take quite a long time to form but can actually remain for hundreds of years and protect what lies beneath. That's where you get the stories of well-preserved saints from. Do you want to take notes?'

I shook my head. 'No, thank you, I've a very good memory.'

'As you wish.' He turned to Carrick and, with more than a hint of challenge in his tone, said, 'Any ideas what might have really killed her to enable someone to write on the death certificate that she died from a coronary embolism?'

'He's a doctor,' Carrick murmured. 'An overdose of morphine or heroin should do the trick.'

'You can't just stick needles in people without them noticing, you know,' Norton replied, now eyeing Carrick somewhat narrowly.

'No, he would have dosed her up with sleeping pills first.'

Norton grunted and said grudgingly, 'I can see you've done your homework. Well?' he asked me peevishly. 'Are you going to come over and learn something or not?'

Thanks, James, I thought, going closer.

First of all, and using the dental records, a positive identification of the body was made by matching them with the teeth in the head.Norton then established, after drilling into the skull – while giving us a running commentary – that the brain, which might have yielded vital information, had rotted away completely. He then turned his attention to the rest of the body. Examination of the long bones and the pelvis revealed no damage, the woman had not been a victim of the kind of violence that would have left marks. The laryngeal skeleton, hyoid bone and hyoid processes in the neck were intact so she had not been strangled.

The procedure continued.

It was when Norton was prodding around in the sludge of the abdomen, after having completed work on the chest cavity and told us that he could identify both heart and lungs – which he had just removed and given to one of the technicians for later further examination – that I began to feel a little faint. I bit the tip of my tongue hard and looked away, anywhere, and met James's gaze from across the other side of the table. He jerked his head infinitesimally in an invitation to go and stand by his side but I shook mine in equally minimalist fashion and took several deep breaths.

'I can identify the diaphragm, remains of a kidney and part

of the large intestine,' Norton was saying. 'There's no sign in the peritoneal cavity of any inflammation. The spleen, stomach and bladder have all gone though.'

More samples were taken plus some from the bones and hair. Norton then sliced into the waxy-looking legs and grunted in satisfaction. 'The muscle's not completely degraded, there's tissue here we can use. He might just have injected her in the thigh.'

Yet more samples were painstakingly removed.

'Are you writing a book about a forensic pathologist then?' Norton said suddenly to me, a grey sliver of flesh halfway to where one of his assistants held out a surgical dish.

'Yes,' I said. I had outlined as much in my letter when I had originally contacted him so either he had forgotten or was just making conversation.

'Is it a murder story?'

Again I answered in the affirmative.

What Norton had found had obviously improved his mood. 'I hope he's not the victim.'

'No, he's the murderer.'

He roared with laughter. 'Well, that's different anyway. I don't read that kind of stuff, I'm afraid. I don't get much time these days to read anything except medical papers what with folk always wanting me to jet off somewhere and tell them how people really died. I've got to go to Greece next week to look at the body of some tycoon who fell into the sea off his yacht. The insurance company are saying he topped himself as someone was going to pull the plug on his highly illegal little empire and he knew it. The family, of course, want to prove it was an accident so they can scoop the insurance money.' Cheerfully, he added, 'It's of no concern to the late lamented of course. Interesting to me though, the prop lopped his head off.'

'Did they find it?' Carrick asked with professional interest.

14

'Too right. It was seeing that floating in the sea that made the crew realise he'd gone overboard.'

'Why didn't it sink?' I asked, my own interest kindled.

'Good question,' said Norton. 'I won't know that until I see it but I understand the deceased was extremely obese. Fat might have kept it afloat or just below the surface.' After a few more minutes had elapsed he straightened. 'You don't both want to stay while I examine the heart and lungs, do you? It'll take a while.'

'I can't. I have to attend a meeting,' Carrick said.

'What's today?' Norton said vaguely, looking at the ceiling as though he might find the answer there. 'Friday. I'll try and get the report to you tomorrow.'

'Many thanks.'

'My first reactions are that you probably have a murder investigation on your hands. From what I've already seen of her heart it doesn't look as though it had a lot wrong with it. But for God's sake don't quote me on that until you have it in front of you in black and white.'

'Are you still able to give me an interview at seven thirty this evening?' I asked the pathologist after Carrick had made the promise.

He frowned. '*Did I* say seven thirty?'

'Yes, you did.'

'Could you make it six thirty? I have to attend a dinner in Bristol – must have forgotten. A professional thing and a bit of a bore but . . . '

This actually suited me as I also had a dinner date and it would give me more time to get ready. 'Fine,' I said.

'You know where I live, don't you? Go to the top of Ralph Allen's Drive, turn right and it's the second on the left with the iron railings,' he said speaking over his shoulder as he moved over to where the samples were being prepared for dissection.

Having already reconnoitred I knew exactly where the

house was and moved to leave, noting with surprise that an hour and a half had elapsed since I had first entered the room.

'Thanks for the invitation to hold your hand,' I said to Carrick as we stripped off our masks, large white plastic aprons and hats and thrust them into a disposal bin.

'I thought you looked a bit pale around the eyes. Did you come by car?'

'No, by taxi from the station. Patrick's driving down but he's calling in to Abbeywood in Bristol to see an old friend before he comes here.'

'The Ministry of Defence place, you mean?'

I nodded.

'I only asked because I wondered if you'd like a lift.'

'Would you drop me somewhere near the nick? Patrick's picking me up in town as I want to do some shopping first.'

'How about lunch?'

'I thought you had a meeting to go to.'

He grinned. 'It's not until four thirty.'

I grinned back. 'I thought you were wishing you were somewhere else too.'

He took me to the Hare and Hounds, a pub with what must be one of the best views in the area, across the Charlcombe valley. It was cooler up here, the unseasonal early Autumn heat in the city centre reminding one forcibly that Bath had been built in the crater of an extinct volcano, hence the hot springs.

I noticed with amusement that this normally stoical Scot – once described by an envious friend of his wife as 'wall-to-wall crumpet' – downed in one a tot of whisky while standing at the bar ordering food.

'Norton's the best,' James said when he returned, bringing

16

me a glass of white wine. 'And you have to have the best in a case like this – nothing must be at all iffy for the defence to start chipping away at.'

'This isn't likely to turn into another Shipman case is it?'

He looked appalled. 'God, I hope not. No, nothing like that. At least, no one's yet mentioned patients.' He gazed soberly at me. 'Was this morning valuable to you?'

'From the point of view of noting techniques and obtaining what I'll call background,' I replied. 'But I felt most uncomfortable – as though I was taking photographs at a funeral.'

'You were undertaking genuine research,' he protested.

'Thanks for trying to make me feel better. I don't think I could ever get used to that kind of thing. You must have to attend quite a few though.'

'They're usually a bit fresher than that,' he said after due consideration. 'If Norton's hunches are correct it'll mean I'll have a pretty watertight case. I didn't mention it earlier but the crash investigator did find that Mrs Bates's car had been meddled with – amateurishly but effectively enough for her to have lost control of the vehicle.'

'Were there any other cars involved in the accident?'

'No. But that means there weren't any witnesses.'

I decided it was time to change the subject. 'Is Joanna really pleased about the baby?'

'It was a bit of a shock because we'd sort of been taking precautions. As you know she'd made up her mind to get this degree in English but hadn't actually thought about what she wanted to do with it afterwards. The afterwards bit might just have to be postponed for a while. Or, as you've done, we'll get a nanny. Right now though, with parts of the old house still a building site, I'll have to concentrate on decorating one of the bedrooms as a nursery.'

They had bought an old farmhouse and were in the process of restoring it.

James's face had assumed an expression I had never seen it

wearing before, what I could only describe as alarmingly soppy. He said, 'Thomas the Tank Engine, I thought.'

'It might be a girl,' I pointed out tersely.

'You're right,' he said, looking a bit taken aback, that possibility obviously not having occurred to him.

'Wait until after the scan,' I said soothingly. 'Or do it in something that doesn't matter what sex the baby is. Patrick's number one person as far as Justin's concerned at the moment because he's really into the Clangers and Patrick can imitate the Soup Dragon. Patrick trades that off for Justin behaving himself, especially at the table.'

'I can see I shall need a lot of tips,' Carrick said, somewhat worriedly.

I really could picture it; a Detective Chief Inspector and a Lieutenant-Colonel having an in-depth conversation about child-care.

'So you've settled down after all the excitement,' Carrick said, a statement with only the merest whiff of enquiry in his tone.

Two months previously Patrick had been involved in a political row when there had been an attempt to incriminate him for the death of a policeman involved in a secret project backed by the Home Secretary of the previous administration. One had to admit that he was well-placed for such a false accusation; when you have been an undercover soldier and worked for MI5 as well as responsible for closing the offending project down – in other words blown most of it to kingdom come – then you are in the front line for frame-ups. The resulting scandal had been a contributory factor to the country now being on the run-up to a General Election.

'Bored,' I said. 'Patrick is, I mean. I'm working on a novel.'

'Oh, of course, the murdering pathologist. I wondered if you were basing the next book on what happened recently.'

'Too right I am. The next book. This one had been planned for quite a while and I've actually written most of it.'

18

After a short pause James said, 'I agree that being Co-ordinator of Defence Studies at Army Staff College is hardly challenging in the light of Patrick's career to date but . . . ' he shrugged expressively. 'Does he not enjoy peace and quiet?'

I took a sip of my wine and then said, 'At home he enjoys playing with the children, potters in the garden, chops wood for the fire, goes fishing or for a ride on Polar Bear, that horse he rescued, we walk on the moor and go down to the pub. All the things quite a lot of families do at weekends. But as far as work's concerned . . . '

'He'd far rather be organising a small but just war somewhere.'

'Absolutely,' I said. 'Patrick's never been a nine to five desk job man. I can see him resigning his commission and doing something quite different.'

'What though?'

'You tell me.'

Our food arrived and we tackled it in silence for a while. Then, half-joking, James said, 'What Patrick really needs is a new project of some kind that will fully engage all his talents.'

I agreed with him but for the life of me still couldn't quite work out what that might be – not legal anyway.

'Well, have a good weekend,' Carrick said as we parted. 'Let me know if I can be of any help with the book – procedures and stuff like that. Oh, and I was told to ask if you'd both like to be godparents.'

'More than delighted,' I said.

Ralph Allen's Drive – he made his fortune reforming the British postal service and then went on to make another one by buying the quarries which were to provide the stone that built Regency Bath – is a steep road that leads up to the village of Combe Down. The houses near the top, with what no doubt are described by local estate agents as breathtaking views over the grounds of Prior Park College, can only be afforded by the very, very rich.

I knew absolutely nothing about Norton's private life; whether he was married or not or if he lived alone. The house – Victorian, detached, immaculate – was of a size that would obviously require the presence of staff. The front garden, with a drive sweeping gently down between mature trees, was attractively conventional but a glance down the side of the house revealed features that reminded me of the gardens at Portmeirion. A semi-ruined stone outhouse or stable at one side of a tiny yard had pots of ferns arranged on the window ledges and, at the bottom of a flight of narrow steps that curved up at one side of it and out of sight to a higher part of the garden, was an unusual and ornate iron lamp. Near the lamp a grotesque mask was set into the wall, water dripping from the gaping verdigris-stained mouth into a lead cistern flanked by more ferns and pots of agapanthus.

I had paused, beguiled and wanting to explore further – I was a few minutes early – when I became aware that I was being watched from an upstairs window. It was only a momentary glimpse of a woman's face – pale, haughty, frowning – and then with an angry twitch of a curtain it had gone.

In a silence broken only by the light breeze rustling through the trees and the twittering of sparrows I turned to survey the way I had come through the front garden: a picture of perfect tranquillity. I wondered if what went on inside the house mirrored its exterior calm and somehow thought not. From what I had seen of Norton he appeared likely to be somewhat contentious.

And that face at the window. Unfriendly. No, openly hostile.

In the next moment the peace was broken. Somewhere on

the other side of the house, where the drive continued and I had obtained a quick view of a modern single-storey building that was probably a row of garages, there was a roar as the engine of a sports car of some kind came to life. Seconds later it appeared, tyres spurting gravel, exhaust belching blue smoke, and headed for the entrance. The drive was plenty wide enough but nevertheless the nearside wheels swerved onto the lawn, carving deep grooves in the soft ground. I thought for a moment that the back of the vehicle might actually clip one of the stone pillars as it went through but by a hair's breadth it missed and careered off. I heard the blast of the horn as someone, or something, got in the way.

'Agatha Christie would sure have loved this,' I drawled and rang the doorbell.

An older version of the woman I had seen at the window answered the door. 'Yes?' she said stonily.

I introduced myself, adding that Professor Norton was expecting me.

'Come in.' She made no comment about the car exhaust fumes that had by now, chokingly, reached us, merely threw open the nearest door on the left in the tiled hall, gestured with her back to me to go in and stalked off.

I entered the room she had indicated. Judging by the quality of the decor and furniture, the pictures on the walls and the pair of large matching Coalport vases on the mantelpiece, the Nortons were not only wealthy but collected fine art. In Victorian times this room would have probably been the withdrawing room – in those days women were kicked out after dinner in order that their menfolk could run riot with the port and tell dirty stories.

I had no further time to admire my surroundings for the door opened behind me and the woman's voice said, 'This way.'

It was on the tip of my tongue to tell her that I had not arrived to survey the drains or track down cockroaches in the kitchen but I desisted, reminding myself that authors' skins, after initial blizzards of publishers' rejection slips, grow very thick and should stay that way. So I merely smiled at her in the fashion that Patrick tells me is hugely irritating and followed her across the hall and past a long-case clock as it chimed the half hour. The woman walked like a model, swaying a little at the hips, as though aware of her slim figure and the expensive black dress she was wearing. We did not have far to go. She flung open another door situated to one side and slightly beneath a wide curving staircase and then went away towards the rear of the house without saying another word. I went in.

John Norton looked up from a newspaper. 'Ah, Miss Langley. Do come in.' He removed the half-moon gold-rimmed spectacles I had already seen him wearing that day, tossed them on to the leather-topped desk nearby and rose to his feet. 'I hope you don't mind but can we keep this fairly short? As you know I'm going out and it seems to take forever to drive to Bristol these days.'

Mentally, I had prepared questions I wanted to ask; about his background, education, training, particularly interesting cases, anything that would help me to convincingly portray what made a forensic pathologist tick. I found I wasn't remotely interested in that kind of thing anymore but was agog to know who the driver of the car was and how the two women fitted into the household and why they were so – well – bloody.

I seated myself in the armchair he indicated. Divested of the protective clothing I had seen him in earlier he somehow appeared far less imposing. I could not really explain the reasons for this as he was actually quite a good-looking man with a head of unruly brown hair, a pleasant smile that revealed good if slightly crooked teeth and boyish sticking-out ears. Then I realised that as all I had been able to see of him that morning were his eyes – like everyone else he had been wearing a surgical mask – which were indeed dark and somewhat unsettling, perhaps a writer's imagination had pictured the rest of his features to be grimly in sympathy.

'I don't quite fit the bill as a killer?' he said, teasing me, in an uncannily close guess to my thoughts. Then, without giving me time to reply added, 'What can I get you to drink?'

I opted for a gin and tonic, mostly to give myself time to think as he went over to a small drinks cabinet. This room was his study and I was trying to commit every detail to memory as I had a suspicion that it might be the most fruitful thing to be gleaned from the interview. The colour scheme was mainly deep rose and burgundy, not particularly masculine but when teamed with Oriental rugs, antique mahogany furniture, including shelves that lined most of the wall space and housed not only books but a myriad of knick-knacks and souvenirs seemingly from every corner of the globe and mostly of a scientific or bizarre nature the overall effect was idiosyncratic if not powerful. I found myself itching to rummage.

'What drew you to this kind of profession?' I asked, wondering if a fist-sized round object on a shelf with what appeared to be a large tuft of black hair on it was a shrunken head.

'Curiosity and science,' he replied unhesitatingly. 'When I was eight I cut up a dead rabbit I'd found on the way home from school to try to discover what it had died of. My mother almost fainted when she saw what I was doing – I'd borrowed her best kitchen knife and the bread board.'

'Did you get into trouble?'

'No, we were a medical family so all that happened after an in-depth teach-in and dire warnings about the dangers of dead bodies and food poisoning was that I had to forfeit my pocket money until there was deemed a suitable sum with which to buy my mother a new knife and board. I got to keep the old ones though and some surgical gloves.'

'Did you discover what the rabbit had died of?'

'It had probably been hit a glancing blow by a car – there was a lot of bruising and internal bleeding. It had been with young though – I can remember feeling quite bad about that even though it taught me an awful lot about the birds and the bees.' He gave me my drink. 'Perhaps that's what set me on the road to helping catch murderers.'

'My character isn't a nice guy like you,' I felt impelled to tell him.

'Oh, I'm not a nice guy at all,' he said in off-hand fashion, reseating himself.

He was drinking straight tonic with ice, I had not helped noticing as he poured. 'Had you ever thought of writing your autobiography?'

He drew in air through his teeth in mock horror. 'No! At least, not until I'm a hundred and thirty years old and there's no one left alive to sue me.'

I suddenly saw what might have been the reason for his mildly militant attitude that morning. 'So your reservations wouldn't be in connection with professional matters but are more to do with your private life?'

He did not quite stare at me open-mouthed but there was a degree of astoundment, as my father used to say. 'Whatever made you say that?'

I could hardly reveal that most women are aware when they're being eyed up. 'I happen to know you're one of the most respected men in your position *ever*,' I murmured. 'So any bother has to be in connection with the ladies.'

He shook his head, smiling, not about to tell me anything along those lines. But his eyes were now glinting with mischief.

Having just realised that the large glass jars on the shelf closest to me contained impossible-to-identify bits and bobs – growths probably – preserved in formaldehyde that he had removed from corpses, I decided it was time I addressed the real purpose of my visit and put to him the questions I needed to ask. He was very helpful, detailing the educational path a hopeful forensic scientist would need to take in order to enter the profession. He even gave me a couple of illustrated textbooks, old and probably out of date as far as he was concerned but containing all the medical terms and procedures I could use in order to make my character and his actions as authentic as possible. Then, aware of his evening engagement, I rose to go, expressing my thanks.

'Are you in Bath all weekend?' Norton asked lightly. 'Only I'm free tomorrow night if you fancy dinner.'

My mind whirled, but only because it was involved with strategy. It seemed I would be mad not to take the opportunity to find out more. 'Yes, that would be lovely,' I said.

'Where shall I pick you up?'

'I think it would be easiest if I took a taxi into the city centre and met you there,' I told him. 'Unless you had somewhere farther out of town in mind.'

'No, that suits me fine. I'll get a taxi too and we can walk. Outside the Roman Baths then? At seven thirty?'

The sky had clouded over since I had arrived and when Norton showed me out it was into a humid dusk that promised thunder. There appeared to be no lights in the drive and the trees blocked out any street lights that might have been visible in the main road. I walked slowly, giving my eyes time to adjust to the gloom. Passing through the trailing branches of a weeping ash low enough to touch those on foot that leaned over the drive like a huge umbrella I was not unduly alarmed when a dark shape emerged from within its spread and clasped me to its bosom.

Not unduly alarmed. That is, I didn't actually shriek loudly in terror.

'I wish you wouldn't do that!' I stormed.

My husband released me and shied stagily, reeling off through the vegetation as though I'd hit him. 'I just thought you might like to be escorted through the dark bits,' Patrick's voice from within the tree said. 'Hey, you're not usually all of a tizz. What did Norton do to you in there?'

'You're not going to like this,' I countered, heart still bumping. 'He's taking me out to dinner tomorrow night.'

Patrick sighed. 'Well, at least it saves you the bother of working out how you were going to break it to me gently.'

2

Buttery, in a virtual haze of garlic fumes and working his way through a plateful of large freshwater prawns, Patrick said, 'So you reckon the woman who opened the door might be Norton's wife and the one who peered at you through the window was his daughter?'

'They looked very much alike,' I said. 'And the elder one was too well-dressed and far too rude to be a housekeeper. Norton didn't acknowledge her showing me into his study as one would a member of staff. No, thank you,' I added when a peeled prawn was offered on a fork.

'If you have a couple you won't notice the garlic should I happen to kiss you later,' he said winsomely.

I beamed at him. 'Not a chance.'

Patrick chuckled and I knew I hadn't heard the last on that subject. It was actually rather a shame. Perhaps if he used half a bottle of mouthwash and was *particularly* persuasive ... He said, 'Perhaps if the person who roared off in the car was a young bloke he was the son and he'd just had a violent row with Mother. That would explain why she was in such a filthy mood. Whoever it was almost hit another car at the crossroads, by the way – just swung right even though some-one was coming the other way and forced them to brake.'

Patrick had picked me up from the Hare and Hounds after phoning me on his mobile and we had whiled away a couple of hours in Bath, mostly by my spending money.

In truth, I was feeling a little guilty at accepting the invita-tion from Norton and was mulling over calling him to cancel it. For, after all, this was the first weekend away that Patrick and I had had together for quite a while and no matter how much you love your home and children a break from both can be bliss indeed.

'I'm not complaining, you know,' he said softly, no doubt correctly reading the reason for the rueful expression on my face.

'I don't like it when my writing comes between us.'

'And you don't usually allow it to, which I very much appreciate. But this is different – even though, as you said, you probably do have enough info for the book.'

'Oh?'

He briskly utilised the finger bowl and dried his hands on his napkin. 'That was delicious. Cheese or a pudding? Or both?'

Built like a racing snake he could, and almost certainly would, have both. 'I might just have some of those profiteroles,' I said, eyeing the dessert trolley as it was wheeled past. '*What* is different this time?'

Patrick smiled like the Mona Lisa but on his austere, albeit good-looking, features the effect was not demure but a touch malevolent. 'I wasn't going to mention it as it really doesn't have any bearing on –' he shrugged, 'anything, really.' He caught the waiter's eye. 'But Norton has a brother by the name of Max. Max is not good news at all.'

'Do you run the names of all the people I get involved with through your computer?' I asked, really wanting to know. Even though he no longer worked for MI5 I has wondered before whether he still had access to what was in effect highly restricted information.

'Yes, I do.'

We ordered our dessert and I asked myself whether I was merely irritated or angry with him for his interference. 'What has Max done?' I enquired coolly. 'Parked on double yellow lines? Walked down Burlington Arcade with his hands in his pockets, whistling and with a large parcel balanced on his head?'

'Would a conviction for pushing drugs here and more of the same thing plus gun-running abroad do for a start?'

I love this man of mine too much to continue being sarcastic. Besides, this was riveting stuff. I stared at him. 'Really?'

'The abroad bit was Indonesia. He had a boat a few years ago that was kept at various small ports on the coast of Sulawesi.'

'That's sort of the South China Sea, isn't it?'

'The Celebes Sea, strictly speaking, but yes, basically you're right. I suppose the bloke could be described as a modern-day pirate but he appears to have only done it on a part-time basis to meet day-to-day expenses. He's reported to have traded with sea-going bandits until the authorities really started to crack down on that kind of thing and then he high-tailed it off to the States and was allowed in mostly on the strength that his great-grandfather had become an American citizen. He and his wife are now back in the UK acting as Mr and Mrs Respectable and looking for a home to buy – in Bath.'

I assimilated this amazing piece of news and then asked, 'Can't he be extradited to Indonesia to answer charges?'

'I'm not too sure there's an extradition agreement with that part of the world but I should imagine they've got their hands full with all the local talent and were glad to be rid of him. He's pretty small beer in comparison with the organised pirate gangs. But I haven't told you the best bit yet. There's a large self-contained flat on the top floor of Professor Norton's house that usually rented out and his brother and sister-in-law are staying there while they're house-hunting.'

I postponed giving that deep thought and asked the question at the top of my mind. 'I assume then that this information was fairly freely available to people like yourself since the war on terrorism started – it's stuff that's circulated around to the police forces, MI6 and so forth?'

'There's no need to be so circuitous in finding out whether someone's popped out of the woodwork and asked me to

29

snoop on this man,' he said with a smile. 'The answer's no. My days of freezing in ditches are over, and anyway, as you know, D12 didn't concern itself with common criminals.'

Our profiteroles were placed before us.

'But you're still prone to lurking under trees,' I said.

'I prefer to be within hailing distance when you go into a pirate's lair.'

'I didn't notice any lights in the top of the house.'

'Why didn't you mention this to me before you went to see Norton?'

'No, there didn't seem to be anyone in.'

'As I said, because it wasn't relevant. But now you've accepted his invitation to dinner…'

'Caution on your part?'

'I'm wondering what's behind it.'

I gave him a very straight look. 'Just because his brother's a bit dodgy it doesn't mean he is too. And hasn't it occurred to you that he might just want to carry on an interesting conversation or, come to think of it, fancies me like crazy?'

'It occurred to me the moment I clapped eyes on you at school that every man on the planet with balls in the right place would fancy you like crazy but, not wishing to sound conceited, I have to ask myself has this bloke read the newspapers recently?'

'In other words it should have crossed his mind that were he to make a pass at your wife – and you've had plenty of publicity recently – you might just roll up and slice him into wafer-thin rashers with one of his own scalpels.' I was not feeling all that crushed, I had to admit I'd been wondering about it as well.

'Yes.'

'So he wants to take me out because he's bored and he and his rude wife are about to be separated. Oh, do get real!'

'It's perfectly possible, and Ingrid Langley does not want to have her name messily involved with someone else's divorce proceedings. On the other hand there might be absolutely nothing in it and he doesn't want to give an unpleasant woman grounds for divorcing him. It's probably just as you said, he merely wants to carry on with an interesting conversation.'

'He *is* a womaniser, though,' I said pensively.

Patrick almost choked on a profiterole. 'Now you tell me! How the hell do you know that?'

'Intuition,' I snapped, irritated by what I deemed to be an over-the-top reaction, cursing my stupidity for mentioning it and not wanting to talk about it any more. 'I think I might just go anyway. I don't see why I should have you check up on everything I do like this and have to put in an application form in triplicate. And if I spot you within a thousand yards of us I'll – '

'Do what?' he enquired stonily but nevertheless with mischief writ large.

'I'll think of something,' I informed him loftily. 'If it happens.'

I was really cursing myself now. You simply don't issue a man like Patrick with that kind of a challenge.

Slightly under twenty-four hours later I knew I had made a bad mistake. Even though I had agreed to meet Patrick after my dinner date with Norton in the Cheshire Cat, a wine bar overlooking the river, I knew I had ruined our weekend, mostly by thoughtless remarks. He had always had my safety in mind and this stemmed, I knew, from the days when I worked as his partner for D12, a small department within MI5 that had been set up to investigate attempted interference with those who had signed the Official Secrets Act and who worked for MI5 or MI6.

So I had spoilt everything and, the previous night, Patrick had taken himself and his garlic-scented breath off to the far side of the bed and had gone straight to sleep. I had lain awake miserably for hours.

Things had not improved by the morning. If anything, the awkwardness had deepened and I had been on the point of apologising, over breakfast, when Patrick's father John had stuck his head around the door and said that Patrick was wanted urgently on the phone. That had entailed ringing someone back on his special-frequency car phone and he was away for quite a long time. When he returned, one look at his face had told me that our weekend was really doomed.

'So where do you have to go?' I had enquired.

'Nowhere today. They want me back early tomorrow afternoon, that's all. The PM's paying the college a visit on Monday and I have to get back to give briefings and starch my best bib and tucker.' This had been uttered with bitter sarcasm: after what had happened to him at the hands of politicians Patrick has very little time for them, whatever their hue. Soldiers always think bureaucrats a waste of space anyway.

'What do you want to do today then?' I had enquired.

'I don't mind. How about you?' he had replied, perfectly disinterested.

Patrick's mother, Elspeth, a slim and still attractive woman in her early sixties, had been closely engaged with the *Telegraph* crossword but had looked up and given us one of her searching looks. 'I hope you two haven't had a row.'

'Not at all,' I had assured her.

'No,' Patrick had said, getting to his feet and heading for the door. 'She's just going out for dinner with someone else and told me not to stick my nose in.'

'Never mind,' Elspeth had said when we were alone, patting my hand. 'It's when they say things like that you know they're still madly in love with you.'

I normally have huge faith in Elspeth's somewhat wacky logic, especially where her son is concerned, but this time was not so sure. I was surprised and a little alarmed by his remark. He can wind himself until he gets into a very bad, if not dangerous, temper. This seemed to be confirmed when he had collected a few personal items, got in his car and driven off.

And now, at a little after seven fifteen in the evening, I had indeed had to order a cab and head for Bath as Patrick had still not returned. John had offered to give me a lift into the city but a clergyman has precious little time to call his own and I had thanked him and declined. So where was Patrick? I was more than a little worried now as he had not taken his weekend bag with him or other things that he would almost certainly need if he had decided to go straight back to Surrey. Bad temper notwithstanding he is not a man prone to going off in a huff and I could think of no other occasion in our entire married life – we have had plenty of rows, having actually been divorced and re-married – when he had behaved in this fashion.

I told myself that the telephone call might have involved other matters. In his time with MI5, sometimes, he had to go to secret locations without telling anyone, not even me, where he was going. I had rather thought that those days were over.

And here was John Norton, all smiles outside the Roman Baths, waiting for me.

I made polite noises, even though I was not late. 'I hope you haven't been waiting long.'

'Only just this very moment got here,' he announced jovially.

The entrance to the Roman Baths, closed at this time of night, is in the Abbey Churchyard. It was a fine, warm evening after heavy thundery rain the night before and the area was still thronging with tourists. In the doorway of the National Trust shop an enterprising youth, probably a university student, was playing the flute.

'I managed to book us in at a little Italian place in Green Street,' Norton said. 'Barolo's. Know it?'

Alas, in a way, I did. Patrick and I have often eaten there. I told him I did and we fell into step.

As I had anticipated, after my unwise comments, I half expected to see Patrick at every inch of the way. That man in the shadows beneath the portico that one went through to reach Union Street ... An indistinct but tall, slim figure standing motionless right in front of the massive carved doorway of the Abbey...

'I don't normally talk shop but being as you were present at the PM I'll tell you this,' Norton went on to say. 'As I had thought there was nothing wrong with the Bates woman's heart, in fact she gave every impression of having been quite healthy up until the time of her death.' In the same breath he added, 'Known Carrick long, have you?'

'Just for a couple of years,' I replied, wondering if he had thought us old flames.

'Watch out!' Norton exclaimed suddenly.

A man giving every appearance of being the worst for drink had walked waveringly but directly towards me causing Norton to catch my arm suddenly and pull me to one side. He shouted angrily again after the man to watch where he was going.

'My apologies for grabbing you like that. I thought he was about to knock you over.'

Barolo's was busy but Norton was obviously a regular and respected client as we were shown to a table in an alcove set slightly away from the general pandemonium that was one of the hallmarks of the place. The thought crossed my mind that his appearance with various other women other than his wife might be a normal part of the scenery. On the other hand it had to be admitted that here I was sitting down to my third meal out with as many different men in roughly thirty-six hours.

'So where is the grim-looking Lieutenant-Colonel who had the misfortune of being plastered all over the media not so long ago?' Norton asked when we were comfortably settled. He seemed to delight in out-of-the-blue questions.

'Patrick was only looking grim *because* he was plastered all over the media,' I replied. 'We were supposed to be spending the weekend here together but I'm afraid duty called.'

There was no doubt about it, even in the soft candlelight I saw the merest hint of satisfaction – and writers are adept at reading nuances of facial expression as they watch people all the time – flit across his face.

'What's the book called?' Norton asked when we had ordered our meal. An opened bottle of extremely good Chablis had been placed before us and, with a deft flourish, the wine waiter had poured some into each glass.

'*Dead Trouble*,' I informed him.

'I like that. It's short so you can remember it easily and yet subtle – there are various layers of meaning.'

'You don't read my kind of thing,' I reminded him.

'That doesn't mean I don't recognise a good title when I hear one. Have you always written crime?'

'No, I started with more general novels that had a good pinch of romance but the darker side of life sort of crept in.'

Half seriously, he said, 'Forensic pathologists don't usually go touting for trade by knocking people off you know. We're kept busy enough as it is.'

'Ah, well the man I'm writing about doesn't kill for that reason. He murders his wife's lover after he finds them together and then tries to make it look like an accident. But the police suspect there's been foul play, even though they don't for a moment think it was *him* and he gets to do the PM. Quandary: how still to make it look like it was an accident?'

'Is he found out?'

'Oh, yes, my copper's the best.'

'I actually find what you've told me quite fascinating.

Would you like me to give you a few pointers on that scenario?'

I suddenly realised that it was the real reason I had come. I had refrained from openly asking a man of his international reputation for help along these lines as, subconsciously perhaps, there had been an awareness that to cheaply pick his brains demeaned him. But the idea appeared to appeal to him enormously and we sat, practically head to head, gradually emptying the wine bottle while he quietly but with relish outlined a couple of quite ghastly and grisly ways, that might even fool his colleagues, in which someone of his calling might try to get way with murder by faking post-mortem findings. This time I did take notes, mostly because of the technicalities.

'I'd be interested to know how your copper cracks either of those,' he finished by saying.

'I shall make it plain that they're uncrackable,' I said. 'He will be exposed by his own careless talk and other police work.'

Norton grinned broadly. I had given him his reward.

'Champagne!' he announced. 'What prizes do you people get for good books? The Golden Dagger? The Diamond-encrusted Handcuffs? Can I come to the awards ceremony?'

'I'll let you know if it happens,' I assured him.

Whether it could be attributed to alcohol or not he became very convivial, a different man to the one I had first met the previous morning. I too was exhilarated: I had been handed first class, if not stunning, material that represented, with diligence on my part, a sizeable chunk of my book. I had already written most of the background. Now, the thing was as good as finished.

A glass of champagne or so later and when I was hungrily embarking on my main course – I had had very little to eat all day – I glanced up to see that a man was watching me from the nearest table some ten feet or so away. He immediately dropped his gaze and gave all his attention to a steaming plateful of pasta.

'Was that your son I saw driving away from your house last night?' I asked, mindful that I owed Patrick a little sleuthing.

Norton, with a mouthful of calamari, grunted. Then he swallowed and said, 'Jason treats motoring as a branch of ballistics. He's written off three cars in the last eighteen months and walked away without a scratch on each occasion. I told him that this is the last one I'll buy for him. If he wants to kill himself in future he can fund it himself – if and when he gets a job. He won't take any notice though, never does. Thinks I'm a soft touch.'

'It must be a dreadful source of worry to his mother,' I remarked chattily.

'Oh no, Frances doesn't care a damn. She wrote us both off years ago.' He was not more forthcoming on this but I now really had the bit between my teeth.

'Would you say then that your profession is high-risk as far as marriage goes?'

Norton gave me an amazed stare. 'Well, it stands to reason, doesn't it? Some women don't like the idea of the hands that are fondling their tits having just been groping around in the entrails of a corpse.'

'I take your point,' I said drily. The man was covertly watching us again and I silently promised myself that if he did it again I would throw one of the somewhat solid bread rolls at his head. I have an extremely good aim.

'On the other hand,' Norton went on, 'it turns others on a treat.'

In a split second's reflection I asked myself the question. No, there wasn't the remotest chance of my fancying this man; there was an underlying coarseness about him, hard to define but nevertheless ingrained.

'No, Jason's more like my brother, Max,' Norton said

reflectively, more I felt in a quest to change the subject because he realised that he had said more than he should have done than a real desire to talk about his son. 'I reckon they both take after bad great-grandfather Charlie. He was a real tearaway. Ran away from home to work on a whaling ship when he had just turned thirteen and ended up making a fortune for himself in the California gold rush. The skeleton in the family cupboard is the rumour that he murdered six men, other miners, in cold blood and grabbed their claims. I've done a bit of research but it's very hard to verify after all this time.'

'You don't get on with Max then?' I asked in an off-hand fashion, thinking that this all fitted in very neatly with what Patrick had already told me.

Norton pulled a face. 'It sounds dreadful if you tell people that you've come to the conclusion that your brother's an absolute bastard so I usually try to avoid talking about him. But I know you're discreet and even if you do put it in the book all the names will be different.'

'I won't,' I said.

'He's a bloody crook, if you ask me,' Norton went on, as though I had not spoken. 'Well, he actually is a crook, for God's sake, he was sent to prison for twelve months for selling drugs to school children when he was in his early twenties. Another one who went off the map without a penny to his name and came back loaded. Hardly ever saw the inside of a schoolroom either – I used to wonder how he ever learned to read and write. Canny, though, money always seemed to stick to him even when he was a lad – usually other people's.'

'And he's back?'

'Back and in my house looking for somewhere to live in the million quid bracket. Married too, to a hard-bitten tart from the States. You know the sort, more face-lifts and liposuction than you'd believe possible. God knows how old she really is. She appears to be around thirty-five but the way she looks at you – I don't know how to put it really – she could have been around for always. Sort of old in a fossil kind of way. Does that make any sense to you?'

It did, and for some reason I shuddered.

I decided against a dessert and just had coffee. Norton, though, guzzled into sticky toffee pudding served with a dollop of clotted cream – the menu was somewhat eclectic – and I found myself looking forward to the end of our association.

'They've come back with masses of stuff,' he said when he had finished, tossing his crumpled napkin on to the table. 'Boxes piled in an empty garage, loads up in the flat, some in a spare bedroom and I'm even tripping over crates in the breakfast room. Max says it's mostly his art collection, whatever that means. But he's got some ethnic stuff unpacked in the flat. Figures, carvings, masks, that kind of thing. Not my kind of clobber, I'm afraid, a bit creepy. Frances said he probably dug it all out to stop us going up there as it's all loaded with ancient curses and for the first time in ages I actually agreed with her. But I'm sure I'm talking too much. Would you like to go now?'

'What kind of figures?' I asked.

'Oh, they're more than half life-sized and made of wood and straw and stuff like that and come from somewhere at the back of beyond and are modelled on the dead. They stare right at you with their beady eyes. Bloody awful, actually. Max always had terrible taste.' He guffawed. 'Especially in women.'

A few minutes later we emerged into the fine night air and I took a deep breath, trying to remember what I had recently read in a newspaper article about the wholesale theft of *tau tau*, the lifelike wooden effigies of the dead of the Torajans of Sulawesi in which they believe reside the souls of the deceased.

'I hope you'll allow me to call a taxi to take you to where you're staying,' Norton said.

'Thank you, but I'm meeting someone in The Cheshire Cat,' I told him.

This seemed to throw him slightly. 'Is that the place down by the river?'

'That's right'

'I insist on escorting you there. There have been several cases lately of women walking alone in the riverside gardens being mugged.'

I knew this to be quite true as James Carrick had warned me about it. I decided to accept his offer reckoning that as long as I left him at the door there would be no suspicion on his part that he had already met Patrick that evening. Not that the latter would still resemble the man who had almost walked into me in the Abbey Churchyard. Had Norton noticed the horribly leery wink? I thought not.

'Thank you,' I said.

He placed an arm lightly across my shoulders and I didn't really mind as he had had rather a lot to drink. In fact I think he was grateful for a steadying influence as we descended the twisting, narrow stone stair at the side of Pulteney Bridge.

'I was rather hoping, you know,' Norton said, 'that you might spend the night at an hotel with me. I don't make a habit of it but you're an extremely attractive woman.'

'Who's nevertheless fairly immune from that kind of old baloney,' I told him briskly.

He stopped walking, forcing me also to halt. 'Perhaps I should have told the truth and admit that I do make the most of any opportunities.' He surveyed my face in the light of the lamp above us. 'But I'm not as tempted as this very often. I assure you you won't regret it.'

In a low voice I said, 'Professor Norton, my husband would be better in bed than you even if you lived to be a thousand years old and had lessons every day.'

He took it right on the chin, smiling at me. 'No offence?'

'No, you're cuddly in a funny kind of way.'

He laughed out loud at this. 'And you're quite a girl, Ingrid, even though I don't believe you about that soldier-boy.'

I was actually glad of his company as there were several gangs of youths hanging around on the walkway through the gardens that border the Avon, shouting and singing, drinking from cans and throwing the empties into the water. A couple of obscene remarks were sent in our direction but that was all.

'I thought they were going to make drinking in public places an offence,' Norton said furiously but not over-loud.

'So did I,' I replied.

And with that someone came from behind a tree and started taking photographs of us.

Half blinded by the flashes I heard Norton shout and then someone else appeared and neatly threw the photographer into the river. A couple of youths endeavoured to interfere and there were two more loud splashes. There was then a short pause while it was ascertained that all three were in no danger of drowning after which I was grabbed and towed at some speed in the direction of bright lights and music. I suddenly realised that Norton was still with us.

'Well?' Patrick snapped just outside the entrance to The Cheshire Cat, letting go of both our wrists.

'I can assure you, Lieutenant-Colonel, that that was absolutely nothing to do with me,' Norton told him, his voice unsteady, probably because he was out of breath.

'It would appear that someone has hired a private eye to spy on you,' he was coldly informed.

'Which is as damaging to me as it is to your wife.'

'Yes, but Ingrid hasn't been screwing around,' was the brutal response.

'You have my word that you will hear nothing more of this.' He turned to me. 'My deepest apologies.'

I surreptitiously reached for Patrick's hand and squeezed it. We have our codes.

'Very well,' Patrick said. 'At least the film was ruined.'

With a final, silent gesture of regret, Norton left us.

I carefully gauged Patrick's mood. While I was fairly convinced that if the friends of those drinking on the riverside came looking for us with revenge in mind he would happily lob the whole lot in the river, I felt that he was no longer angry with *me*.

'Do you still want to go for a drink?' I asked him.

'Yes, I'm stone cold sober,' he retorted and plunged within. I followed and found a table in a corner while he went over to the bar.

'I'm not drunk.' I said a few minutes later, an orange juice having just been plonked in front of me.

'No, you've just got a bloody stupid look on your face. Just like this lot,' he added, gesturing at the décor of the bar; painted, grinning Cheshire cats in every conceivable colour.

'He insisted on buying champagne.'

Patrick just stared stonily at the wall behind my head.

'I'm sorry,' I whispered, tears pricking my eyes. 'I've made a fool of us both.'

He took a swig of his wine and breathed out hard, almost snorted. 'You haven't made a fool of us. Perhaps I just haven't seen you with another man before. Perhaps I'm over-reacting.'

'I didn't find him remotely attractive.'

'So why was he here and with his arm around you?'

'Because several women have been mugged in the area lately and because he was a bit sloshed. Patrick, when did you last *eat*?'

He looked surprised. 'God knows. This morning?'

'When you had coffee and two slices of toast. This place has quite good food. Shall I order you something?'

'No. I'd rather go home and raid the fridge.'

42

There was another silence between us and then Patrick stretched out a hand and gently stroked my nose with one finger. 'Sorry.'

'I found out quite a lot about Max.'

'Look, I was really only interested in the bloke from the point of view of your safety.'

'I know that now, but what he told me is interesting.'

We went back to Hinton Littlemoor – by 'home' of course Patrick had meant the rectory – where Elspeth, who had been on her way up to bed, produced in just a few minutes and as if by magic a huge helping of casseroled steak and kidney with dumplings.

'Better?' I enquired when it had disappeared.

Patrick smiled at me by way of an answer. The he said, 'So how did your evening go?'

'Extremely well. He gave me loads of info of a highly technical nature that meant the book's as good as written. Are you going to tell me why you went off like that?'

He hesitated for a moment or two before saying, 'You're aware that I still have links with MI5?'

'It had crossed my mind that you had,' I replied, evenly. 'So I take you had a summons to go somewhere today as well as orders to return to Camberley tomorrow?'

Patrick nodded, watching me. 'In a nutshell they want me back – full time.'

'I see,' was all I could think of saying just then.

'As you know all kinds of things were mooted before I left. They wanted to keep D12 going and then changed their minds and it was merged with another department. Then I was offered a small unit that would liaise with others abroad in connection with combating terrorism. Minds were changed again as the entire thinking on that subject has now been completely restructured after what happened on September 11th – small units for that kind of work are now out of the question.'

'And small covert units are precisely what you're good at. Patrick ...'

'I think I know what's going through your mind. I promised when we took on Matthew and Katie that in future I'd stick to a job where I wouldn't be in any real danger...' He too broke off.

We have four children: Justin and Victoria are ours and quite a bit younger than Patrick's brother's two whom we adopted after he was killed about twelve months ago. I said, 'But you're going out of your mind with boredom arranging lectures, planning training, giving briefings, going to formal dinners and being nice to politicians. So what's going on?'

'They *are* going to resurrect D12 – as a separate unit.'

'With you in charge?'

'That seems to be what's on offer although everything's still a bit vague. With a commensurate salary. In other words my present pay plus all the usual and unusual allowances.'

'In other, other words, danger money,' I said sharply.

'I said I'd trot the idea by you.' This with his most charming smile. 'And ...'

'What?'

'They want you too.'

I just stared disbelievingly at him.

3

I was not sure what Patrick had expected my reaction to be to this revelation but when I merely stared at him, hardly believing my ears, he left the kitchen and I heard him go into the living room – the hinges on the door squeak a little – and, after a short pause, there was the distinct sound of the top of a whisky bottle being unscrewed and liquid splashing into a glass.

Things were going from bad to worse. Between us, that is. Slowly, I got to my feet, tidied the kitchen and put the used plate and cutlery into the dishwasher. I was desperately tired after yesterday's practically sleepless night but knew that if I merely went to bed without making some kind of effort to sort something out then Patrick would drink far too much and probably spend the night on the sofa. After that would come a monumental hangover, ill-mannered and hardly fair on Elspeth as she was still mourning the death of Patrick's brother, Larry. John would probably lose his temper because he is overworked on Sundays as there are not sufficient numbers of team clergy and he expects his home-life at least to run smoothly. The weekend would not be so much doomed as extinct.

There was one obvious way to reverse the downward spiral. It would actually address what I guessed was the crux of the problem.

Patrick glanced up when I entered the room and then went back to the magazine he was pretending to read. I kicked off my shoes, reclined – no arrayed myself – on the sofa and silently appraised him. His hair, still thickly wavy even though with more than a sprinkling of grey among the black, needed cutting as usual although it was how I like it best, long enough to run my fingers through, curling down onto his neck in the most sexy fashion. Right now, his expression taut, there was no hint of the boy with whom I had fallen in love all those years ago at school although I knew that when he smiled . . .

Patrick took a fierce swig of his whisky and, not looking at me, said, 'Would you like a drink?'

'Can I have a sip of yours?'

He regarded me blankly. 'You don't like whisky.'

'I do at New Year and in emergencies.'

'It isn't either.'

'This is an emergency.'

He came over. 'Ingrid, are you feeling okay?'

He looked concerned but his eyes still had sparks of anger in them. I looked into them. Mesmeric eyes; grey irises with a dark rim, flecks of gold. This wasn't going to be too difficult after all. I wasn't remotely tired. I sat up to pull my evening top over my head, removed my bra and then held out a hand for the glass. But I took his wrist instead and drew him towards me, removing the glass from his fingers.

'Someone might come back downstairs,' Patrick said a little breathlessly a couple of minutes later when things were getting torrid. In other words a shade this side of us not being able to stop even if a Royal Marines' band marched in.

I gently pushed him away, got off the sofa, removed the rest of my clothes, crossed the room to the french doors, opened them and wafted out into the garden, a long shaft of light behind me, my shadow in its centre, creating a path across the lawn. The grass was already moist with dew but I did not care and sat down on a narrow path that wound through tall shrubs to find that the ground was still warm after the day's sunshine.

'Remember the first time?' I said when, literally hot on my heels, he had followed me, closing the doors, and curtains, behind him. 'On Dartmoor?'

It was now very dark but I knew Patrick was shedding

his clothes as fast as a man can, exclaiming softly as he encountered a prickly bush. I was sitting with my arms around my raised knees and in the next moment he had dropped down by my side and was kissing me, one hand exploring absolutely everywhere. I unclenched my arms and pulled him close, we sank back onto the grass and then it was like that first time on Dartmoor; urgent, fervent and quite, quite sublime.

'In bed,' Patrick gasped a few minutes later, only just able to speak, 'I propose we do that again.'

But we stayed where we were, and then made love again, more slowly this time. I had told Norton the truth.

Unfortunately it did not remain a secret and when we went down to the kitchen cum breakfast room the next morning to find Elspeth frying bacon and tomatoes, she surveyed us with a gaze that was burgeoning with suppressed mirth. One immediately became aware though that if she had heard any strange noises in the garden the previous night she would not make any comments with John present for fear of embarrassing us. Elspeth is nothing if not tactful.

'What time do you have to set off, Patrick?' she asked.

'There's no rush,' he assured her. 'Around ten should be fine.'

'Oh, good, you've plenty of time to eat your breakfast then. Toast as usual for you, Ingrid?'

'Is any of that going spare?' I enquired, eyeing the fragrant panful and thinking my hunger must be something to do with all the fresh air and exercise.

'But of course! In fact I put an extra plate in the oven just in case.'

To me, Patrick said, 'You take the car and I'll catch a train. It's far easier for you that way – that's if you don't mind picking me up at the station next weekend.'

When I am away from home my car is left for the use of our nanny, Carrie, whenever possible. 'Sure?' I asked.

'Sure. And I'll tell them the other thing we discussed is off.'

'We didn't 'really discuss it.'

'I don't think there's a lot of point, do you?'

'I think we ought, at least, to talk it over.'

John, who had greeted our arrival and had had his breakfast, now emerged from behind the newspaper. 'So it's no use my asking if you'll fill a couple of gaps in the choir for the ten fifteen then.' He was addressing Patrick, I cannot sing a note.

'Counter-tenor or bass?' he was asked, Patrick being a more than passable former in mad moments but actually preferring tenor.

'Both at once if you like.'

'Why not? I can still be away at just after eleven.'

John rose. 'But before that I have to take Matins over in Wellow. See you later. Oh, and you might put the hose away next time you have one of your nocturnal frolics and have to wash the grass and leaves off yourselves. I almost fell over it just now.' He grinned at us, eyebrows waggling. 'Catch your deaths at your age.'

Elspeth exploded with laughter, the door closed behind John and Patrick and I glanced at one another sideways. Finally, Elspeth stopped cackling, saw that we were looking at her in not too amused fashion and quickly put the bacon and tomatoes into the Rayburn to keep hot. Then, she turned, and almost resentfully, said, 'Surely you don't think you're the only ones ever to have made love in the garden?'

The water from the outside tap had been exceedingly cold.

Patrick and I were married at Hinton Littlemoor. The first time, that is, and it was a wedding that most young women would dream about; the historic church filled with flowers, a horse-drawn carriage, a military guard of honour, the village green setting. Today, quite a few years later, I sat at the back of the church and thought about it. Since then prayers have been offered here for Patrick when he was horribly injured during the Falklands War, at a time when we had split up and, much later after we had remarried in a London Registry office and Justin had been born, there had been his christening. Births and marriages but, so far, no deaths. Not yet.

I did not want to work for MI5 again and I did not want Patrick to either. He and I have done our bit for Queen and country and had come very close to the death thing on several occasions.

The service was almost over and, as we stood for the final hymn, I heard the latch on the heavy door click as someone entered. Then, in the middle of the first verse, James Carrick came and stood beside me. I glanced at him questioningly but he shook his head and intimated that we could share my hymn book.

'Go in peace to love and serve the Lord!' John finally encouraged us from the altar steps.

'In the name of God, amen,' responded the congregation.

Patrick, mainly because he was the tallest, walked at the head of the choir carrying the cross as they came in procession down the aisle and went into the vestry, John bringing up the rear. We again knelt, faintly hearing John reciting the words of The Grace.

'I have to talk to you both,' Carrick said when we were on our feet.

'Patrick won't be a moment,' I said.

'Outside,' he said shortly and walked off.

With a group of others in the vestry Patrick was extricating himself from the folds of his robe.

'Is little Victoria going to be christened here or in Devon?'

one of the village matrons was gushing at him though the open doorway.

'She was baptised the night she was born,' Patrick replied. 'Dad drove down to Plymouth as she was premature and it wasn't thought she'd survive.'

'Oh, poor lamb, poor little lamb,' said the lady, catching sight of me and saying severely, 'You can never be too careful, can you?' as though I had been bungee-jumping right up until the last minute.

'James wants to talk to us,' I said to Patrick.

'James is here? It'll have to be quick – I shall have to get going.'

'I have an idea he's on business.'

'Well, don't look at me. I haven't done anything. Unless we infringed some kind of by-law last night when we – '

'Patrick!'

'Used the hose-pipe,' he concluded blithely. 'What are you looking so alarmed about?'

James was pacing slowly up and down in the lane, just outside the lych-gate, his hands rammed into his trouser pockets jingling loose change. When he caught sight of us he gestured across to where he had parked his car, went to it and got in the driving seat.

'Good to see you, Patrick,' he said, not smiling, when we reached him. 'I'm afraid I want to talk to you both – at the nick.'

'At the nick?' Patrick echoed. 'Sorry, old chum but I've got to get back to Camberley, starting just over an hour ago.'

'Do I ask you nicely again, or not?'

'What on earth's happened?' I asked.

'Norton's dead. Someone's killed him – very messily. And I know you were with him last night because he actually wrote the time and place to meet you in his diary. And there's a separate matter concerning an assault – or rather three assaults.'

Patrick groaned, gaze skywards, and loped off in the direction of the rectory. 'You'll have to wait while I make a phone call. I'll tell them I've broken my bloody neck.' He turned to add, 'It's not separate at all, you Jockanese nit-wit.'

'Please ignore that quite uncalled-for remark,' I said to James.

'Don't be daft,' Carrick said quietly. 'The man once saved my life.'

The news finally sank in. 'Norton's *dead*?'

'His wife found him comprehensively knifed this morning. In his study. He probably died around midnight.'

I got in the front passenger seat, shivery with shock, hardly able to take in what he was saying. 'It was probably at around ten thirty to a quarter to eleven when he left us.'

Carrick nodded. 'That would tie in with witness's statements with regard to the three men who were thrown into the river.' His anger surfaced. 'Why is it that as soon as you two hit Bath all hell breaks loose?'

'How did you know it was us?'

'The camera didn't quite hit the water and the description of Patrick was quite a good one. Someone said that for a moment he thought it was a rehearsal for a new James Bond film.'

'Norton would probably be alive now if I'd agreed to spend the night in an hotel with him,' I whispered.

Carrick looked appalled. 'He asked you?'

'I wouldn't have mentioned it if he hadn't, would I?' I retorted.

'Sorry. It was just that I – ' Something else occurred to him. 'Did you tell Patrick?'

I met the ice-blue gaze. 'No. But I'll have to now, won't I?'

He beat his hands a couple of times on the steering wheel. 'Bloody hell. This is all off the record and I shouldn't be asking you questions like this here but was the reason for Patrick's anger this guy taking photos?'

'Of course. He just popped out from hiding and started to take pictures of us. I think it might have been the same man as the one I noticed in the restaurant who kept looking at us.'

'Any idea why?'

'No, unless Norton's wife hired a private eye. Has he made a formal complaint?'

'He scarpered. '

'Oh.'

Patrick came back after another couple of minutes had elapsed, got in the back and without saying another word Carrick drove us into Bath. When we arrived we were interviewed separately, Patrick first.

'I do realise that this is difficult for you,' was Carrick's opening remark when it was my turn and before the tape recorder had been switched on and he had formally opened the interview. 'But . . . '

'You have your job to do even where friends are concerned,' I concluded for him.

He nodded soberly in response to this and then got down to business. 'First of all I'd like you to take me through your visit to Norton's house on Friday evening.'

As already intimated I have a very good memory and could remember the conversation I had had with him practically word for word. But I could still hardly believe that the man with whom I had so recently been out to dinner was dead.

'Take your time,' Carrick said.

I mustered my thoughts.

'Did he give you the impression that he was anxious about anything? Was he edgy?' Carrick asked when I had stopped talking.

'Not at all. His answer that he would probably end up by being sued if he wrote his autobiography was the nearest he got to anything like that. And he was very tongue-in-cheek when he said it.'

'You're a writer. How would you sum up the guy?'

'Dedicated, hard-working, highly reliable professionally but not with other men's wives, a bit of a lad but deep down quite ordinary, if not what used to be referred to as common.' After a pause I went on, 'I think it would help me help you if you gave me a few more details of how Norton died. Unless I really am a suspect.'

Carrick frowned momentarily and I recalled the light-hearted conversation I had had with Patrick about the possibility that he might slice Norton into rashers with one of his own scalpels if he made a pass at me. James, who knows Patrick better than most, was being very, very careful.

'It was a bloodbath,' he said after quite a long silence. 'Almost as though . . . ' His voice petered out for a moment as, obviously, the scene came vividly to his mind. 'Almost as though someone had done a PM on him.'

I decided not to dwell too closely on the implications of that immediately. 'So murder definitely was the name of the game, not robbery?'

'I can't think that robbery was the original motive. Nothing appears to have been disturbed but the room's so full of stuff it's anyone's guess if anything's missing. The wife's fairly useless in that respect and says she hardly ever goes in there. Apparently there's a cleaning woman and she's not back from a weekend trip to see her brother in Brighton until tonight.'

'What about Norton's brother, Max, and his wife?'

'What about them?'

'Were they in the house last night?'

'No, they were away too – spent the night with friends in Bradford on Avon.' Then, seeming to realise that he was the one being grilled he said, for the benefit of the tape recorder, 'Miss Langley doesn't look very well. I shall give her a rest and a cup of tea.' He switched off the machine and asked the WPC sitting next to him to fetch us both one.

When we were alone I said, 'I was in that room. Do you want me to take a look to see if – '

He interrupted with, 'Ingrid, I can't . . . '

'Why not? You use criminal profilers who are not actually part of any police force. What's wrong with someone who was recently at the scene of the crime having a look and who might just notice an aberration?'

'You're a possible witness,' he pointed out.

'Sometimes, surely, you have to bend the rules slightly.'

'Yeah,' Carrick acknowledged slowly. He chewed the end of the pen upon which he had been carrying out a fairly sustained dental assault without apparently noticing what he was doing. 'I still don't want you to go into that room. Even though the body's been removed it's – '

'James, I'm sure I've seen worse things than that.'

He sighed. 'I'd forgotten your MI5 days for a moment. I'll think about it.'

'How did the killer get in?'

'There's no sign of forced entry. According to Mrs Norton, who said she went to bed as usual, her husband usually locked up. They don't share a room – not surprising after what you told me.'

'Is she upset?' I asked baldly.

'Well, I could hardly say the woman's devastated. Horribly shocked of course, after finding him. It was enough to turn anyone's stomach. She said she had no idea anything was amiss and didn't notice the bloody footprints on the hall carpet as it's red. His killer must have quietly let himself out afterwards. No fingerprints – whoever did it was wearing gloves.'

'There must have been blood on their clothing though.'

'Almost certainly.'

'There were long curtains at the windows – right down to

the floor – but they seemed to cover most of one short wall. Was there a door behind them too?'

'Yes. Narrow french doors. They were locked on the inside.'

'What was the actual cause of death?'

'I haven't had the PM report yet but there had been a severe blow or blows to the back of the head. He never stood a chance.'

'Patrick didn't do it,' I said.

James tossed the pen down on the table between us. 'I know that. Someone with his training doesn't have to butcher people.' Looking a bit driven he continued, 'When I re-start the tape I shall have to ask what you did when you got home last night and whether anyone was with you and could remember what time you got back.'

'No problem at all,' I said. 'Patrick hadn't eaten so his mother fixed him something and then went up to bed. John had already gone up. Patrick and I went into the living room, I took everything off and then we rushed out into the garden and made love under the *Viburnum bodnantense* "Dawn".'

For a moment Carrick didn't know where to put his face. Then he yielded to his first reaction and laughed. Wiping the grin off his face with an effort he said, 'That's one of those alibis that has a twenty-four-caret ring of truth to it.'

Just then our tea arrived and when the tape-recorder had been switched on again I related the previous evening as accurately as I was able and then gave an account of the walk from the restaurant to The Cheshire Cat. I ended by saying, 'Do you think this is anything to do with his work? The Bates case? And that Greece job sounded as though questionable people and a huge amount of money might be involved.'

A finger was waggled admonishingly at me. 'Kindly allow the Jockanese nit-wit to work in his own fashion.'

'At least tell me if Patrick's going to be had up for assault.'

He made me wait for a moment or two before saying, 'As I

said earlier, the photographer did a runner so I can't press charges if he hasn't made a complaint.'

'You'll need to ask Mrs Norton about him,' I interposed quickly.

'I already have. What did this guy in the restaurant look like – assuming for a moment that it was the same man who took the photos?'

'He was quite unremarkable. Gormless-looking in a way. I didn't see him standing up but would say he was of medium height and slight build. He had short, pale brown hair, not much of it, and quite thick glasses so I couldn't tell what colour his eyes were. He was wearing grey trousers, a green finely-checked shirt and a V-necked grey pullover. Oh, and black slip-on shoes.'

'Mrs Norton denies all knowledge of private investigators or photographers. As for the others who Patrick threw in the river . . .'

'Well?' I blared at him when he stopped speaking.

Carrick smiled reflectively. 'Rumour has it that they're members of a gang consisting of several brothers, cousins and others we've nicknamed the Neanderthals on account of their long arms and conspicuous lack of skull contents. They inhabit some kind of rat-hole in Bristol and live on the pro-ceeds of mugging, drugs-pushing, and attacking old ladies to steal their handbags. Any members of the public who feel strongly enough about their presence in this lovely city of ours and wish to deter further visits have my blessing to chuck them into anything that happens to be handy.'

And with that he brought the interview to a close.

'Did he tell you if the other two little shits have made formal complaints?' Patrick enquired, the questioned delivered in an undertone, as by this time we were in a nearby pub, but nevertheless impassioned.

I told him what James had said, not really blaming him for leaving Patrick on the hook but also recognising that he had acted in self-defence. I went on, 'He has to take the professional attitude, you know that. You'd be just the same if the shoe was on the other foot.'

The man in my life swore under his breath and then buried his nose in his beer tankard.

'He made it quite clear it's none of our business now,' I said.

'Go home and forget about it,' Patrick reiterated dully.

'Yes. I didn't tell him you were keeping tabs on me last night though. Did you?'

'No, I thought it might muddy the waters. D'you reckon you would recognise that photographer again?'

'Only if it was the same man who was in the restaurant. I didn't get a good look at the one by the river as I was dazzled by the flashes. Look, I really think we should keep out of James's hair.'

'What was his reaction to the stuff on Max?'

'Why are you asking me? You spoke to him as well.'

'It was all very formal: his way, I think, of distancing himself from the fact that he and Joanna are close friends of ours. No, I was read the Riot Act after I'd said my piece and then railroaded out.'

I realised, belatedly, that Patrick was actually rather offended. 'He just said he would interview them. But they were staying with friends in Bradford on Avon last night.'

'A bit convenient, wouldn't you say?'

Placing a hand over one of his for a moment I slowly said, 'I would say you have real bee in your bonnet over this Max. Let James sort it out.'

Patrick smiled ruefully. 'And bless his tartan reach-me-downs he'll explore all the obvious things first like the bitch of a wife, ditto daughter, bastard son and then all the murderers Norton helped to shove in the slammer during his career and then. . . ' He broke off and shrugged. 'No, I do the man no credit at all. He's a bloody good copper.' The fine eyes regarded me closely. 'Do you want to go home?'

'You mean Devon?'

'Yes, I've a fortnight's leave.'

'I thought you were supposed to be – '

'I told them to poke it.' Then, obviously still thirsting for blood, he outlined a few picturesque and more than slightly obscene fates that might befall a certain politician if he himself were to be present in Camberley the following day.

'You really want to go for this D12 thing, don't you?'

'I'd need to know a lot more about what's being proposed first but, basically, yes.'

'There would have to be a much better structure.'

Patrick slowly revolved his empty glass on the mat a few times and then looked up, fully aware that this was the mother of his children laying down the first of several ground rules. 'And?' he enquired softly.

'If you're in charge you shouldn't have to take all the risks.'

'Without wishing to sound conceited that might happen only when they've cloned me several times.'

'Heaven forbid!' I exclaimed and he laughed out loud at my fervour. But, undaunted, I continued, 'So are we talking about an undercover unit with exactly the same brief to investigate interference, foreign or otherwise, with those involved with national security? There were at least twenty-five of us in our heyday so this time you and who else, for goodness sake?'

'Something much smaller is envisaged with the department that took over the work continuing with the more routine stuff. They're having problems.'

'It sounds as though they're out of their depth and need a trouble-shooter.'

'Basically you're right. Another drink?'

'I think I'll have a vodka and orange.'

'You haven't had one of those for ages.'

'No, but that's what I used to drink in those days so perhaps it will get me in the right frame of mind to talk about it.'

He went over to the bar.

I did not want even to think about it, that was the problem. Those few years when we had worked for D12 had been a nightmare, interspersed with a few, a very few, fantastically good times. We had laughed quite a lot as well, sometimes, and cried. We had also been beaten up, drugged, shot, kidnapped, trapped in crashed cars and tortured. Despite and during all this we had conceived two children, a bit of a miracle after Patrick's Falkland's War injuries, and adopted two more. Was the price I would have to pay for future marital and family peace not mine at all but Patrick's? Was it fair to expect a man who was only happy when he was fully physically and mentally stretched to endure a desk-job for the rest of his working life? Even if he left the army and turned his back for ever on MI5 what would he do then? Security consultancy work like so many of his peers? Run an adventure and survival school for bored city executives? No, as James Carrick with unnerving accuracy had put it, in desperation Patrick would finish up by going abroad somewhere to run a small ethical war.

Perhaps it would be better, assuming that he stayed in one piece, if he followed his inclinations, and with official backing, not to mention remuneration, right on my doorstep. There did not actually seem to be much choice.

When he came back I said, 'There's something I have to tell you. I'm not sure that it's very important now but I think you ought to know anyway.'

'Fire away,' he said evenly.

'Norton asked me to spend the night at an hotel with him. Obviously, I refused.'

After a meaningful silence Patrick raised his glass. 'To us,' he said.

We drank and it was never mentioned again.

'If I understand this correctly,' I said thoughtfully after this significant toast, 'You'd like us to explore other possibilities of this case, the ones that James might not address immediately, with a view to getting back into the swing of things – a sort of dress rehearsal for working for MI5 again.'

'Well – yes,' he said.

'Make a start by investigating Max?' I suggested. 'Break into their flat when they're out, eh? Have a look in all those boxes and see what he's really been up to?'

'Sometimes, Ingrid,' Patrick murmured, 'I love you to bits.'

4

'I thought I might find you both here,' said James Carrick, arriving all at once and drawing up a chair.

'What can I get you to drink?' Patrick asked solicitously.

'Let me get you one,' Carrick offered.

'No, I'm driving.'

'In that case I'll just have orange juice ˙ I'm working.'

'Ice?'

'Please.'

I gazed after Patrick as he left the table, and said, 'Thus endeth a short lesson in mutual forgiveness.'

Carrick nodded. 'It's difficult for both of us. But I thought he was . . .'

'So did I. But it appears that he's as good as told those in charge to go boil their heads. Anyway, he's now on leave.'

I thought for a moment that I had revealed too much but James just smiled, his mind obviously light years away from the subject of possible maverick investigators. 'I've thought about it,' he said.

'You'd like me to have a look in Norton's study?'

'Yes. When could you do it?'

'Now?'

'That would be extremely helpful.'

'Can Patrick come too?'

'I'm not too sure I can justify that – to higher authority, I mean.'

'But I'm quite nervous and his strong, supportive presence would enable me to carry out my public duty.'

'You're a scheming woman, aren't you, hen?'

In the event, SOCO did not finish their preliminary investigations until a little after three thirty that afternoon and when Carrick, Patrick and I threaded our way on foot between the vehicles parked in the drive the area was still partially cordoned off with fluttering blue and white incident tape. My previous journey to this house seemed to have taken place years ago, if not in another lifetime.

James asked us to wait with the constable standing just outside the front door and went in. A couple of minutes later he reappeared and told us we could enter.

'I'd like to go in alone,' I said.

'Are you sure?' James asked.

'Yes, no distractions. I was almost alone before as Norton's wife virtually ignored me.'

'Please don't touch anything or tread within the chalked areas in the hall or study where we've encircled footprints and other possible evidence.'

I went into the room I had first entered, the room on the left, the windows of which overlooked the front garden. Carrick had not revealed whether it was thought the murderer had come in here, he had only said that the trail of footprints suggested that whoever it was had let themselves out of the front door. Although everywhere had obviously been dusted for fingerprints there were no chalked or other marks on the pale blue carpet so I assumed it was safe to roam around.

Nothing much seemed to have changed. There was a Sunday newspaper on a low table, unopened and pristine, one of the armchairs was in a slightly different position to what I remembered, pushed back nearer the wall, in fact I could see the indentations on the carpet where the castors had previously stood. Perhaps someone had shifted it slightly so Mrs Norton could seat herself at a slight distance from the crowd of police and their activities.

I turned and left the room. There was nothing to be learned in here.

Carefully avoiding the marked areas on the carpet I slowly

walked down the hall and past the long-case clock. I wondered how many other hallways it had stood in and people's lifetimes it had impartially ticked away. There were a few portraits in oils on the walls that I had not really looked at closely on my first visit. They were the usual stiff Victorians who gazed down impassively, adding to my feeling of a watching and waiting presence. Were they Norton ancestors or had the paintings been bought at one of Bath's many antiques shops? I had an idea it might be the latter.

The door to the study was wide open and the butcher's shop smell issued out and encompassed me. It became obvious, right from the moment I entered, that in this room I would be unable to walk around freely as Carrick's team had created a no-go area of a large percentage of the floor-space. As I already knew, the colour-scheme was of deep rose and burgundy, shades that I had expected would conceal the full horror of which Carrick had hinted. What I had forgotten was that a lot of blood would actually show up as black.

I was standing in a slaughterhouse.

The efflux was everywhere, glistening in places, drying matt in others, as though someone had thrown a bucketful of blood into the room. And I knew that even though everything possible had been done to remove matter relating to the corpse Norton had been disembowelled: there were trails of slime and mucus on the carpet and on the spines of the books in the shelves behind the desk. And another unmistakable smell.

On the floor his dead outline had been carefully marked out before the body was taken to the mortuary, a life reduced to a white line, as though a child had drawn around someone lying on the carpet. This is the stark truth of murder; it is not only about killing but reducing a human being to mere chalk marks, a personality to so much carrion.

Something told me that Norton had been seated in the same chair as I had, although this too was in a slightly different position, and that whoever had killed him had entered the room without him hearing them and struck him from behind. I could not sit in it even if I had wished to as it was now in the no-go area but I stood where it had been and stooped slightly so my field of vision was at roughly the same level as it had been on the Friday evening. Then, after a couple of minutes, back aching, I straightened and made my way behind the desk as far as I could and scanned along the shelves.

'Are you all right, Ingrid?' Carrick's voice called from the hall when I had just about completed what I was doing.

'Come in if you want to,' I replied.

Both men did, Patrick stopping abruptly just inside the doorway, eyes wide, a muttered exclamation on his lips.

Indicating the shelves I said, 'I think that some of this stuff has been moved around a bit as though someone's had a search through it. Or has your team done so?'

Carrick shook his head. 'We've not yet examined anything on the shelves and I want to be present when it's all gone through carefully.'

'And the shrunken head's gone.'

'Shrunken head!' both men said in unison.

'I wasn't sure what it was when I first saw it. But when I stood up I could see it more clearly. Come to think of it the specimen jars are in slightly different positions from what I remember too.'

'Norton could have shifted things around himself looking for something,' Patrick pointed out.

'Aye, he could,' Carrick said on a gusty sigh. 'Many thanks though, Ingrid, for coming in.'

'You said there was no sign of forced entry. Surely that means that Norton, or someone else, let his killer in.'

'It's still possible he got in through a window that hadn't been properly locked. I haven't had a chance to talk to the SOCO team yet.'

Craning his neck, Patrick was reading the labels on the jars. 'A shrunken head was a little out of context, wouldn't you say? I mean, all the other stuff seems to be in connection with genuine research.'

'I think he had quite a sense of humour,' I said.

He looked at me quizzically. 'Are they funny though?'

'No, not in *themselves*. It's macabre but the sort of thing a forensic pathologist might just have knocking around. Someone might have given it to him. Or, who knows, he might have been studying how it was done.'

Patrick said, 'Umm,' in the way people do when they're not convinced. Then, 'Suppose it belongs to Max?'

'Ingrid mentioned Norton's views on his brother – and the fact that he had a native art collection,' Carrick said. 'Interesting. I'll ask him.'

'You might like to run an international check on Max,' Patrick continued. 'I did. Ingrid's annoyed with me but I always check out the complete strangers she shuts herself up in dark houses with. It's a husband thing. Can we go?'

'I take it your conscience made you give James that lead about Max,' I said later.

'It was never my intention to keep him in the dark about the man,' Patrick responded.

'If you're still keen to have a nose around the flat we'll have to mount a watch on the house to wait until Max and his wife go out. That won't be easy in the present circumstances. And even more complicated with someone living in the rooms below,' I added, regretting having suggested it in the first place. 'Unless you were thinking of just storming in and taking the place apart having tied them to a bedpost . . . ' I ground to a halt on perceiving the beatific smile now upon his face. 'Patrick, we can't!'

'Think.' And when I did not comment further he

continued, 'Of course we can. We have it on very good authority that this guy is *bent*. He's done business with foreign pirates involving guns and drugs to keep himself in pink gin and cavier. There's probably a couple of Kalashnikovs and God knows what else stowed away in those boxes of his and no doubt he knows how to use them. Nothing short of an armed raid will do. We'd be daft if we settled for anything less.'

'James isn't stupid,' I said mulishly, although knowing that he was right. 'He'll know it was us.'

'If they do report it to the police, which they probably won't if there really is a load of illegal goodies up there, there'll be nothing to connect it with us. We'll leave Hinton Littlemoor, saying we're going home. Only we won't. And we'll wear masks.'

'Weapons?' I enquired, aware that his Smith and Wesson, which no one has ever asked him to hand back, was in the secret cubby box in the Range Rover.

'A knife should do – just to frighten him a bit. The British are terrified of knives.'

With good reason as far as Patrick was concerned, I thought. I said, 'Don't forget his wife.'

'Who might be even worse than he is. Yes, you're right.'

That hadn't been what I had meant at all and well he knew it.

'I've a surprise for you,' Elspeth said when we got back to the rectory. 'I've asked James and Joanna for dinner tonight so you can all have a nice get-together.' A huge joint of beef was in a roasting tin on the table before her into which she was rubbing dry mustard and ground black pepper.

Soldiers are used to having to change plans right at the last minute and of course Elspeth had absolutely no idea what had already transpired that day.

Patrick beamed at her and said, 'Great!'

She regarded him. Elspeth is the only person in the world who can make him actually wriggle. 'I take it you weren't planning on leaving tonight.'

'To be honest,' he said, 'we'd been thinking of doing just that.' He eyed the joint. 'But another few hours of your wonderful company . . . '

'Don't you mean cooking?' she said with pretend ire.

He kissed her cheek, laughing.

'Well, it's far too large for just us four,' said Elspeth. 'And you can only eat so much cold meat and cottage pie.' She giggled and then said, 'I won it in the pub raffle.'

A little later, when Patrick and I were alone, he said, 'This is even better. We'll give them plenty of wine – not Joanna as she's expecting but she can drive James home – everyone goes to bed semi-plastered and then we sneak out and raid Max's place. Superb alibi.'

'I'm heavily relying on you to ensure that we don't need one,' I said.

Even though, when we had worked for MI5, we had acted with full official backing – well, for most of the time – there had never been any desire on our part to advertise our presence to the local police force. ID cards can be, and sometimes were, shown in order to establish *bona fides* but when you are working undercover this is positively the last thing you want to do. So when Patrick and I warily approached the Norton home that night our procedures were not only well-rehearsed, but second-nature. We were outwardly calm although hyper-alert and I only bumped into Patrick the once when he halted suddenly under the confounded weeping ash tree.

We intended to enter through the rear of the house for the very good reason that, as the top storey had almost certainly at one time been servants' quarters, direct access to it would be via the back stairs. This would also, if our guesses were correct, lengthen the odds of us coming into contact with anyone who lived in the rest of the building.

The impromptu dinner party had been a huge success, more than adequately rewarding Elspeth's considerable efforts. Joanna, glowingly pregnant but still retaining her slim figure, had permitted herself a small glass of the excellent red Burgundy Patrick had bought and Patrick and I had also been fairly abstemious on the grounds that we were sharing the driving early the following morning. Everyone else had imbibed well, even John, who had jokingly asked if it was a rehearsal for Christmas Day.

He and Elspeth would sleep well and hopefully hear no night-time goings and comings.

I was too experienced to ask questions about things like burglar alarm systems or locks as Patrick is an expert at bypassing them. The only danger was if the back door was securely bolted, a detail that would force us to enter by a window. As we emerged cautiously from beneath the tree it became obvious that people were still up on the ground and first floors as too many lights were on merely to have been left on for security reasons. The upper floor was in utter darkness.

Dressed in dark-blue tracksuits, thin gloves to avoid leaving fingerprints and with camouflage cream on our faces in lieu of masks – despite what Patrick had said both they and balaclavas impair sight and hearing – we silently made our way down the side of the house and into the Portmeirion-style courtyard. I already knew that the drive was dark but oddly, we encountered no security lighting in the close proximity of the building. I was fairly unconcerned anyway as those sold for domestic use have a habit of switching on every time a cat or even a hedgehog wanders by and people indoors grow to ignore them. They deter casual but not determined intruders. The real problem would be the presence of dogs although there had been no sign of any on Friday.

We did not ascend the curving flight of steps but bore sharp left, skirted the top of another flight that plunged downwards to what was probably a cellar and, avoiding tripping over a low plant trough by a whisker, arrived at a large door. There was a single step up into a porch and another small disaster was averted when I just managed to catch a broom, the bristles of which I had trodden on, before it fell over. In the next moment Patrick had turned the door knob. The door was unlocked.

Within, all was in complete darkness. Patrick switched on his pencil-slim burglar's torch, the light from it picking out the details of a medium-sized room, probably a one-time scullery, the floor strewn with outdoor shoes of different sorts and sizes, a car wheel without the tyre, a set of ramps and a metal box on its side, some of the tools it contained spilling out. I closed the door and we stepped carefully through or over these, making for the stone stairs visible beyond a wall-mounted and very full coat rack. An old fancy chimney pot at the bottom of the stairs served to hold walking sticks, fishing rods and a keep-net. These were all smothered in dust, fair comment perhaps on the Norton family's exercise habits.

At the bottom of the stairs we stood quite still for a few moments, listening. Faintly, a radio or television studio audience could be heard laughing and then a door banged and afterwards there was complete silence. Patrick touched my arm and we started up the stairs. I was on the second stair when there was the sound of a lavatory being flushed, much closer than the previous noises, and footsteps that sounded as though they were rapidly approaching the room we had just left. As soundlessly as possible we fled upwards and did not pause until we reached a narrow landing on the first floor.

Someone came into the room below, switched on the light and a man's voice swore loudly. Then he exited, slamming the door but leaving the light on.

Patrick whispered, 'The maniac driver, no doubt. I wonder what he's looking for?'

Cautiously, we began to ascend the next flight. A short but wide passageway had led off the landing, furnished only with a chair and an old chest of drawers and ending at a door at the top of two steps. A slit of light had been visible beneath it.

The stairs were narrow and curving here and Patrick paused to switch off his torch as we passed a tiny window. Peeping out as I went by I could just see the row of garages on the other side of the house, one single wall-light illuminating the parking area in front of them. The Nortons certainly were not extravagant with lighting.

As if to emphasise this a dim illumination became visible as we neared the top of the flight of stairs. Patrick raised a warning hand and I stopped and let him go on ahead. Seconds later he beckoned me on again and I joined him on a much larger landing that had several closed doors off it. The light was coming from a tiny table lamp set on a carved chest against one wall and was obviously the kind of light people leave on in case anyone wants to visit the bathroom during the night. I could hear women's voices coming from behind the nearest door.

We went up again, the steps even more narrow and cramped. There had been no carpet on any flight and it was extremely difficult to walk on the stone treads without making a noise. We came to another tiny window on a tight bend. And then Patrick froze, crouched, listening. In the next moment he had set off again at speed and I followed, desperately trying not to make scuffing sounds with my clothing against the walls.

At the top there was a flash of light as he swung the torch

around briefly and then utter darkness. Not unused to this kind of thing I groped around to my left when I arrived and encountered him and then my hand was grabbed and I was pulled into what appeared to be a space between two large cupboards. It was dusty and I fought back a sneeze.

There was no mistaking it: someone was very quietly coming up the stairs behind us.

There was a neat and virtually soundless *pas de deux* during which Patrick and I changed places. Several tense seconds elapsed during which I held my breath. But my partner was engaged in the opposite and I could hear him scenting the air like an animal. There was then another seemingly endless silence.

A dark shape emerged from the deeper darkness of the stairwell and rose until it was on a level with and slightly beyond where we were standing. Then, Patrick pounced. I could see no detail but knew that one hand would be clamped over the mouth, the other arm like a band of steel around the throat.

There was a muffled sound that could only be described as a squeak. Unaccountably I then sensed Patrick relaxing, releasing his hold. The tiny beam of light from his torch shone into the face of his catch.

Joanna.

Recriminations, explanations and the like cannot be conducted in silence and virtual darkness. Possibly working on the principle that Carrick's wife and former CID sergeant was now in for a penny, in for a pound Patrick, no doubt seething, left us and went over to the front door of the flat. There was a short pause while he examined the locks – from where I was standing they looked antiquated – and then his set of skeleton keys was in his hand and with swift movements of a strong wrist he was inside.

I detained Joanna with a hand on the sleeve of her jacket and we waited.

No burglar alarm, angry shouts, strangling noises or evidence of bloody mayhem.

'There's no one here,' Patrick returned to whisper through the open doorway.

We went in, closing the door.

Patrick switched on a light in the hall having closed all the inner doors. This did indeed reveal that Joanna was facing an ice-capped volcano. She did not appear to be too worried about it.

'James knew you were up to something,' she reported, of necessity, quietly. 'But obviously he can't tail you.'

'So he sent his wife and brand-new family?' Patrick asked, or rather hissed.

'No, James doesn't know.'

'I can't believe he won't miss you and that bloke-bending perfume you're wearing.' This with slight alarm.

'So we'd better get on with it, hadn't we?' she responded sweetly.

'I shall do the searching. Both of you keep watch.'

I did not argue, aware that he did not dare risk one Titian hair of Joanna's head being harmed. This was not to say that I did not resent it. Joanna though snapped, 'I'm sure I'm quite capable of doing that on my own. Besides, you'll get it over with a lot faster if Ingrid helps you.'

'Are you going to report back to James?' I had to know.

'It depends on what you find.'

Patrick usually has to have the last word. 'I just hope you realise the consequences if we're caught,' he said to her back as she turned to go back onto the landing. I went to follow but then he shrugged and beckoned me closer. 'She's right – it'll be quicker if you give me a hand.'

One side of the carpeted hallway was piled with cardboard boxes and wooden crates. Some of the former were unopened cases of French and South African wine, the packer's seals still intact, and Patrick quickly sorted through them and lifted them to one side. Obviously he was going to waste no time taking trouble to leave things exactly as we had found them. He does not normally use his throwing-knife for such tasks but took it from his pocket, sprang the blade – I have never got used to the ghastly slicing click – and started cutting the string around the others.

I was actually glad to be wearing gloves as what some of these boxes contained was anyone's guess. True enough, as I started on the first that Patrick had opened it was obvious that it was very damp and a smell of decomposition rose up from limp, stained cardboard. Dubiously, I began to lift off a layer of bubble-wrap.

'You'll have to work a bit faster than that,' said Patrick without looking up from what he was doing.

'There's something dead in here,' I said, on the verge of gagging.

'So they shoved in something off-putting to stop anyone looking any further,' was the ruthlessly pragmatic response. 'Tip the whole bloody lot out onto the floor. For God's sake woman, we haven't much time!'

I tipped the whole bloody lot out onto the floor. Like large hairy potatoes the shrunken heads rolled to all corners of the hallway, shedding a few ears like pieces of dried apple skins in the process and releasing a stench that defied description. Somehow, I desisted in throwing up and, or, completely freaking out.

'Patrick,' I gasped. 'These look like Europeans!'

He had paused to spare an interested glance. 'They might go that pale colour when they're put in the shrink stuff. Don't worry about it. Is that all that was in there?'

Not for the first time, I realised the kind of sights that soldiers' eyes have seen. 'Yes.'

He hefted across another box to me and, having cut through all the string on the others, burrowed into one of them himself. 'I'm convinced the placing of these is deliberate. Some hooch and a few nasties near the door to act as bait and then put the frighteners on common thieves, the more important stuff farther in, higher up. No, this one's full of carved wooden antelopes – airport art, if you ask me.'

My next box contained just travel brochures and maps.

It seemed to take hours but methodically we worked our way through the contents of the boxes in the hall and then, by the light of a bigger torch Patrick had found in the kitchen and having drawn the curtains, two crates in a bedroom which were difficult to open and yielded clothing wrapped around several thousand American dollars in used bills, four old but apparently in working order handguns, a positively ancient Lee Enfield rifle and a motley collection of slightly rusty but otherwise sharp knives, one of which was stained with what looked like blood but could have been anything.

'Norton said there were cases of stuff in his part of the house,' I recalled. 'And in a garage.'

'You may depend the others indoors won't contain anything important,' Patrick replied. 'We might have to come back to break into the garage. Now, the living room.'

'Nothing stored in the other rooms?'

'Nothing out in the open. We simply don't have time to look under floorboards and places like that. Check with Joanna, would you?'

Joanna, understandably, was getting impatient. 'You've been *ages*,' she whispered. 'We really ought not to stay any longer. Someone's still up downstairs – I can hear them moving around.'

'Sure it wasn't us?'

'No.'

When I relayed her concerns back to Patrick in the living room, where he had risked switching on a small lamp – the curtains were made of thick brocade material and also lined – he looked at his watch and, in the obligatory undertone, said, 'It's just after one forty. If Max and his wife have gone out to eat they would have been back by now, ditto theatre or cinema. They might have gone to a club in which case they'll be a while yet.'

It was on the tip of my tongue to interrupt and query if one did those kind of things when one's brother had been savagely murdered but stopped just in time when I remembered that Patrick had, not so long ago, lost his own brother in ghastly circumstances. And from what we had heard about him Max Norton could not be described as a caring sort of man.

Patrick was saying, 'But get ready to abandon ship if Joanna gives the alarm. I've checked and there's some good solid ivy growing just outside the windows of this room. Brittle, I know, but it would have to do.'

He went straight over to yet another stack of boxes against the wall behind the door, and set to work. Some of them were more wooden crates, others strong cardboard, a few odd-sized ones seemingly purpose-built for particular items and made of plywood. They contained china dinner services, glassware, a couple of Chinese vases and one highly obscene piece involving carved male figures.

Patrick tut-tutted, chuckled and rammed it back into its packing. 'That's the lot. Nothing.'

The other rooms had been barely furnished but this interior was opulent with pale cream carpeting and a magnificent Chinese rug in the centre. The colours of other soft furnishings in the room echoed those of the rug; soft apricot, pale green and terracotta. But the collection of primitive art dominated all.

Mostly fashioned from dark-coloured materials; wood, stone and hide, the figures and artefacts turned what would have been a restful retreat into some kind of gloomy museum, almost a burial chamber. The sheer power of some of the items was a tangible force. I walked across the rug to look more closely at a group of five figures about four feet in height. They were standing on a low shelf facing into the room and were all different for they had been carved from life, or rather, death. One was a woman, the others men. They stared at me with their sea-shell and bead eyes. Hair had been fashioned from different types of grass, now disintegrating, but the clothing was real and had perhaps belonged to the people the figures represented. They had a faint musty smell.

I had remembered more details of the newspaper article I had read. Almost certainly stolen, these were the *tau tau* Norton had mentioned; grave guardians, effigies of the dead made by the Torajan people of Sulawesi. The Torajans believe that the ghosts of the departed reside in the figures, something I could easily believe as they stared back at me with their bead eyes, not smiling.

Patrick was listening again. 'A car's coming down the drive! Get Joanna!'

But Joanna had heard it too and had already come to warn us.

Patrick turned off the lamp and opened the lower part of one of the large sash windows. Like the rest of the house it was well-maintained and slid up with only a soft rumbling sound. Through a narrow gap in the curtains he looked out, withdrawing quickly when the beams from car headlights swung around the drive in front of the house. They were switched off and we heard the engine murmur into silence.

'As soon as they've gone from sight we go,' Patrick said. 'Climb down the ivy for about six feet and then there's a drainpipe from the guttering up top that slopes across the wall to the right to a bigger pipe. Put your feet on the pipe, hands on the window ledge above it or whatever else you can find. Then shin down the large drainpipe to the ground. You'll have to go like blazes to try to avoid your weight breaking the ivy or pulling it from the wall. I'll go first. Got that?'

'Roger,' Joanna said.

I made off with one small item I had noticed just before the light went out.

5

'Serve her right if she has quads,' Patrick said later that night.

He did not mean it of course, this was natural male ire after the mother-to-be had walked away without a scratch while he himself had sprained his ankle – his own left ankle, that is, the right one is of man-made construction following his injuries suffered during the Falkland's War – falling the final ten feet after losing his grip on the large drain pipe. It is actually very difficult to climb up or down anything when you have no sensation in one foot. I had not escaped unscathed and had a grazed hand plus the makings of a few bruises. We were also both utterly filthy.

By the time we had sneaked back into the rectory, using a route that Patrick has never told his mother about but which would not be attempted lightly by a burglar, and showered, it was a little after three a.m. I collected all our dirty clothing from the floor where we had dropped it and shoved it into plastic bags, having first removed something from the large pocket of my tracksuit jacket.

'I thought you looked a funny shape,' said Patrick from in bed. 'Oh no, not another one. You really do have a fixation about those damned things.'

'It's the one that was in John Norton's study,' I told him.

'You can't possibly be sure of that. They all look the same.'

'No, they don't. This one has a missing front tooth and the hair has a piece of red string knotted into it.'

He was not impressed. 'I'll think about it in the morning. Please go and wash your hands again and then come to bed.' Angry with himself for falling off a house, afraid of no longer being fit for any new and demanding job, horribly afraid of being too old, Patrick then flung himself under the covers.

But it was already the morning and it seemed as though I had hardly closed my eyes when Elspeth knocked and brought us some tea. I then realised I had left the shrunken head on the dressing table.

She noticed it, of course: Elspeth, like her son, is a noticing person.

'Oh, how fascinating!' she exclaimed in ringing tones and I felt Patrick start as he awoke from an, unusually for him, heavy sleep. 'Where on earth did you get it? I read once how they break all the skull up and remove the pieces and then sew it up again and subject it to some kind of heat-treatment – in one of their hot stone ovens, I expect. I wonder if they mashed up and drew out the brain with hooks up the nose first like the Egyptians did when they were mummifying bodies? You won't be long will you?' she went on, dumping down the tea. 'I've got some really wonderful black pudding from the Sausage Shop in Bath and you know how quickly it gets overcooked.'

'There's probably a WI recipe leaflet that tells you all about it,' Patrick muttered when she had gone and we both laughed until we cried.

'Seriously though,' Patrick said. 'Last night was a fiasco. Oh, we found some weapons and dosh but nothing really important.'

'I think the important stuff was right there in front of our eyes,' I said. 'There were things from Easter island – carvings of what I seem to remember are called bird-men, and stones engraved with signs and pictures of animals. And those *tau tau*, the ones Professor Norton told me about. They've nearly all been plundered from where they originated and sold on the blackmarket. Perhaps the whole collection's stolen property.'

'It's not exactly in the same bracket as drugs and arms-dealing though, is it?'

I decided to let time prove me correct or otherwise and

said, 'You realise Joanna isn't the kind of girl not to tell James about our little sortie last night?'

Inspecting his sprained ankle he said, 'I'm expecting him to arrive hooting and skirling on the breakfast table.'

'James, how nice to see you!' said Elspeth, as though she had not seen him in months instead of just the previous evening. 'Tea or coffee?'

'I hope I'm not intruding,' said Carrick stiffly, having accepted a cup of coffee.

'Of course you are,' Patrick told him, but smiling.

Carrick sat down, giving Patrick the kind of look that probably hadn't been aired since Bannockburn. 'A little bird told me that . . . ' he began heavily, throwing a worried glance in Elspeth's direction.

'Do you want me to go?' she asked, having previously coped with MI5 in strength in her living room, Patrick arriving home more dead than alive on more than one occasion and, as she herself had once put it, 'armed men in the onion bed'.

'Not at all,' Patrick told her. 'Anyway, you're agog to know where Ingrid got the shrunken head from.' To me he said, 'I think you ought to go and get it.'

This I duly did, placing it next to the cruet.

Patrick said, 'Have they made a complaint?'

'No, Bath appears to be brimming with people like that,' Carrick replied sarcastically.

'That means Max and Co have something to hide.'

James gazed, frowning, at the head for a moment and then looked at us. 'I'll say it the once. Four words. Go home – stay there.'

Possibly to cover her slight embarrassment Elspeth picked up the shrunken head by the red cord in the hair and peered at it. Then into the silence that Carrick's words had engendered she said, 'It's very heavy seeing the bones have all been removed, isn't it?' Prodding, she added, 'Although, come to think of it the top's quite crunchy. Is this thing highly important forensic evidence?'

'Not *now*,' Carrick told her with arctic politeness.

A pair of scissors was already in her hand. 'May I . . . ?'

'Mother's a doctor's daughter,' Patrick said to James, obviously having trouble in keeping a straight face.

Carrick said, 'If you put it back together exactly as it was before.'

'Naturally,' Elspeth said, a bit offended.

'Okay,' Patrick said to Carrick. 'We went in there and we examined the contents of about two dozen boxes, crates and what have you before we were disturbed. We found quite a lot of rubbish, several old handguns, a Lee Enfield rifle that probably last saw service in the Kyber Pass first time around and several thousand American dollars in used bills. Ingrid reckons that some of the native art collection in the living room might be stolen property. I have to say that I expected to find something a lot more meaningful than that but we couldn't transfer our attention to stuff that's apparently in the garages as they came back before we had a chance. I'm saying "they" but I'm not sure of the actual identity of the people who arrived by car. I didn't think it wise to stop and find out. I'm convinced though that we would have discovered something if we'd had more time. This bloke's got real form.'

'I'm sure it's just gravel that's been put in to keep it in shape,' Elspeth was saying to herself, having laid the scissors aside to unravel the red cord first.

'You've put me in an extremely difficult position,' Carrick said. 'For one thing Joanna was there. How the hell do you think I'd explain that away?'

'That was hardly our fault,' I said. 'Anyway, she said you had a fairly good idea we were going to do something. She was right in the house with us before we realised it.'

Carrick ran his fingers through his thick fair hair and I suddenly remembered that he had a lot of Viking blood in his veins as his mother was from Orkney. 'Damage control then,' he said. 'You go home and stay there. I pray they don't make a complaint and carry on with the investigation as though nothing has happened. But you look here, Patrick,' he almost spat, eyeball to eyeball with him. 'You may have worked under a cloud of deception when you were with MI5 but I don't. I run a bloody tidy nick. Get under my feet one more time and I'll – I'll throw the book at you.'

The pause before the somewhat lukewarm threat, I felt, was a lot to do with Elspeth's presence, otherwise the air would have been blue. She, though, appeared totally oblivious to all this, over in the better light by the window carefully unpicking crude black thread stitches with the point of the scissors.

'I'll do a deal with you,' Patrick said winningly. 'You concentrate on the murder, I'll find out what Max is all about.'

'No,' was the uncompromising reply.

'What other info about Max was on your computer?' I asked Patrick, an unwelcome suspicion that Patrick had not told the whole story having suddenly lurched into my mind.

He turned and gave me one of his unsettling Mona Lisa smiles. 'Once upon a time Max had some dodgy friends and attracted the attention of MI5. For a while he was under suspicion in connection with weapons and explosives coming into this country for the use of an IRA terrorist cell. He had a boat in those days too apparently, a different one.'

'This was before he packed up and went off to the South China Sea.'

'Yes, he lived in Brighton then – had an antiques shop that didn't make any money.'

'Did they manage to pin anything on him?'

'No, there was no real evidence.'

Carrick realised that he'd been slightly sidelined. 'Look – '

'There,' said Elspeth. 'No, it's all very boring I'm afraid. I don't actually think it's a real human head at all but made of some kind of animal skin. And just with some rather odd-looking stones inside to keep the shape.' She tipped them out on to the table with a clatter.

Carrick said something vivid-sounding in Gaelic.

Patrick picked up the largest one and weighed it in his hand. 'At least two carets there, wouldn't you say?'

Uncut diamonds.

'Ye gods, there was a whole box full of heads!' I exclaimed.

'They might have been the real thing,' Patrick pointed out. 'Especially as you said they stank.'

Elspeth sat down. 'How much are they worth?'

'It depends on the quality and I'm no expert,' Carrick said. 'But if they're really good anything from a hundred thousand pounds upwards.' He wrenched his hands through his hair again. 'How the hell am I going to explain this.'

'It's easy,' Patrick said. 'MI5 have been notified of Professor Norton's murder because his brother's name is still on file and they've sent an investigator who, as he operates under a *carte blanche* brief, has searched for the shrunken head which, among other things, his wife saw in Norton's study on the first occasion she met him but which went missing after his death. Max Norton is known to have a large collection of primitive art.' He leaned back, arms folded, grinning.

'I'd never get away with that,' Carrick said.

'You will, old son, because it happens to be true, or soon will be. All I have to do is confirm ASAP that I want my old job back.'

You had to admire the man, for although assisted by circumstances, he had out-manoeuvred the pair of us.

'The only iffy bit after your wheeler-dealering then,' I said coolly, 'is whether you stay married or not.'

Slowly, Patrick pushed the diamond he had been examining across the table towards me, holding my gaze, those wonderful grey eyes sparkling with amusement. And damn him, love, better than any diamonds. I picked it up to kiss it goodbye, laughing, and put it back with the others.

'Well, thank goodness for that!' Elspeth said. 'There's never a dull moment with you two.'

Carrick groaned.

'I have an idea you planned this as soon as you received the intelligence details about Max,' I said.

'No, hardly. Be fair, Norton hadn't been murdered then. Obviously though my interest was kindled – habits die hard.'

We were at home in Devon and, the previous day, I had done all the driving as Patrick's ankle was painful. But it was not sufficiently serious to require medical attention and he intended to rest it for a couple more days before heading for London and an interview. This also meant that James Carrick could have a well-deserved breathing-space to oversee his murder inquiry before Patrick returned in any kind of official capacity. He had given me no further details but I knew he was itching to get to grips with a man who may or may not have assisted a terrorist organisation. Privately I thought it doubtful that he would be permitted to. National security presented far more pressing problems than a small-time smuggler.

I was far from sure that James had forgiven us but a bottle of very good single malt whisky was on its way to him by courier with a sincere letter of apology, penned by me and signed by both of us. It seemed preferable to stay right out of his way although the awkward question of the shrunken head stuffed with uncut diamonds had yet to be addressed.

I voiced these concerns out loud.

'I reckon he'll change his mind pronto as far as our involvement without official blessing's concerned,' Patrick said. 'Right now that thing's too hot for him to handle.'

Top of my list of priorities was to get on with *Dead Trouble*, which I intended to dedicate to John Norton, an undertaking that might have been my way of pushing to the back of my mind Patrick's new venture. And begorrah, themselves wanted the distaff side of the partnership back as well. I thought I could handle that – Patrick and I had made a successful team and I had ended up with oceans of plot material – providing the assignments we undertook did not become so life-threatening as they had in the past, if only for the children's sake.

Patrick had asked me how I felt about us working together again and I had told him I hadn't had time to think about it properly, which was true. But I have never really been the sort of person who benefits from brain-storming sessions, I simply come back to the answer gut-reaction presented me with in the first place.

Breaking into his own thoughts I said, 'I still feel the same about this as I did when you first mentioned it. I'd rather have you in my sights, so to speak, than you be in someone's else's and all I'm left with is to stay at home and worry about you.'

'I can understand that.' After a pause he added, 'I did make it clear that I'm not interested in having a much younger member of the team to train as I did with Terry last time.'

'It's a good idea to have three of us though. You could still ask him – he's older and wiser now.'

'And a family man with a very good job. He wouldn't be interested. He's *not* interested. I rang him a few days ago.'

'How about Steve?'

'Living in the States with a woman ten years older than himself with five children by previous marriages.'

'I do wish you'd tell me things – these people are my friends too.'

'Sorry, but I only found out myself very recently.'

85

'You've been sounding out several ex-D12 operatives then.'

Patrick nodded. 'Nathan's no good from our personal point of view as he's trained purely in surveillance. He's already working for the main department anyway and we can borrow him if and when we want to.'

'I think we ought to recruit someone older and level-headed, someone we trust and is already experienced.'

'To be frank I don't think we know anyone who fits the bill.'

'How about Tim Shandy?'

'Tim!'

Tim – actually christened Tristram by obviously eccentric parents but known as Tim to everyone – was an old friend of Patrick's whom it was thought had died fighting as a mercenary for the Croats in Bosnia. But he had only been very badly injured, maimed in body and a little in spirit. We had met him again recently when he had proved to be of immense assistance to me when I had tracked down the real murderer of the Anti-terrorist Branch Commander.

'He's not at all conventional,' Patrick said. 'And as a one-time tank regiment brigadier I can't see him taking orders from *me*. Not only that – ' He broke off, staring into space, frowning thoughtfully, and then said, 'You've reminded me of something. Years ago, not long after we were recruited and D12 was looking for all kinds of people, Daws asked me if I could recommend anyone and I mentioned Shandy's name. That was before he blew a fuse, resigned his commission and went off to vent his wrath on what he called "the Great Slobbo's filthy hoards". Perhaps it's just as well nothing came of it as saying Tim's not conventional is putting it mildly. Sometimes he's right off the planet. He's only really happy when he's rigging up vast explosions, for God's sake!'

'He's probably quite different now he's back with his family,' I said soothingly. 'And I'm sure he needs the money. He and his wife have that huge Elizabethan manor house they're trying to restore. And two growing sons to bring up.'

Patrick's gaze had come to rest on me. 'You rang him?' he asked, the tone beguilingly light.

'Yes, this morning,' I said, not adding that two could play at making secret phone calls. 'He's recently undergone plastic surgery to straighten his face out a bit. He sounded pleased – said his mouth no longer goes up in what he calls his sideways leer. I asked him in the most vague terms if he'd be interested in working with us if you should ever happen to approach him.'

'And?' Patrick prompted when I stopped speaking.

'He said he'd like to come and talk to us about it before he committed himself to anything or you even decided that he might be the man for the job.'

Patrick grinned. 'I had an idea you'd got something up your sleeve. Ingrid, you do know that he's blind in one eye?'

'It seemed to make not a whit of difference when we worked together.'

'When's he coming?'

'Tonight.'

'Bloody hell.'

But Tim rang a few hours later to say that he had forgotten that there was a school concert in the evening and as one of his boys played the cello in the orchestra he simply could not fail to attend. He would, if it was convenient, come the next day. So when the doorbell rang the following morning and Carrie answered it I was fully expecting it to be him, very very early.

'It's Chief Inspector Carrick,' she called up the winding stairs to my little writing room under the eaves.

Mentally, I swore. I really like James but was deeply and fruitfully involved with *Dead Trouble* and when I'm working I loathe interruptions. 'Could you please say I'll be five minutes and tell Patrick he's here? He's over in the barn.'

Patrick and I actually live in the barn conversion across the courtyard when the children are at home – although we eat most of our meals together – as the cottage is too small for everybody. For some time I had seriously been contemplating taking myself, my desk and word processor over to the spare bedroom there, if only for the sake of a little more peace and quiet – you can't keep shushing lively youngsters – thereby releasing one more room that would enable Matthew to have his own bedroom and not have to share with Justin.

Feeling guilty about James I scrawled a few ideas on a notepad and went down.

The men were standing in the centre of the courtyard, James immaculate in a pearl-grey suit, white shirt and blue tie, Patrick in old jeans and army 'woolly-pully', extremely dirty having been half-way through giving the woodstove its annual big clean, an undertaking that also entails getting on the roof of the barn and sweeping the chimney. On learning of this proposal I had tartly remarked that such a task would hardly rest his ankle but had been solemnly assured that it was exercise and therefore therapeutic.

'I thought it would be good to thank you for the whisky in person,' James said when he saw me, breaking off a conversation apparently about stoves, wood, for the use of, and, judging from Patrick's gesticulations, why you have to sweep the chimney of some from the top down.

No, obviously, Carrick hadn't made a two and a half hour road journey merely to voice his appreciation of the gift.

Patrick glanced at his watch. 'Lunch?' he suggested hopefully. 'At the pub?'

'I was rather hoping to speak to you in private,' Carrick said. 'This is a working trip as well, I'm afraid.'

'No problem,' I told them. 'Ham and salad rolls with canned beer here?'

'Saves me having to get changed, I suppose,' Patrick muttered. He caught my look. 'Okay, I'll have a good scrub under the parish pump first.'

We were all hungry and talking happened after we had eaten.

'Thank you,' Carrick said. 'I didn't have time for breakfast.' Setting his empty plate down on a side-table he continued, 'You know that before Joanna and I got married she had a private-eye business over the herbalist's shop in Milsom Street?'

'Yes,' Patrick and I said together.

'She sold it to a guy by the name of Briggs. Briggs employs a guy called Frank King. He's the one who was tailing Professor Norton that night and who took the pictures. King isn't as stupid as he looks when he chooses to, in fact he's ex-Drugs Squad Bristol CID and specialises in blending into the background looking like all kinds of morons. Frances Norton hired Briggs's company to dig dirt on her husband. Briggs reckons she wanted the house *and* all his money. Rumour has it that she's having it away with a one-time friend of Norton's.'

Digesting this for a moment Patrick said, 'You get the most amazing client confidentiality with this outfit, don't you?'

Carrick laughed. 'Never hire a private detective. Briggs is ex-CID too and I've seen cleaner gutters than the state of his mind. He's actually one of my best sources of information as he's kept all his snouts – certain people can't even have a bath without him knowing about it.'

I said, 'So what did Frances Norton say when you confronted her with this?'

'I haven't yet had an opportunity to as I only got the info late last night. I mentioned it first because I want you to know that your name, Ingrid, won't be bandied about in connection with Norton by Briggs, King, or anyone else connected with them. Otherwise they all get thrown in the river – from Clifton Bridge.'

No doubt assuming that he himself would be expected to carry this out, Patrick opened his mouth to protest.

'Relax,' Carrick said. 'I'm joking.'

I got the distinct impression that had Patrick volunteered . . .

James went on, 'There were no surprises as far as the PM results on Norton were concerned. He was killed by several blows to the back of the head made by a heavy blunt object of some kind. We haven't found the murder weapon. Then, as you already know, his killer carved him up – apparently with an extremely sharp knife or open razor. There's no need for me to go into details but it goes without saying that we're either talking about someone seriously mentally unbalanced or with a sizable grudge.'

Patrick asked, 'Did the pathologist stick his neck out and say whoever did it had medical knowledge?'

'He said in his view the murderer knew about gutting animals.'

After a short silence that had followed these words Carrick continued, 'I also thought you might like to hear how I got on with Max Norton and his wife. Her name's Sharleen, by the way.'

'Yuk,' I said.

'You're right, she is rather off-putting,' James commented. 'I only managed to talk to them yesterday as they seem to have been out all the time – either that or haven't been answering the phone or the door bell. A suspicious bloke like me would call that being deliberately elusive. But when I called with Bob Ingrams, he having rung for the umpteenth time, they were all smiles and falling over themselves to explain their absence. They said they've been dealing with business affairs and frantically house-hunting as they're terrified Frances Norton will sell the house literally from under them now her husband's dead and they'll be left without anywhere to live.'

'No love lost there then,' Patrick said. 'I wonder why they agreed to let them live there in the first place.'

'I got the impression from Max that his brother needed the money from the rent. To keep that son of his in motors perhaps. Anyway, to cut a long story short they were with friends in Bradford on Avon the night John Norton was murdered. There were several other couples there as well as it was someone's birthday party so it seems as though they have a good alibi. Bob's checking that out now. I know what you're going to say Patrick; that that proves nothing as Max probably wouldn't have done the deed himself but – '

Patrick butted in with, 'I've never actually said I thought Max was responsible for his brother's murder. But he's involved with crime. Does he look like his brother? Are we talking about mistaken identity?'

'He's about the same height and build and with roughly the same colour hair but he's younger and his hair's more fashionably cut. He's far better dressed too: Frances Norton did mention when I asked about the rather old clothes John had been wearing that he was always a shambles.' James looked at me. 'Does that tally with your observations?'

'He was wearing different suits on the occasions I saw him,' I said. 'Well-tailored but they all looked a bit past their prime. Do be aware though that wives nearly always think their husbands look a shambles at home. Patrick does.' I smiled at him. 'For example, everything you have on is going in the bin. The zip's been gone on those jeans for ages.'

Patrick hurriedly checked that he wasn't indecent. 'Not the pullover,' he protested. 'It's really useful.'

'You can shoot peas through it,' I told him mercilessly. 'Sorry, James. Please go on.'

'There's not a lot more to say really. Neither of them had any theories as to who could have killed him. I have to say I believed them, especially as they've only just returned to the UK after quite a few years away. I also have to admit that I thought Max looked shifty as God knows what scams he's been involved with, or still is for that matter. But as far as his brother's death goes . . .' He shrugged.

'Did they say anything about having a break-in?' Patrick asked.

Carrick shook his head. 'No, which I agree is extremely strange, especially as something valuable was lifted. And everywhere looked tidy. There wasn't any stuff lying around or anything like that. As you said, the whole place is jam-packed with native art but you'd need an expert to tell you whether any of it's stolen property. I fully intend to talk to them again and try to rattle them a bit.'

'What about the son, Jason?'

'He's a got a real chip on his shoulder and made no secret of the fact that he and his father rarely saw eye to eye. But I can't see him killing him, for after all Daddy was the sole source of his income and he made no secret of that either. The situation's no better with his mother, something she was only too keen to tell me about and I think his chances of carrying on free-loading at home are now zero.'

'Does Jason have an alibi for the night of the murder though?' Patrick asked.

'A cast-iron if not bloody brilliant one. He was involved in a minor shunt with his car and was actually in Bristol city centre nick being interviewed in connection with being over the limit. He got very stroppy and they chucked him in a cell and kept him there all night. He'd had another row with his mother, mostly about money again and his lack of a job. You yourselves saw him leave home the previous evening as though all hell was after him.'

'And the daughter?' I enquired.

'Name of Arabis,' Carrick said succinctly. 'She's all bitter and twisted because she reckons her father was the root cause of her marriage break-up by refusing to bail out her and her husband's failing business. She admitted when I pressed her that he'd helped them out before. When the bank pulled the plug they lost their home and that's why she's living with her parents. Her husband went off with someone else.'

'They were both very forthcoming, weren't they?' Patrick commented. 'Folk don't usually own up so easily to such dislike for murder victims.'

'Oh, I wouldn't say it was easy,' Carrick replied. 'Perhaps I finally got a bit fed up with their arrogance and evasive answers. Perhaps on the other hand I took a leaf out of your book.'

Patrick smiled depreciatingly at this and said, 'I take it that apart from not yet having had time to question Frances Norton on the latest developments you have no red-hot suspects.'

'That's right. No fingerprints, a few footprints in blood made by size ten trainers of a kind made by the million in China. Oh, we found one single fair hair, not mine or anyone else's in the house, the DNA from which doesn't match anything on the computer. Could be anyone's. It could have come in on Norton's clothing. But if we end up with a fair-haired suspect . . . who knows?'

'If you apply the golden rule and ask who benefits,' I said, 'who does?'

'The wife does unless he's left all his money to a cats' and dogs' home but then again she might have got her divorce and it seems a bit precipitant to have him done to death before giving her private sleuth time to get results. As for digging into the cases Norton was working on – well, that's going to take time. But I think I can rule out the Bates affair – the PM you attended, Ingrid – Doctor Bates is a five foot six weed who takes size eight in shoes and by all accounts he's stony-broke so could hardly afford to hire a hit-man. No, that just doesn't gel. The Greek job is far more complicated but again it seems pretty stupid to me to bump off the guy about to investigate the ins and outs of the death of someone who fell off a boat. I mean, another pathologist simply takes over, doesn't he?'

'Norton was regarded as the best,' I said. 'And the case is difficult with a lot of insurance money at stake.'

Carrick shook his head. 'I hear what you're saying but I don't think it's to do with his work. I shall still have to look into that side of his life of course.'

'With no shrunken head left unturned?' Patrick said.

'That's what I wanted to talk to you about. D'you reckon you could get that thing back in there?'

'You'll have to elaborate a little before I can answer,' he was told. 'D'you mean by dropping it down one of their chimneys or firing it from a giant catapult at the top of Beechen Cliff through a window?'

Carrick stared at the ceiling for several seconds and then said, 'I sometimes forget you're a soldier. No, the same way you removed it. Only this time with a bug hidden in with the diamonds.'

'There's no real problem. But it's a bad strategy. The first thing they'll do is rip it open to see if the rocks are still there and thereby find the bug.'

'But surely if the head's hidden somewhere they'll think they forgot to look there the last time and blame themselves. It was only left lying on a shelf, wasn't it?'

'Yes,' I said, 'but I can't believe they'd forgotten where they'd put such an important item. And if we hide it we might not find it for ages and the bug would be a waste of time.'

'Listening devices don't work very well hidden inside cupboards and drawers,' Patrick explained. 'That's why they're put under the flat surfaces of furniture fairly low down or out of sight on walls behind it. It would be better to bug the phone both for calls and to pick up conversation in the flat but you know as well as I do that you'd need to obtain permission to do that and I guess you don't want to because the evidence you have isn't exactly on the line. And as far as we're concerned I'm going to London tomorrow but won't even hear about the new position I'm after for another few days at the earliest so I can't do anything officially and there's no guarantee that I'll get that particular assignment – assuming that anyone's even interested in making it one.'

'Thanks for blowing me out of the water so neatly,' Carrick said. But he was sort of smiling as he spoke. 'I'll forget it then.'

'I do understand both your need to get rid of it, preferably back to where it came from and also, by your actions, make something positive happen with regard to your murder investigation.'

'What would you do?' James asked.

'I'm used to working to a completely different set of rules so whatever I said probably wouldn't be of much help to you. Where is it, by the way?'

Carrick pointed to his leather briefcase. 'In there. I brought it down to ask you to carry on as you thought fit.'

After a little silence Patrick murmured, 'You told us to go away and stay away unless we were acting in an official capacity.'

'I really have no choice,' Carrick said stolidly. 'I'm too much of a rule-book copper.' Then he blurted out, 'The bloody thing's burning a hole in me.'

Checkmate.

Patrick did not smile, let alone look pleased, as aware as I am that the Scots are a proud race. 'To policemen with integrity,' he said, raising his beer glass.

'I shall still have to question Max Norton and his wife again,' Carrick said.

'You do whatever you feel is appropriate,' Patrick told him. 'Act normally. You don't know what we're doing and you've never clapped eyes on the head. I ask only that you apprise me of anything you think is relevant to my investigations and I'll forward everything I learn that I think will lead you to Norton's killer. If we arrive at the same point we'll have achieved something.'

'He hasn't blond hair,' Carrick said. 'Nor has his wife.'

'No, but the bastard's involved all right. I can always smell conspiracy.'

Carrick leaned over, opened his briefcase and removed a round bundle. 'Joanna put it in a cloth bag. Whatever the hell it's made of is going off and we thought putting it in a plastic one would only hasten the process.' He passed it over quickly into Patrick's waiting hands. 'Do what you like with it. Bury it in the garden if you want to – diamonds and all. I never want to see it again.'

Patrick took the object from the bag and held it up by the hair. The same smell of putrefaction that we had encountered in the upper flat wafted from it. 'I reckon this *is* the real thing,' he said, gazing into the tiny and sunken but oddly glittering eyes. 'What a shame it can't talk.'

'Man, you're unreal,' Carrick whispered.'

6

Shortly afterwards Carrick left even though we had invited him to stay and meet Tim Shandy: pressure of work prevented him from spending any more time away.

'Suppose I put this in the fridge,' Patrick suggested, tossing the bag containing the head up in the air and catching it again.

'In several very well-sealed freezer bags,' I insisted. 'I'll clear out one of the salad drawers for it. I have two questions. When do you propose to endeavour to sneak it back and are you going to bug it? I'm asking mostly from the point of view of my writing schedule.'

'I'm not going to sneak it back. I intend to pay Max Norton a visit and offer to be his minder, returning his stolen property intact as proof of my efficiency and good intentions.'

'Don't you think he might just, for one tiny moment, suspect you'd made off with it in the first place?'

'No, I reckon he'll be flattered.'

We gazed at one another for a few more seconds and then there was a mutual smile. I knew exactly what he intended to do.

I said, 'I can't be in on this. We might bump into Frances Norton and she'd recognise me.'

'If we go late at night there's no real danger of that happening. Change the style of your clothes. Spike up your hair, be a bit scruffy for a change.'

We had been for a walk in the main part of the garden, which is behind the barn, and now went indoors. Just inside the door Patrick stopped. Carrie had just left with Victoria in her pram to collect Justin from the village school and, knowing we were in the vicinity, she had left the front door unlocked. From Patrick's manner I knew he thought something was wrong.

Sometimes, visitors remark on the rather odd positioning of some of the mirrors in the cottage but this is a deliberate ploy on our part for the Gillards are still on several terrorist organisations' hit-lists. Standing in certain positions one can see into the other rooms, even up the stairs, and, gazing along the short passageway that leads from the dining room, which one walks directly into having entered through the front door, Patrick could see, courtesy of a long gilt-framed mirror set at a slight angle on the wall at the end, right into the living room. He chuckled.

'I can see you, you old fox!' he called out.

Tim Shandy emerged, grinning. 'I swore Carrie to silence,' he reported gleefully. 'But I did ring the bell first in the proper manner.' He gazed about. 'I should have realised when I was here before that this place is as secure as a fortress. Boiling oil and trapdoors, eh?'

We all shook hands and I did not comment just then on the improvement plastic surgery operations had made to his face. As he had intimated himself, his mouth was no longer dragged up and to one side by scar tissue which had given him an unfortunate leer and the area around his blinded eye, complete with a new eyebrow, now looked the same as his good one. More obvious was his increased self-confidence, for Tim had been a man who until quite recently had only gone out at night. He was, I knew, in his middle fifties and Patrick's jocular description had been an accurate one as his hair was a sandy rufous colour. With a slim gangling frame and standing very slightly taller than Patrick's six feet two inches he made a commanding figure and I wondered if the pair, who were very good friends, could actually work together.

We would have to find out.

Patrick handed him what he was holding. 'What do you make of that?'

Shandy regarded him with his one bright blue eye. 'Is this

the first test in whether I make the grade?' he said with a broad smile.

'Then you can have a cup of tea,' Patrick said comfortingly.

Tim took the head from the bag with his large but graceful hands. 'I never knew your Great-aunt Mildred was waylaid by head-hunters,' he said wonderingly. 'They're extremely collectable in certain quarters, you know.'

'That one even more so. It's full of uncut diamonds.'

Tim whistled softly. 'It stinks like a Serb's backside. So if I suggest we remove the rocks, bung the rest on a nice hot fire and retire to Patagonia I've failed?'

The fascinating and grisly business in Bath sometimes – usually late at night, I had only to close my eyes to see, in every detail, the interior of that bloodied room – had to wait and, the next morning, Patrick departed for London. He and Tim had talked late into the night, long after I had gone to bed and, early next day, shortly after Patrick had left by taxi for the station, Tim also departed as he had business in Truro with an architect who was going to help him with restoration work on his house.

I did not hear from Patrick for almost a week.

This was not necessarily alarming. In the days when I had been his working partner it had occurred quite frequently. I was assuming that he had been provisionally accepted and was having to undergo re-training. Was he fit enough? In his middle forties was he too old?

It was early evening on the sixth day when the phone rang and it was Patrick using his mobile. The line was terrible and I just managed to hear him ask me to meet him outside Bath railway station at eleven that night before we were cut off. He had used a pre-arranged code-word.

It was just as well I had made a few preparations.

Arriving a little early I parked the Range Rover in a side

road some distance from the station and walked, loitering at the front of the building, elegant with its wrought iron pillars and tracery supporting a glass canopy. I leaned on one of the uprights in what I can only describe as a tart pose; head back, chest thrust forward, one leg – I was wearing a micro-skirt and long leather boots – crossed in front of the other. I did not want to look like Ingrid Langley.

Half an hour later and when three men had tried to pick me up another approached, slouched to a nearby pillar, leaned on it in an attitude of utter exhaustion and lit a small cigar. I suppose I gawped at him.

'What the hell's happened to you?' I said, finally.

His eyes focused and he said something under his breath. He peeled himself off the pillar and came over, wincing as he walked. We stood face to face and then Patrick blew out a long plume of smoke and said, 'God, woman, I didn't recognise you with that wig on.'

'It isn't a wig,' I told him. 'I've been thinking of going blonde for a while now.' More quietly I added, 'There's a man over there who's hanging around still hoping I'll go to a cheap hotel with him and might cut up rough when I go off with you. The river isn't exactly handy.'

'Furthermore I don't have any energy,' was the terse reply. So he merely sprang the blade of his throwing knife by way of saying hello to any interested parties as we walked away.

I had plenty of cash with me – you don't flash credit cards around with your real name on them while playing this game – and we went to a dark basement bar we knew of where Patrick not so much sat down as collapsed. I bought him a pint of Murphys as I had an idea he was in Irish mode, if indeed in any particular mode at all, and a half of shandy for myself as right now I wanted to remain extremely sober.

'If James's bunch raids this place I'll kill him,' Patrick said when the beer had gone. Then he made an odd sound, perhaps a chuckle, almost a sob. He looked terrible, nothing to do with any disguise. There was at least two day's growth of stubble on his face, which was gaunt and very pale. He looked as though he hurt just about everywhere.

I asked no questions just then. There was food available, of a sort, and I ordered us both sausages and chips. I gave him most of mine after he had wolfed down his own. The colour began to come back into his cheeks.

'Didn't they feed you?'

'No, the only concession was to be dropped off where I wanted to be today.'

'So you've been on some kind of expertise and survival exercise.'

'Not really. It was more of a does this Lieutenant-Colonel who's been swanning around at Staff College really want to do the interesting stuff again? If you make him sleep rough, chuck him into Crazy Well pool a few times and set enough Marines sergeants on him you tend to find out.'

'You've been on Dartmoor! Right on our doorstep!'

He actually smiled. 'It's a big, private place to take people apart, isn't it?'

'What was the verdict?'

Bleakly, he replied, 'They ran out of Marines.'

I took that to mean that he had passed. 'I hope I don't have to do anything like that. I've been swimming and running but –'

'No,' he interrupted. 'You don't think I'd allow that to be part of the equation, do you?'

'Nobody took any prisoners during the training for D12 first time round, you included.' He had stared, stony-faced with all the others when it had been my turn to be stripped naked and interrogated and ignored my entreaty to kill the rabbit for me that was to be our supper, even feigned deafness at wifely shrieks of terror when my abseil down a cliff had gone horribly wrong and I had ended up descending head instead of feet first.

'You'll just have to have a medical and perhaps prove your heart and lungs still work. This job isn't going to be the same as it was last time or I wouldn't want to sign up for it. I've done my last gunfight at the OK Corral. God, I'm still hungry.' He rubbed his hands tiredly over his face. 'There's one drawback though. I still won't have complete free-rein. There'll be three of us all right but with someone overseeing everything, just like when we worked for Richard Daws. I have a sneaking feeling it *will* be Richard Daws. I intend to sleep on that one – nothing's in writing yet.'

We went to a cheap hotel.

I did not sleep, my thoughts churning around in my head. I wondered if we were doing the right thing, or whether Patrick was trying to turn back the clock and would face only disappointment. If indeed we were to work together again, would we be permitted to take on Tim Shandy? During that afternoon and later, after dinner, Patrick had quizzed him gently and not so gently, weaving arguments, seeking reactions, provoking and testing. I had witnessed similar encounters in the past and he had made it look surprisingly easy to push people into either losing their tempers or breaking down in tears. Not for nothing had he once worked for MI5 as an interrogator and he had made strong men cry. He is an actor; he should have gone on the stage, it would have been a hell of a sight less hazardous.

Tim, obviously realising what had been going on, had apparently not lost his sense of humour.

As always seems to happen I dozed off just before dawn, waking with a backache from the dreadful mattress when Patrick mumbled into my ear, 'Did you remember to bring it?'

'Of course,' I answered.

He commenced to snore quietly. Then, seconds later, 'Do we *have* to be all of a heap in the middle like this?'

'The bed's programmed that way,' I told him. 'It's only ever been bonked in.'

Suddenly he was awake. 'We could – '

'Not with those bristles.'

Over coffee and croissants in a nearby brasserie, the smell of stale, burning, frying oil in the hotel having put us off breakfasting there, Patrick said, 'Today we devote to Max.' He was almost his old self and with not as many bruises as I had expected. 'Tomorrow we go to London, yours truly having spruced himself up a bit, for the final assessments. Then we shall know where we stand and can plan accordingly.'

'Max might not be at home today,' I said.

'No, but I shall find him. I might ask a policeman.'

He was already working out strategy, I could tell by the far-away look in his eyes, so I ate the rest of my breakfast in silence, feeling a bit like a gangster's doxy. Patrick was already slipping into his chosen persona; one he had used before based on a man we had both met and who, for simplicity's sake, I shall describe as an Irish terrorist. Once the mind-set was in place the rest followed and, entering the restaurant as Patrick Gillard he emerged as someone else. This was no vaudeville Irishman, there was hardly a trace of an accent, here was a man who now quietly exuded cold-blooded menace.

I do not enjoy his company when he is like this.

'So what do I call you?' I asked when we were on the way to pick up the car, which hopefully was still where I had left it the previous day.

'Just stick to Patrick. There's no need for us to bother with surnames.'

'And I'm your what? controller? current lay? People like you don't include girlfriends on missions.'

He shrugged himself a little deeper into his black leather

jacket and brooded, a sign I had hit on something he had overlooked. Then he said, 'you're the widow of a man who ran a Real IRA cell over here and have dedicated yourself to the cause after Special Branch shot him one night when he had an argument with them over his car being parked on double yellow lines packed full of explosives.'

'But that means I'd sympathise with Max's past gun-running activities.'

'Don't worry about that. Leave it to me. And you and I are an item. Just act sexy. And stupid.'

Going blonde seemed to have been a mistake.

There was the unspoken realisation that while it did not really matter what kind of car we arrived in we did not want any of the Nortons to be in a position to note down the registration number. So again, the Range Rover was left in a side street, in Combe Down, some distance from the one-time vicarage and we walked. Patrick had contacted James Carrick on his mobile and, after telling him what we intended to do, asked him to check if Max Norton and his wife were at home – we had already decided that a late-at-night visit was unnecessary. Bob Ingrams, Carrick's sergeant, had rung back to say that they were in and had covered his call by making an appointment for the DCI to ask them a few more questions later in the day.

'Just march straight in?' I asked when we were heading down the drive.

'We know where to go,' was the reply, answering a different query and in different, difficult mode.

Quietly, quickly we went to the rear door of the house, went in, crossed the old scullery and hurried up the stairs. I was not expecting him to ring the doorbell when we arrived, but he did and when it was opened, by a women, barged his way in, thrusting her aside. She yelled abuse, Patrick rapidly went from sight and, moments later, there was the sound of a gunshot.

'Cool it!' I shouted to the woman, who had her large mouth open for another shrieked tirade. The devoted-to-the-cause-dumb-blonde then frog-marched her into the living room.

Patrick was prising his knife out of the gold-filigree decoration on the tooled leather top of Max Norton's writing desk. The sleeve of Norton's jacket, shirt cuff and, judging by his language, a small fold of skin were involved as well. The gun, one of those shiny little things that American women keep in their handbags, had understandably dropped from his grasp and, just after I entered Patrick scooped it up with his other hand and slipped it into a pocket. He closely inspected the tip of his freed knife for damage, frowning, and then sat down and surveyed us all with the demeanour of a man bored because he wasn't just then strangling someone with his bare hands.

Max Norton emerged from his shocked daze. 'You some kind of nutter?' He realised his wrist was bleeding, reached over, slowly, took a paper tissue from a box on the desk and held it to the cut. I had thought his brother slightly coarse: here was a coarser, tanned, slimmer version.

Patrick said, 'I had a little bet with myself that your first words would sound like something out of a low-budget soap. Is the woman your wife Sharleen?'

Norton nodded.

Without looking at her Patrick said, 'Sit down.'

She sat, with a little assistance from me when I thought she was about to argue.

'Is anyone in downstairs?'

'God knows.'

'If they should come up and query the sound of the shot you will tell them that you dropped something in the kitchen, which I happen to know has a tiled floor.'

'You were the bastard who broke in!'

Patrick glanced at me and I removed the head from the bag

I had been carrying it in and put it on a corner of the desk. 'All present and correct,' he said. 'Count them if you want to.'

Max Norton did, ripping out the stitches so frenziedly with a small pair of scissors he took from a drawer – having wisely asked Patrick's permission beforehand – that the diamonds scattered, some falling to the floor. He scrabbled for them and then briefly examined the empty head for any further contents before hurling it in the direction of a metal wastepaper basket in corner of the room. It missed, hit the wall and disintegrated.

I felt a little sickened at the man's callousness: this object had once been part of a human being.

'Word has got around,' Patrick said, playing with the knife, 'that you're back. Still, you can't keep running for ever, can you?'

'I didn't run,' Norton protested.

Patrick gave him a shark's smile. 'Okay, we'll save your pride and just say things got a little hot.'

'I don't owe you people anything!' the other shouted.

'Keep your voice down. And I think you've missed the point. I don't represent any particular organisation. I'm freelance, although, admittedly, with certain loyalties and a subscriber to certain sources of intelligence. The people who broke in and stole your property won't give you any more trouble in that direction, I assure you.'

'What do you want?' Norton asked sullenly.

'I was going to offer to be your bodyguard as obviously you need one rather badly – in return, of course, for a splendid salary – but having met the pair of you I don't think I could stomach the job. I can make more money by selling information to interested parties and protecting them from unwelcome publicity, for example by ensuring they don't become involved with police investigations into crimes they didn't commit. Especially murder inquiries. I have such an assignment. Your brother met a nasty end, didn't he?'

'I had nothing to do with John's death and I don't have to help you,' Max snarled.

'Oh, but you do. Otherwise I shall make sure a snout tells the police why you didn't report the burglary. In other words all about the weapons and loot stashed away here, not to mention the fact that most of the stuff in this room was taken from its rightful owner or illegally removed from monuments and excavations.'

'You haven't a shred of proof.'

'It shouldn't be too difficult to find it. Carrick's good, you know. I've been on the wrong side of him a couple of times so I know what I'm talking about.'

'I'm surprised then that he's still drawing breath.' This was from Sharleen, who spat the words at him like bullets from an automatic weapon. As John Norton had said, she could have been aged anywhere between nineteen and ninety and her skin was so stretched across her face, presumably as a result of face-lifts, I wondered she could even blink.

'Oh, it makes no sense to kill policemen,' Patrick whispered. 'I just concentrate on shits I can make a little money from.'

There was a short meaningful silence.

'So the first thing I want to know,' he went on, 'is how that shrunken head, which was on a shelf in your brother's study when he was visited by a female novelist on the Friday evening before he died, was missing from the room after he was murdered and then turned up here, right in this room. And be warned,' he added, perceiving the reaction writ large in Max's expression, 'I have all kinds of contacts and not all of them are on the wrong side of the law.'

Max cleared his throat. 'There's nothing odd about it. The head's mine and I confess I smuggled the diamonds through customs hidden inside it. John was interested in that kind of thing, how it was shrunk, I mean. He asked me if he could have a look at it as he'd seen it here. He kept it for a couple of days and gave it to me back on the Saturday morning.'

'And you let him have it even though it was worth a mint of money?'

'I did ask him not to mess around with it.'

Sarcastically, Patrick said, 'So all those other heads packed in a box in the hall are loaded with diamonds too.'

'No, of course not.'

'Then why the hell not give him one of those instead?'

'I had an idea they were going mouldy. The box had got damp. When we were burgled and they got chucked all over the place I saw that they were useless from an investment point of view and threw them out.'

'Whose diamonds were they before you appropriated them?'

'I bought them fair and square,' Max said furiously. 'I made some money abroad and it's a good way of carrying it around.'

'I asked because one possibility is that someone really is after your hide and they got the wrong man. Just about all the law enforcement agencies in this country and a few abroad know of your gun-running and other activities and, as I said just now, your cronies from those days won't want it to look as though through an old associate they're even indirectly responsible for murder, especially something so messy and dramatic. It's unprofessional. You would just disappear quietly and that would be that. How many people have you upset who relish bloodbaths?'

'I could do with a drink,' Max muttered.

'Answer the question.'

'The answer's none. I know no one like that. You have enemies, don't you?'

The query was ignored. Patrick's gaze drifted around the room and came to rest on the grave guardian figures from Sulawesi. 'Tell me about your days as a pirate in – '

There came a thunderous knocking on the front door of the flat.

'It – it can't be those downstairs,' Max stuttered when both he and Patrick had shot to their feet. 'They wouldn't knock like that.'

'Is it locked?' Patrick demanded to know of the last one in, me.

'No,' I said, aware of the old-fashioned nature of the door furniture.

Whoever it was was coming in and Patrick's knife was poised in his hand.

'Police!' a man's voice shouted just before James Carrick erupted into the room. He appeared to be alone and had a rather wild look on his face. 'I have reason to believe . . . ' he was saying as he came through the doorway. 'Ah, yes. You're under arrest.'

He was looking at Patrick. Then he looked at me. 'You too.'

Uppermost in Patrick's mind, I knew, was our require-ment to leave without either of us being taken into police custody or anyone getting hurt. He was also thunderstruck, needless to say. With this in mind he approached the DCI and I was not sure then exactly what he intended to do. He had to preserve our own cover and might also have been feeling charitable enough to want to go along with whatever the hell it was that Carrick was up to. So perhaps a swift picking up and depositing in the general direction of the long-suffering wastepaper basket was on the cards before he and I ran like hares.

When the two were just out of range of one another Carrick lunged forward and hit him. It was a fairly beefy jab just below the ribs – he's broad-shouldered and plays rugby – and when Patrick understandably stopped as though he'd walked into a wall, more surprised than anything, Carrick then followed it with a very nicely judged right to the side of the jaw. My husband went down sprawling on to the sump-tuous Chinese carpet. He was rolled briskly over on to his front and his arms handcuffed behind him.

Sharleen took her cue from this and went for me like a rabid alley-cat. Her crimson nails had raked down my arm before I could defend myself in any way and then she grabbed hold of my hair and yanked hard.

'You old trout!' I yelled and my hand was raised to hit to make her let go when it was caught and twisted up my back.

'We wouldn't want to be had up for assault, would we?' James said silkily in my ear. Then, 'Pack it in!' he shouted at the aggrieved Mrs Norton. 'Or I'll take you in too.'

She spat in my face and went over to stand by the window.

'The bastard threw a knife at me!' Norton raged. 'I'll have him for grievous bodily harm, threatening behaviour and – '

'Save it for later,' Carrick interrupted, releasing his hold on me. 'I'll come back at the pre-arranged time.'

I wiped the spittle from my face.

Patrick was able to get to his feet unaided but I slipped an arm through a fastened one as he was a little unsteady. Carrick walked ahead of us all the way down the stairs as though we weren't there. His own car was outside, he had no back-up and the only visible witness to our subdued departure was a thin black cat. We were closely supervised into the rear seats and then Carrick got behind the wheel and we were driven away.

Not straight to the police station in Manvers Street however.

He drew up in the completely empty car park of a church about half a mile down the road, got out, opened the door nearest to Patrick and unlocked the handcuffs.

'The bastard took a shot at me,' said Patrick stonily, feeling the side of his face gently with one hand while taking the tiny weapon from his pocket and handing it to Carrick with the other.

'I've had to change my plan,' Carrick said, getting back in the car again without commenting on the weapon. 'And there's a bloke from MI5 at the nick who wants to see you pronto. He seemed to know I knew where you were. I don't like it when bods from your lot know that I know where you are. When he realised I wasn't going to be helpful he said he also knew you were investigating Max Norton and under no circumstances did he want you to. He really impressed that on me and as I'm working on the theory that Norton's involved in a few scams the Met still have on file it suits me fine and I'm going to ask Bob Ingrams to look into it. But I don't want to frighten Norton off. So I'm keeping him sweet for a bit while I investigate his brother's murder. Did you give him back the head?'

Patrick not feeling particularly sugary towards Carrick just then, I answered in the affirmative.

'I'll tell the Nortons you're wanted by the anti-Terrorist Branch,' James continued. 'And that you're out of my hands because it takes precedence.'

'I'm really glad this has all worked so nicely for you, James,' I murmured and must have spoken too quietly for him to hear, for again he said nothing in reply.

'The super's away so we can use his office,' Carrick said when we were walking towards the rear entrance of the nick, the car park being behind the building.

Patrick stopped walking and when we had all halted he said to Carrick, 'That *wasn't* necessary.'

Carrick's somewhat fevered gaze seemed to clear and took a step back. 'Sorry, but I didn't know how else to play it,' he said desperately. 'For all I knew you would have done just the same to me and made a dash for it. Besides, there's this guy who – '

'There are four points I'd like to raise with you,' Patrick interrupted, speaking through his teeth. 'First, I don't have to be brought in on a stretcher just because somebody from MI5 wants to talk to me. Second, your keeping some little turd of a gun-runner happy now seems to take priority over our friendship. Third, whatever this bloke from London says you've just sunk my investigation without trace. And fourth, and I really hate saying this to people, James, you seem to have forgotten who I am.'

A couple of minutes later a frigid trio traipsed into Superintendent Buller's office where Carrick invited us to seat ourselves while he tracked down the man from London, whom he seemed to think was in the canteen.

'In the canteen? Patrick said wonderingly when James had gone. He rubbed a hand ruefully over his unshaven chin. 'What the hell did he do that for?'

I said, 'Looked at dispassionately I think he told the truth and did a somewhat heavier version of what were about to do to him. In other words he's getting more like you every day.'

He glared at me.

'I did say looked at dispassionately,' I said. 'But he was a bit over the top – I actually thought he looked rather upset about something. He didn't really do much damage though, did he?'

'You're almost saying that it's only my pride that's been hurt.'

'Was I?' I asked in surprised fashion.

The man from MI5 entered, apologised for keeping us waiting and sat at Buller's desk. He then apologised again, this time for being over-dressed, full military uniform, as he had to go on to another, formal engagement.

If Patrick had been in uniform too he would have had to get to his feet and salute. As it was he sat very still, thunder-struck for the second time that morning.

Tim Shandy cleared his throat. 'I realise this is a bit of a shock to you both. It was only sprung on me late last night.'

'It's all beginning to slot into place,' Patrick said after a short pause. 'I have an idea that when I recommended you to Colonel Daws he did something about it only you ended up working for an outfit like 14th Intelligence. I could hardly believe it when you first told me you'd resigned your commission and were going off to fight for the Croats as a mercenary. You were keeping a very close watch on the Serbs in Bosnia, weren't you? Only you were horribly wounded and couldn't just be collected and flown out without jeopardising secret operations.'

'They didn't know where I was,' Shandy said. 'And nor did I for quite a while. The rest though . . '

When, after making his own way home, maimed – and if the truth were known, probably having suffered a nervous breakdown – unable to face wife and children, career and friends, he had hidden himself away at a club exclusively for wounded officers in London. Until, hearing through a services' grapevine that Patrick had been arrested in the connection with the death of a policeman, he had taken to the road with a tent and a few belongings in a knapsack and made his way, mostly across country, to Devon. It had been the beginning of his full recovery.

Patrick said, 'So now you're back with the covert stuff.'

'Yes, I do believe I'm your new boss,' said Shandy.

7

'You wouldn't by any chance be the one who asked those at Lympstone to see if I was still keen for the job?' Patrick enquired and although I had an idea that the emotions raging through him included anger, disappointment and embarrassment his tone merely denoted polite interest.

'I'm sure you would have done the same in similar circumstances.'

Patrick nodded slowly and there was another silence broken by his saying, 'To ensure that I'm completely in the picture perhaps you'd be good enough also to tell me if you asked Carrick to get me away from Max Norton come what may.'

It was Shandy's turn to nod.

'Why?' Patrick breathed.

'You filled me in with the situation when I came down to Devon and I've just about had time to do some more digging. Years ago Norton used to be as thick as thieves with several people, terrorists, whom you personally have since helped to shove in the slammer. A couple are out now and they'd blow your cover and you to high heaven as well. I don't want your mutilated body dredged from a river somewhere.'

All this was taking quite a bit of getting used to.

'Can't you take orders from me?' Tim asked gently, his large hands undertaking a little invisible knot-tying, a mannerism to which he was particularly prone.

'Of course,' Patrick replied.

'But you won't necessarily do as I tell you.'

'No.'

Another silence.

'But that's not because I always used not to do as Daws told me,' Patrick went on. 'You and I have a different, better, relationship.'

'That's exactly the kind of working relationship I was hoping to have with you.'

'I'm sorry,' Patrick said quietly. 'But, no. Sir.'

Shandy jumped to his feet, undid his uniform jacket, yanked it off, screwed it into a ball and hurled it into a corner of the room. 'Bugger rank!' he bellowed, dropping back into the chair again. 'You tell me how you want to play it!'

Patrick leaned forward, obviously choosing his words with care. 'Daws, who used to head D12, and who as you know also happens to be the Fourteenth Earl of Hartwood, liaised with Number 10. He was the one who handled the civil servants, under-secretaries, spin-doctors, Uncle Tom Cobbley and all – and had the ear of those right at the top. He belongs to all the right clubs. He tended all the grapevines, something I understand he still does and has consented to carry on overseeing the entire department, only not in quite such a hands-on way, and act as our adviser. As far as I'm concerned all that is absolutely splendid. It's obvious that we three, the trouble-shooters not actually accountable to whoever's going to be in charge of the rest of the outfit, just to Daws, are only going to be given the difficult jobs. But I always ended up with them anyway and in that sense I *was* D12. I have the experience and with all due respect you don't. My condition for taking this on again is that, for a while anyway, you work for me. As you say, bugger rank.'

Some of this I had not known before and I wasn't offended that neither of them, so far, had asked for my opinion. Sometimes, it really is better for a woman to keep her mouth shut, mainly for the perfectly good reason that it can then be more effective when she does open it.

'I was in the middle of an actual operation,' Patrick said, only speaking to Shandy. 'By my reckoning Max Norton is unfinished business and, from what you've just told me, has been for some years.'

It was only then that I realised the extent of the blunder that Shandy, partly for reasons of friendship, had made. Bad judgement in hauling someone away from what they are doing by dint of persuading a policeman to go in and 'arrest' them – although I was fairly sure now that Carrick had acted in what he thought were our best interests – hardly boded well for the future. Tim, probably, had also gone in for a little ill-thought-out one-upmanship due to lack of confidence that he could keep Patrick reined in. Patrick, whom I already knew thought that it was Shandy who needed keeping an eye on, was hardly to be blamed for his present attitude. We weren't just talking about wounded pride.

'This old fox is perfectly aware that you weren't working on anything remotely official this time,' Shandy pointed out a trifle mulishly.

Patrick said, 'Only insofar as Carrick, who once upon a time was a friend of mine, asked me to return the shrunken head to where we'd found it on the strength that it was too hot for him to handle. He actually told me to do what the hell I liked with it because it was burning holes in his tidy little world. He's now changed his mind with regard to tactics as the Met might get involved but as I'd done my little bit to get him out of the brown stuff his socking me on the jaw is apparently quite all right. I'm not going to argue with you, Tim. You have twenty-four hours to think it over. Meanwhile I'm going home.'

And with that Patrick rose and went over to the door. 'Coming?' he said to me.

I also rose and left but on the way out I retrieved the jacket, gave it a little shake, folded it in half and then placed it on one corner of the desk.

Neither of us spoke as we walked to the station, which is not far away and where the nearest taxi rank is, and took a cab back to where we had left the car.

'Wouldn't it be sensible to stay at Hinton Littlemoor?' I

ventured. 'Or aren't we going to London tomorrow in view of what's happened?'

From his position in the driving seat Patrick said, 'It's not often you lose a job and your two best friends in one day, is it?' Before I could speak he continued, 'I just want to get the hell out of here. Let's go home – and have a very long debriefing in the pub.'

'I'll drive,' I said.

It seemed to me that we were floundering through life, directionless. On top of that I felt that what had happened that morning was literally a crying shame. Dartmoor mirrored both of these sentiments by welcoming us with torrential rain and a full gale. There was also that local phenomenon, hill fog, in other words you are trying to find your way home through low-flying clouds while someone turns a hose-pipe full on the windscreen.

Having no inclination whatsoever to turn out again and go to the pub and knowing that damage control with regard to the man in my life could largely be represented by home fires, a modest amount of good whisky and a good dinner of traditional hue I raided the freezer as soon as I got in, found some braising beef, thawed it in the microwave – sometimes you have to take these short cuts – and prepared a casserole. With herbs heroically gathered from the garden, half a bottle of red wine, new potatoes, mushrooms to be added later and a few dumplings to simmer on the top for the final twenty minutes it promised to be everything for which I was hoping.

'Shall I light the wood stove?' asked a dressing-gown clad figure, fresh from the shower, mercifully clean-shaven, wet hair sticking up on end.

I had quickly checked that all was well with Carrie and the children over at the cottage. Carrie had been cooking too, putting a chicken in the oven for their dinner and had turned to present me with a very warm face and, grinning while she curtsied, bird and all, 'invited' us over later for coffee. I get on extremely well with her.

'You'd be miffed if I said it wasn't cold enough,' I said. 'Yes, please do.'

'This is more like it,' Patrick said when, dressed and with a tot of his favourite single malt, he sank into an armchair to gaze favourably upon the flames dancing behind the glass panels of the doors of the woodstove.

It was now dark and I finished closing the curtains and lit a couple of candles to augment the soft light from small table lamps. Rain was still battering against the windows.

'Perhaps everything isn't completely finished,' he added. 'Sorry, I forgot to open a bottle of white wine for you.'

'Whisht!' I said, Patrick half-way to his feet. 'I've done it. No, you're right, it might not be. I've been thinking about James though – I've never seen him with such a wild look on his face.'

'I have. Sometimes he's a truly wild Scot. Don't you remember that episode with the broadswords? No doubt he'd had a very bad morning too. Are you going to come and sit down?'

'Just casserole fussing for a couple more minutes.' I returned to the small kitchen that is separated from the living room by a screen of bookshelves and plants in time to see through the window the lights of a vehicle just turning into the courtyard. My heart sank. Please God make it someone collecting for charity who would bother Carrie, not visitors for us. I swore under my breath, when a minute or so later, someone rang the doorbell.

'A thousand, thousand apologies,' Tim Shandy was saying as he came through the door, the water cascading from him even though he had only had to travel a few yards in the open air. 'A thousand apologies for everything.' Invited to make himself at home he sat down when he had given Patrick his coat and exhibited extreme mortification.

'How now, old chum?' Patrick said gently. 'You shouldn't have driven all this way in such lousy weather to apologise. I'm sure you and I can survive a small skirmish.'

Shandy hardly appeared to hear. 'James Carrick too. He's feeling very bad about it, you know. God, if only I'd known. But I think he actually got the call after he left me to go and find you.'

'What call?' Patrick said.

'His wife lost their baby this morning. He went straight off to the hospital afterwards and I understand that she's all right. Fairly early days, someone said. But when you said he'd belted you...'

Patrick dispensed a tot of whisky for Tim and topped up his own. 'That's dreadful news. I'll phone him.'

'Leave it until later,' I pleaded. 'Let him be with Joanna and not have to talk about it with anyone else yet – especially someone he thinks he's got on the wrong side of. Tomorrow would be far better.'

'Ingrid's right,' Tim said. Then, humbly, 'What do you want this big-headed old fart to do? Kneel and offer you his sword?'

'I'd far rather you joined us for dinner,' Patrick said.

I headed for the kitchen, washed some extra new potatoes and then raided the cottage kitchen for another bottle of wine, two avocado pears, a lemon, a pack of prepared green salad plus an 'emergency' chocolate gateau and some smoked salmon from the freezer.

'It's hungry weather, isn't it?' Carrie said, obviously not having heard Shandy's car above the wind and rain.

It transpired that in exchange for dropping his investigation into Max Norton, temporarily at least, and allowing the police

119

to carry on with their investigation into finding his brother's murderer Patrick got everything from Shandy, as far as his immediate wishes for D12 were concerned, that he wanted. The arrangement, more sensible than anything suggested so far, was that there would be a probationary period that would apply to them both, with frank exchanges of views the norm, or rather, as Shandy put it, anything short of blunderbusses at twenty paces. Patrick also intimated that, as my first wish was to get on with *Dead Trouble*, it would be perfectly all right for me to stay at home and do so and he would go to London with Tim the following day. There was a lot of preparatory work for them to do. I decided that life was too short to waste time wondering if I was being sidelined and whether I cared or not and, the following morning, waved them goodbye and then lugged over my word-processor from my writing room and set up shop in the newly-vacated spare bedroom. There, I hit the wall.

It's sometimes referred to as writers' block and usually happens when you've written yourself into a cul-de-sac. The way out can sometimes entail binning what you've recently written or, and this is usually more complicated, altering an important supporting structure of the plot or even the ultimate outcome. My problem was that everything about the book seemed cut and dried, all I had to do was provide the embroidery, so to speak.

I blamed my complete change of surroundings and, grimly, took myself and everything back to the cottage where I sat down again and endeavoured to empty my mind of all extraneous thoughts.

Nothing.

I had reached the part of the story where my main character, whom I had already decided was *not* based on Professor Norton, was about to undertake the post-mortem on his wife's lover, whom he had murdered. But all I could see in my mind's eye was John Norton himself as he had appeared that Friday morning to perform the post-mortem on Nadine

Bates, his unsettling dark eyes peering at me over his gold-framed half-moon spectacles. However much I fought against it the image refused to be banished. Finally, I went downstairs to make myself some coffee.

I had the cottage to myself, but for Pirate, our tortoise-shell cat, who was curled up asleep on a chair. The three eldest children were at school or playgroup and Carrie had taken Vicky with her into Tavistock.

I took my coffee into the living room and stared out of the window. The heavy rain and wind had ceased but the thick hill fog persisted and the outline of the barn opposite, only some ten yards across the courtyard, was indistinct. Those eyes . . . I could still see them. They were not necessarily the eyes of an honest man, other men's wives notwithstanding.

'Suppose . . ' I said out loud. 'Suppose it wasn't just great-grandfather Charlie and Max who were bad lads but John too? Suppose, years ago and before he went into forensic science he got up to no good?' I already knew that Norton had been in his early thirties when he had first entered the profession. What had he done before that? Did I owe it to him to find out – even if I did discover he had been the worst kind of crook – and thereby possibly discover something that would lead to his killer?

Yes, I did. The book would have to wait.

I realised when I went back upstairs to shut everything down that my sense of urgency with regard to the unfinished novel was actually a sub-conscious need to solve Norton's murder. For a little while he and I had shared the research into this story that I had created and he had thrown himself into it with great enjoyment and enthusiasm. That made him an inextricable part of it. Although I had not actually liked him a lot I found myself desperately wanting to find out who had so horribly done him to death, thereby, in a way, putting him to rest.

I went off to pack a small suitcase, feeling oddly happy.

Fortunately, both men had gone off in Shandy's car and, half an hour or so later, I threw everything I thought I might need in to the Range Rover and set off. I had left Carrie a note. As we are away quite a lot she has the use of credit cards for shopping and other expenses so I don't have to worry about leaving her with a supply of cash. I would have preferred to have seen her and the children again before I left but did not want to delay my departure and thereby end up driving after dark in the present weather conditions.

What was I going to do about James Carrick, who was, after all, the official investigating officer?

I decided to do absolutely nothing about him. If I discovered anything useful I would then bring him in to what I was doing.

As a gesture to the processes of conventional law and order I would stay right away from Max Norton and the horrendous Sharleen. For the present. Until I had exhausted other possibilities. Actually I was agog to know if Carrick had confronted him with the small firearm – a Derringer? – with which he had taken a wild shot at Patrick. Surely the DCI wasn't going to ignore it in the name of keeping Norton sweet for a while.

I arrived in plenty of time in Bath to find myself a good hotel – no slumming it this time – and then made an appointment for the following morning at a hairdresser's to have my hair dyed back to its natural colour, black. Going blonde, somehow, had not achieved anything other than disguise and as I had also worn a lot of tarty make-up for that particular visit to one branch of the Norton family I was hoping that they would not recognise me should they be around if and when I paid another call to the house. I was hoping though to be able to talk to Frances Norton and her offspring well away from the old vicarage.

If they would consent to talk to me at all, that was.

I could not ignore James completely of course and rang his work number as soon as I got back to the hotel. Bob Ingrams told me that he was on compassionate leave until the next day. I then thought to ask if John Norton's body had been released to the family and he told me that it had and the funeral was in two day's time.

Perfect.

Joanna answered the phone when I rang the Carrick's home number. I was extremely concerned that her escapade with us, shinning down drainpipes and so forth, had had something to do with the miscarriage but she assured me that it was not so, there had been some kind of abnormality. She then went on to ask me from where I was speaking. I told her.

'Oh, wonderful! Please come over and eat with us this evening. We'd love some company.'

'Are you sure?'

'Absolutely. James can cook the dinner – it'll give him something to think about.'

I am not a hard-boiled pragmatist but this seemed to be an opportunity not only to mend a few fences with a friend and try to ease his grief a little but possibly to learn more in connection with my investigation as well.

'You didn't tell me that Ingrid had gone blonde!' Joanna cried when she saw me.

'I assumed it was a wig,' Carrick replied without any enthusiasm for the subject. He regarded me sadly, the sadness mostly to do with the neat flooring of Patrick.

I kissed him in a noisy jokey way. 'Himself's nay bothered,' I told him. 'About anything.'

'He rang me around lunchtime,' James said. 'But I still feel bloody awful about it. I must have gone a bit off my head.'

'Not to mention the fact that the pair of you are too volatile just to rub along in boring fashion. He told me about the time you once had a go at him with a broadsword.'

A small smile appeared. 'So I did. In Scotland. I thought he'd applied undue pressure to a lady I'll refer to now as an important witness but she'd shut her own hand in a drawer after drinking too much champagne. Patrick grabbed a sword too and flailed all hell out of me.' He grinned reflectively. 'It was great.'

'Be prepared,' I said, smiling back. 'He's like an elephant and never forgets.'

'You fancied her,' Joanna said. 'I was there, stoopid! Remember? It was just before you proposed to me.'

'Oh, God,' James sighed. 'So you were.' He went back into the kitchen.

'Thank you so much for coming,' Joanna said fervently in a low voice. 'It's done him the world of good and he'd only have hit the whisky again.'

We proceeded to hit a bottle of very good Chablis. And no, Joanna is not hard-boiled either and had had a little weep when we had spoken on the phone. But with some men if you go to pieces then they do too.

It was James who brought up the subject of John Norton's funeral and I told him that, as I was in the area, I would probably attend.

'We haven't got very far with catching whoever killed him,' he admitted. 'Okay, a tremendous amount of work's been done. House to house enquiries haven't borne any fruit although they don't usually when the area involved consists of large detached houses with high hedges where most people haven't a clue who lives next door and don't care a toss anyway. No one heard or saw anything out of the ordinary and no one suspicious-looking has been seen hanging around. And after checking through his past cases I think we can now eliminate a connection with his work. As far as current jobs went I looked into the Greek one, which incidentally has been handed over to an American with as good a reputation as Norton's, and seemingly there's nothing amiss there. The Bates case is

124

cut and dried as he's now changed his plea to guilty. That, of course, I have Norton to thank for but any pathologist worth his salt would have reached the same conclusions.'

'What did he do when he was younger?' I asked, making my voice sound disinterested.

'No idea, not yet anyway. I haven't had time to dig into that yet. What makes you ask?'

'He told me he didn't enter the profession until his early thirties, that's all.'

'Well, he was obviously at university, medical school, whatever, for quite a chunk of his late twenties. Oh, Frances Norton said he and Max used to mess around during their holidays with a boat Max had.'

'Perhaps it's in the blood what with great-grandfather Charlie running away to sea.' I dared not ask any more questions. But where had the boat been berthed? Was it the same boat that Max had used for gun-running purposes before he went abroad? Or, come to think of it, had the brothers been in some kind of scam together?

'I remember you mentioning that now.'

'He reckoned Max takes after him as he was a bad lot.'

'I confiscated the Derringer,' James said after a pause.

'Just as well Patrick's pretty fast on his feet,' I said, unjustifiably irritated with him all of a sudden.

Two days later, quite deliberately, and knowing deep down that John Norton would have approved, I set out to take his funeral arrangements by storm. A couple of phone calls, one to my agent Berkley Morton, ensured that the photographer from the local paper was augmented by several others from the nationals. A television news team were kicking their heels just outside the entrance to the crematorium courtyard but poised themselves to surge forward when the hired car I was driving approached.

I had dressed for the occasion, having treated myself to a long black wool coat that would do very well for several winters to come and a rather rakish black hat with a single red silk rose tucked into the brim. The high-heeled shoes were higher than I wear normally and I was planning on walking in slow and stately fashion, mostly to avoid disaster.

Flashlamps blazed and a microphone was thrust into my face as soon as I got out of the car. 'Miss Langley, is it true that Professor Norton was helping you with research for your next novel?'

'Yes, I was with him the day before he was murdered,' I replied, pushing the mike away a little. 'He was very helpful with his advice, and the very least I can do is to come today to pay him my last respects.'

'When's the book coming out?'

'Some time next year, I hope.'

'I understand he was a real ladies' man,' went on microphone man with a leer. 'Would you agree with that?'

'I know nothing about his private life. My relationship with him was purely on a professional basis,' I said.

The hearse then arrived and we had to step back out of the way. In the cars that followed I was pleased to see Frances Norton recognise me and then proceed to stare incredulously, and Max and Sharleen merely glance and then carry on with their conversation, taking no further interest.

'Come to cause a bit of a stir?' said a voice at my elbow.

'Why not?' I said to James Carrick without turning round. 'His wife and family are just going to send him to the fire and then go away and forget all about him. It won't hurt the nation to be reminded that some people command the respect and admiration of others.' Although I was afraid this might sound pompous it was actually from the bottom of my heart. I had not meant to say it though. I saw with alarm that one of the reporters was standing very close to me and that his recorder was switched on. No, to hell with everything, even if I was jeopardising any chance of a subsequent conversation with Frances Norton. To hell with everything again, I was crying and someone was getting it all on camera.

'Would you like me to escort you?' James asked gently.

I took his arm.

Afterwards, having watched the coffin obscured by that final curtain, we went back into the murky morning and I stood at Carrick's side, wondering if he was aware that we were both engaged in the same task; that of carefully scrutinising all those present. Murderers have been known to attend their victim's funerals.

Frances Norton obviously felt driven to say something. 'Thank you, Chief Inspector, for coming,' she said, strolling over. 'And Miss Langley. How remiss of me not to have recognised a top author when you came to the house. I hope John was able to help you.' Then with a formal little nod she rejoined her son and daughter. I saw that Arabis had indeed been the one who had looked at me from the upper window, a younger, flabbier version of her mother.

Frances had forgotten something. 'Do please come to the house for refreshments,' she called across to us but speaking, I was convinced, to Carrick alone.

'Thank you but I'm afraid I can't,' he said. 'I'm expected at a meeting.'

'I'd love to,' I said and the woman's face set into a mask and she turned away.

'But if you . . . ' James said.

'Should happen to find out anything interesting,' I said, finishing what he had been about to say. 'You and your bloody convenient meetings.'

'It's true. We're being blessed with a visit from the Divisional Crime Officer.'

I patted his arm. 'Don't take any notice of me. I'll report back with anything interesting.'

'That woman doesn't like you.'

'Does she like anyone?'

8

Perhaps Frances Norton did suspect me of having been the cause of a surprising amount of media interest in her husband's funeral and that was the reason for her increasingly chilly behaviour towards me when I arrived at the house. That was the whole idea: if I got her really mad she might just say something she would rather not have done. To most of the fifty or so friends and relations present I was a complete enigma of course and if they thought me an old flame of the deceased's then so much the better.

I noticed, after the widow had ignored me completely, returning to a conversation with another woman after one stony glance, that Arabis was in charge of an extremely modest buffet in the blue drawing room.

'Well, it doesn't look as though you want anyone to stay for very long,' I observed, helping myself to a glass of white wine, warm, and a ham sandwich, dry. 'Five rounds of sandwiches and a dozen sausage rolls won't go very far among this lot.'

'Why the hell did you come anyway?' she whispered furiously.

'I'm a crime writer and crimes interest me,' I replied. 'Has it occurred to you that whoever murdered your father might well be right here in this room?'

She opened and closed her mouth a couple of times, and then managed to say, 'You're mad!'

'Not at all. A family friend whose wife had an affair with him, for example. An underworld crony of dear Uncle Max. You or your husband, whose business wasn't bailed out. Is he here with his new floozy, by the way?'

'No!' she honked.

'And there's always your brother with the plug pulled on his handouts. A nasty temper by all accounts.'

'Carrick told you all this, I suppose. I shall make an official complaint.'

'Forget it. Most of the information came from your father.'

I was enjoying myself hugely, partly on account of the fascination of watching her trying to cope with the felicitations and sympathy of the others present in between being hostile to me as they clustered around us, hopeful of refreshment. Not all were successful.

'Shall I go and make some more sandwiches?' I offered.

She thawed by one millionth of a degree. 'We didn't think so many would turn up.'

I found my own way to the kitchen where Jason appeared to be on a similar errand, rummaging in the fridge.

'Oh, it's you,' he said when he saw me, relief writ large that it was not his mother. 'Seen any beer around?'

'No,' I said. 'Grab anything that's edible – there's an army to feed out there.'

Obligingly, and seemingly having had more than one beer already, he tossed a load of stuff on to the worktop. 'You're that novelist – Ingrid someone or other. Were you the old man's latest lay?'

'No, and if you carry on talking about your father, or me, in that fashion I might just box your ears,' I said, approaching him.

Jason went a little pale and backed off. 'Hey, hey, calm down.' And when he deemed himself safe said, hesitantly, 'Are you always like this?'

I gave him a good hard stare. 'Only when little shits rubbish their own fathers.' I sorted through the heap and handed over bread, a carton of spreadable butter, cheese, tomatoes, the last of the ham and a bag of washed salad. 'Get busy. Work fast. Do something useful for once in your life. Are there any cakes or biscuits around?'

He appeared bemused but started work. 'In the big tins on top of that cupboard. Yeah, I remember catching a glimpse of you now when I stormed out of the place that night. I'd had a row with the old – er – with Dad.'

He looked like him too, somewhat rakish good looks, though with a touch of refinement from his mother's side.

'Know any real mobsters?' I continued. 'Someone who might just be prepared to indulge in a little butchery if they thought there was a copper or two in it for them?'

He stopped spreading. 'Hey, that's dreadful! You think I – '

'Hurry up, everyone's hungry. You might not have done it on purpose but you're the kind of idiot who blabs when he's had too much to drink and goes in rough pubs because it makes him feel like a real grown-up. I really wish my husband was here,' I raged at him, getting emotional again. 'He'd feed you into that food processor over there, slowly, until you told the truth.'

'Jeeze, I'm really glad the guy isn't,' Jason moaned under his breath, spreading and slicing like a mad thing. 'I'll tell *you* the truth. I didn't kill Dad ⋅ I'd been arrested after a minor prang with the car. I didn't arrange with anyone to have him killed. I really am going to get a job. I didn't have a chance to tell him but I've been for an interview for one that seemed to go quite well. Now I'll never be able to tell him anything ever again, will I?' And he burst into tears.

I finished making the pile of sandwiches, a couple of minutes' work, and took them, together with another plate I filled with small cakes, to the crowd in the reception rooms. When I returned to the kitchen Jason was drying his eyes on a paper tissue.

'Tell me what your father did before he studied to be a pathologist,' I said.

Jason looked at me in surprise. 'You need to talk to Arabis, she's older than me.'

'I'm asking you.'

'Well, I was only a little sprog, wasn't I? From what I can remember he was mostly away. Studying, Mum said. So I guess he was at uni somewhere. He must have been a senior student come to think of it, he didn't take up forensic science until he was in his late twenties.'

'So how did the family live? Your father can't have been earning then.'

He did not appear to mind my probing. 'God knows, but there's always been plenty of money. Until lately that is when he started to put the screws on me, especially about motors.'

'There's a very slim chance too that he wanted to keep you in one piece. But can't you shed any light at all on what went on? Somewhere along the line your father might have met someone who years later was a party to his death. Children have a good nose for sniffing out things adults don't want them to know. Were there no scandals? Huge family rows? Strange visitors? The police coming to call? Come on, think!'

Jason noisily blew his nose. 'Honestly, I can't think of anything.'

'And what about Max? Your sister didn't react earlier when I reminded her that he had a dodgy past. Where was he all this time?'

'I think he had an antiques shop in Brighton when I was quite small. Then he went off and has only just come back.'

'He had a boat, didn't he?'

'Over here, you mean? Yes, but I never went on it. Dad did though.'

'Competitive sailing?'

'Ah! I know,' said Jason and plunged into a lower cupboard. He emerged clutching a four-pack of beer, wrenched one of the cans from it, opened it and took a long drink. 'Just remembered the emergency hiding place,' he said, coming up for air. 'Sorry, what did you say?'

'I wondered if they went sailing for sport.'

'No, Dad hated all sport. He used to say he'd rather do anything himself, even go for a walk, than watch idiots tearing around a field chasing balls and stuff like that. Sailing round bouys wouldn't have been his thing either. I have an idea he and Max used to cross the channel to buy loads of cheese and sausage in French ports. That kind of thing just wasn't so readily available then as it is now. They went for booze and fags as well probably and hid them from Customs if the truth was known.'

'Do you know where the boat was kept?'

Jason thought about it and then shrugged. 'Brighton perhaps, as Max lived there. But it's only a guess, I haven't a clue really.'

Frances Norton came in and performed an elaborate pretence of surprise at finding me still on the premises.

'She's been helping me make more sandwiches,' Jason said somewhat lamely.

'Well, I'm sure we can dispense with your services now,' said the lady of the house poisonously.

I sat down on a pine bench and made myself comfortable. 'I'm trying to find out who murdered your husband.'

'That's what the police are for,' she snapped.

'Who go through the proper channels and have to adhere to all kinds of rules and regulations and when they get round to asking the really awkward personal questions there has to be a female officer present. Questions along the lines of your planned divorce and the business of the private eye to get your late husband on film with his latest dolly-bird. I take great exception to your arranging a little ambush for me that night when he was very kindly escorting me to where I was meeting my husband. As long as you dug dirt on him it seems you cared not a damn for anyone else's reputation.'

She opened her mouth to speak but I banged in with the big one. 'What are you going to say when Carrick asks you who you're sleeping with?'

'Get out!' the woman yelled but she was speaking to Jason, not to me. And when he had gone, only pausing to snatch up the rest of the pack of beer, she continued furiously, 'You may feel you have grounds for complaint against me, Miss Langley, but I can assure you that – '

I carved her up. 'A bit convenient, wasn't it, John being killed just when he might have started to investigate what you were up to? You wanted his money and the house but if he'd hired a private detective as well, to discover who your close friends were, you would probably have lost the lot. Do you know some cronies of Max's from the bad old days who would cut someone's throat for the price of a drink?'

'Of course not!'

'And then there's the business of the shrunken head stuffed with diamonds that was in John's study the day before he died but mysteriously disappeared and then turned up again in the flat upstairs. Are you in league with Max?'

'Get out of my house!'

'Are you aware that he's left a trail of crimes behind him in the Far East? Crimes like piracy and gun-running?'

I knew I was taking a huge risk with Carrick's investigation by telling her these details and if she really was involved in any kind of criminal activity with Max she would immediately warn him and he would, as they say, scarper.

Shakily, Frances Norton sat down beside me on the bench. 'Miss Langley,' she whispered. 'I want you to know that I loathe Max and this woman he has returned to this country with – they're not really married so I refuse to refer to her as his wife. I have always loathed Max. He represents to me all that is utterly rotten in my husband's family. And I can see it in Jason, and in Arabis sometimes. I really regret having involved you in my quest to prove that John was seeing other women. I assure you that I did not mention your name in connection with him when I arranged with a private detective to have him followed. Once I loved my husband but when he repeatedly – repeatedly – had affairs, some little more than one-night-stands with any female he met and fancied, then love dies. But I did not having anything to do with his murder. I'm not that kind of person. I intend to put this house on the market tomorrow and all I want is a small home somewhere and peace and quiet well away from either of my children. I think it's high time they learned to support themselves. Does that make me so terrible?' She wiped an invisible tear from her eye.

I rather felt she deserved an Oscar nomination but made no response to the question, saying instead, 'Jason told me that John and Max used to go out on Max's boat. Did you used to go along too?'

'Once or twice and then never again. I suffer dreadfully from sea-sickness. Jason had no right to talk to you about what we did.'

'It would be the sort of thing to interest a boy though,' I said, really surprised by her attitude. 'Dad out on a yacht while has to stay at home.'

'It was more of a motor cruiser I understand, not a yacht.' In an off-hand tone she added, 'There was no question of the children being left behind while we went on holiday. I have an idea Max used it for – er – business purposes.' She stood up. 'I really can't stay out here talking any longer.'

'And what about years later when Max had another boat in Indonesia?'

'I had nothing to do with that! Nothing!'

She almost ran from the room.

I left, hoping for a chance to speak to Arabis but she had made herself scarce. Most of the guests seemed to have left by now and as I walked through the almost empty house and down the hall – it had a brand new carpet I now noticed – it was with a feeling of sadness and helplessness. This thing, this crime, this situation where a man had been murdered by someone with experience of gutting animals was bigger than I was. And I had forgotten to ask the name of the boat.

* * *

The real expert, the one possessing the facility to remain cool while facing maniacs flourishing flensing knives, or whatever, was still in London. A call to Devon confirmed that he was not at home and his mobile phone was switched off, always a sign that he was deeply entrenched in work. I assumed that Patrick would not actually have to serve out notice at Camberley and would merely be transferred from one posting to another, a neat arrangement that would ensure someone else would have to go and collect his uniform and quite a few of his clothes, probably me.

I decided to be scrupulously fair and rang and told James about the boat. He was politely interested and said he had already started to delve into the murder victim's past.

'Frances Norton's scared,' I finished by saying. 'There's a skeleton in the cupboard all right. I also think she lied about a few things.'

'Umm,' said Carrick. 'D'you reckon the library would have a copy of *Lloyd's Register*?'

'Sure to,' I told him.

But I already knew that it did not possess one that listed owners' and their boats some twenty years previously as I had checked. We exchanged a few pleasantries and then rang off. Having a sudden idea I then phoned Patrick's navy friend who works at Abbeywood. I happened to know that the establishment has a very large technical and nautical library. Half an hour later he rang back with the information that Max Norton's boat – in his words a thirty foot poser's gin-palace – had been called *Painted Lady* and before Brighton Marina had opened and it had been transferred there it had been berthed at Shoreham, a short distance in a westerly direction along the south coast. In the mid-eighties it had suffered a serious fire and been scrapped. Most interesting of all, as far as I was concerned, was that John and Frances Norton had been co-owners, together with someone calling himself Harvey Vindepays, a phoney name if ever I had heard one.

She lied, she lied.

It was the perfect night to park near someone's home and watch what went on as it was dark with no moon and dry and still. Parked virtually out of sight of the house on a level with the church, in the deep shade of a large tree and with the window of the car wound down, I would be able to hear anyone leave and walk across the gravel either to the parked cars or towards me and out through the gateway. All those who had attended the funeral earlier in the day seemed to have left: a quick recce on foot down the drive having told me that there were now no cars parked in front of the house. I had explored no farther for fear of being spotted. The place had now assumed its normal gloomy appearance with hardly any lights visible within.

It was too good to be true, of course, when, three-quarters of an hour after I had arrived I heard a car start up and Frances Norton's silver Ford emerged from the driveway, she having obviously gone out by the back door. I followed, wondering if this was merely a shopping run to re-stock the much-depleted fridge and after we had both fought our way through Bath's truly dire traffic problems – a real struggle to keep her in sight but leave two or three cars between us – my guess was proved correct when we both ended up at Sainsbury's. I followed her home again after she had loaded the boot with carrier bags then listened to the car radio for an hour before deciding to call it a day, the house having returned to its sepulchral gloom. My hand was on the ignition key when Jason roared home in a whirlwind of shrieking tyres and flying gravel and I left, praying that Justin would not evolve likewise. Not a chance, not while Patrick drew breath.

The following morning there was a surprise; a couple of vans from a security company parked by the front door and men installing security lights around the exterior of the building and others going in and out carrying small cable drums and cardboard boxes, presumably putting in an alarm system indoors. It seemed strange that some kind of security system had not been in place already in such a wealthy enclave but I could imagine John Norton not being really bothered with such things. Perhaps he had been too involved with his work to worry about personal possessions. One could hardly blame Frances Norton for feeling vulnerable but surely she had told me she was going to put the place on the market this very morning?

I sat in the car for a couple of hours, content that high hedges shielded me from the view of those living in the properties opposite, and saw hardly anyone. Two women arrived on foot carrying flowers and went into the church. A little later another two drove up in a Landrover Discovery, unloaded a vacuum cleaner and a basket containing dusters and polish and also went within. A postman worked his way along the road. Then a car, a small red hatchback, drew up a short distance in front of me. It was difficult to see how many people were in it because of the head-rests. No one got out.

I played at consulting an Ordnance Survey map I had spread across the wheel, my little ploy for having parked there if anyone came by, glancing up every few seconds at the car in front of me. I decided that it only contained the driver; the vehicle, a rather old one, had a very slight list to starboard. Still nothing moved.

Sometimes, for no apparent reason whatsoever, you get shivers down your spine.

Then, suddenly, the engine of the vehicle came to life and the car accelerated away. I waited until it had turned left at the nearby crossroads and then threw my map aside and went after it. It immediately became apparent that whoever was driving was in a huge hurry, the vehicle going like an Exocet, already almost out of sight down Ralph Allen's Drive. To follow with any hope of success in keeping it in sight would not only draw attention to myself but no doubt incur the wrath of Carrick's colleagues in Traffic Division. This was pointless if all I had been watching was a doctor or vet who had received an emergency call on his mobile.

What my father had referred to as my cat's whiskers, a certain intuition, had intimated otherwise.

To return to the house straight away invited suspicion so I went back to my hotel, had lunch and then made my way to Manvers Street. Sergeant Derek Woods, on the desk, knows me and is also aware that Patrick and I are somehow still *involved*.

'The guv's out,' he reported, his voice briskly businesslike but with the soft West Country burr that is so attractive. 'But I could put out a call for him.'

'Please don't bother – I'll wait,' I said, adding, 'I take it it's more than your life's worth to check a car registration number for me.'

'And this isn't someone who's just carved you up?' he said, grinning.

'Of course not!'

Carrick then solved the problem by turning up, at some speed himself and obviously in the thick of something. Hardly pausing to listen to what I said he took the proffered sheet of paper upon which I had noted down the number of the red car from my outstretched hand and scorched off in the direction of his office, Bob Ingrams, his sergeant, wallowing in his wake. Woods and I had hardly had time to exchange a little light chat when he returned.

'Agnes Meggnessen, Chichester, West Sussex,' he reported tersely, slapping the scrap of paper on the counter. 'Eighty-three years old, retired shop-worker. Is that all you wanted to know?'

Truly, he *was* getting more like Patrick every day. 'Yes, thank you, James,' I replied with a big smile. 'She's one hell of a driver for her age though.'

'Perhaps she's the old mum of that chap who hosted Mastermind,' Woods said, possibly trying to alleviate the lumpen atmosphere. He failed: both Carrick and I gave him a dirty look before going in our respective opposite directions.

It was obvious that I could not mount a permanent watch on the Norton's home but I returned at early dusk and parked in my usual place reckoning that if anything interesting was going to happen it would be during the hours of darkness. The weather remained on my side and it was another fine, still evening.

There was a flurry of traffic during what passed for rush-hour in this part of Bath and then everything settled down again but for the occasional foray to the local post office cum store just along the road. There was no sign of life at the Norton residence at all and I had begun to wonder if Frances had kicked out her offspring and left the country when Jason's car arrived. Through the driver's open window as it went by a street light I could see that Frances was driving. It went from sight down the drive in the direction of the garages and nothing moved at the house for a further two hours.

It was almost dark when I heard a car start up and the same vehicle emerged. My problem was that I could not now see who was driving but as the progress could not be described as frenetic I assumed that Frances was again behind the wheel. I followed at a safe distance.

Fifteen minutes later we were heading out of the city in the direction of Bristol. Thankfully Frances had not taken any complicated short cuts through the maze of minor roads in Bath so I hoped was not suspecting anyone of tailing her. The roads were busy and my real worry was losing her at traffic lights. This did happen once but I succeeded in catching up, mostly because she was driving so sedately. I had an idea she was terrified of all those unaccustomed ccs under the bonnet.

In my handbag, my mobile phone played *Colonel Bogey*, a ring tone that could be laid at Patrick's door, but I ignored it: I could not stop now. Frances had speeded up slightly, perhaps she had got the hang of the car and I almost lost her when she went round a roundabout twice. Had she merely missed the turning or did she mean to lose me? We were in the suburbs of Bristol now and I dropped back when the car I was following turned into a quiet tree-lined road. It turned right and when I again had it in view was turning left some two hundred yards ahead. Another quiet street lined with the ubiquitous cherry and birch trees.

I pulled up quickly and parked, the driver having stopped and left the car to hurry towards the gate of one of a group of semi-detached houses. There were no other cars parked outside and I wondered to whom the old lady in Chichester had lent hers. A son or daughter? And if male, was this person the unlikely-sounding Harvey Vindepays? I started the car again and cruised past the house. There were no other vehicles parked in the drive in front of the single garage either but that meant nothing, the red car I had seen could very well be inside it.

'Or the red car has absolutely nothing to do with any bloody thing,' I muttered, having turned the Range Rover round and parked well away from lamp-posts. I dug in my bag for my mobile and listened to the recorded message.

'Hi, it's me,' said that well-remembered voice. 'Please ring me back ASAP and let me know if it's convenient for you to come to HQ tomorrow to talk about your future role. Speak to you later.'

I whispered some expletives through the open window into the night air having tossed the phone in the general direction of my bag then retrieved it and dialled his mobile number.

'Patrick Gillard.' There were other, jolly-sounding, voices in the background. A team bonding session at a fashionable restaurant?

'Ingrid Gillard,' I said. 'The answer's no.'

There was a pause while, I'll swear, he left the table and sought somewhere a little quieter and with more privacy. 'No? Why ever the hell not?'

'I'm already on a mission and I don't want to be taken off it. You know, just like you told Tim the other day?'

'It'll only take a few hours.'

'Look, you did ask me if it was convenient. It isn't. I might be on to something here.'

Speaking very quietly Patrick said, 'I'm actually in slightly exalted company, one of whom, who isn't Tim, needs an answer. If I tell you my credibility's on the line here . . . '

A hand came through the open window and snatched my phone.

Furious, I was about to hurl myself from the vehicle to give chase, thinking of nothing more complicated than theft when the car door was yanked open and I was dragged out.

Two men.

I kicked one in the crotch and then hit him hard on the ear with clenched fist after, predictably, he doubled over. The other kept a hold on one of my arms, made as if to lunge at me with his other hand and I saw the glitter of a knife. I poked him in both eyes with my fingers, feeling the bite of the knife-blade on my wrist as I did so. Then something hit me on the head and everything became fuzzy.

Only start screaming when all seems lost.

I can make a lot of noise when I want to and picked myself up, not aware of having fallen, and let rip. Both of them came at me at once, one attempting to pin my arms to my sides, the other trying to land a punch on me as I flailed around. A

142

fist grazed past my cheek, the fingers then becoming entangled in my hair. I really screamed then, from the pain, really saw red and, tearing myself free from the other man, chopped him across the side of the neck. He went down like a ninepin on to the road. Then I was hit on the head again. Everything went black.

That it was possible, in deepest Merrie England, to lie in the middle of the road, bleeding gently, and for no one to notice, or choose to ignore one's plight, was a reality that penetrated my fuddled consciousness slowly. Self-protection finally forced me to crawl towards the kerb and away from the traffic but, come to think of it, there wasn't any. Painfully turning my head I saw with a shock that the car was still there. Staring dumbly and stupidly, blood trickling down my face and soaking into my tee-shirt, I realised that some kind of wall coping stone beside me was probably what I had been hit with and the small dark shape lying on the tarmac near the driver's door was my mobile phone. On all fours I headed for it and salt tears added to the general ruin when I found that it was still working. Somehow I found the right buttons.

'Patrick Gillard.'

Such was my relief I was quite unable to speak. Perhaps I sobbed.

'Ingrid? Is that you? Ingrid!'

I suppose I sort of gasped.

'God, woman, I thought you'd hung up on me. What the hell's happened?'

I could see it – my imagination always presents me with vivid and quite irrelevant pictures at the wrong moment – Patrick surrounded by the great and good over coffee and liqueurs, everyone in black tie, while he shouted down the phone to his wife, the newest recruit to the department, whom everyone now thinks has just pranged the car.

'I want you to know,' I said, shaking like a leaf in a Force Ten, 'that I'll come to London tomorrow if I can. Meanwhile, would you please call the police for me. And an ambulance.'

The man I had struck across the side of the neck was still lying near the gutter where he had fallen. He looked rather dead.

9

I awoke from drug-induced sleep into broad daylight,
discovered that my head and one hand were bandaged and
that two pairs of eyes were watching me: the heavy brigade.
The headache being particularly savage I endeavoured to
return to pleasant, painless nothingness.

'How are you feeling?' Patrick's voice enquired.

'I will come to London tomorrow,' I told him, surprised
that my own voice sounded so weak and slurred.

'James would like a word. Are you feeling up to it?'

I opened my eyes again and surveyed them both. Patrick
looked rather pale. Then my gaze strayed to two superb
arrangements of flowers by the side of the bed. 'For me?'

'Faith, they're right and the woman really is gaga,' Patrick
murmured with a strong Irish accent. He half rose from his
chair, saying to James, – 'Fancy a pint?'

'You're an absolute bastard,' I told him.

He subsided again, smiling broadly.

'I really do have to talk to you if you feel well enough,'
Carrick said, frowning as he no doubt disapproved of
Patrick's methods of making me sit up and take notice.

'I did a little more investigating and followed Frances
Norton into Bristol,' I said as he got out his pen and notebook.

'Why?'

'I don't feel well enough to go into full details now,' I said.
'I'll just tell you that I found out she and John were co-owners
of a boat Max once had. It could well have been the one he
used for smuggling guns and stuff for the IRA.'

'And when you parked in Granville Road you were
mugged and someone tried to steal the car.' This was a statement, not a question.

'No, I think this was all about stopping me from nosing around. The two men stole nothing. At least, did they make off with my bag?'

Carrick shook his head. 'I'm working on the theory that you fought them off so effectively you scared them away.'

'I'm pretty sure that wasn't the case. I was stunned, probably by a third person who sneaked up behind me. They hit me twice – I think. There was a stone in the road that looked as though it had been pulled from the top of a garden wall. So they could have stolen anything they wanted.'

He looked very uncomfortable. 'Ingrid, if you were anyone else I wouldn't tell you this yet. When the police arrived one of the men was dead – your handbag was beneath the body.'

This was what I had been dreading. I looked at Patrick and staggeringly, he solemnly winked at me.

'Can you remember much about the attack?' James asked.

'Just about everything,' I said.

'I would be very grateful if you could tell me as much as possible while it's still fresh in your mind.'

I gave him as good an account as I was able. When I had finished he said, 'Show me exactly how you hit this man.'

Patrick volunteered to act as victim and came over and I demonstrated, feebly, how I had used the edge of my hand, in a fashion that Patrick himself had taught me, in a chopping movement.

'Which would render him unconscious and inflict bruising but nothing much more,' Patrick said. 'James, Ingrid isn't strong enough to break anyone's neck. To achieve what the pathologist was talking about you'd have to get the guy's neck in the crook of your elbow and force his head back, sharply.' This asserted by someone whom I had once witnessed do just that. The sound it had made had been like that produced by breaking a stick of seaside rock between gloved hands.

'Who was he?' I asked.

'A local hoodlum with convictions for mugging, theft and burglary,' Carrick said.

'So who broke his neck?'

'I've set up a murder inquiry,' the DCI answered shortly. 'Did you see this third person whom you say hit you on the head?'

'Objection,' Patrick said. 'Ingrid was hit on the head – twice according to her and the medics – by someone using the coping stone your SOCO lot found in the road with several of her hairs on it and microscopic traces of skin that have subsequently been DNA matched with her. If she had seen whoever it was she would have said so.'

I gave him a big smile to tell him that I was eternally grateful but also that he need not be quite so protective. Perhaps his conscience was bothering him.

'I didn't see whoever it was,' I stressed, looking at James. 'But . . . ' In my mind's eye I was back in that quiet street in Bristol. They had had scarves over their faces . . . and in the background out of sight somewhere had been another person . . . the someone who had remained hidden because perhaps they had been crouched down on the near-side of the Range Rover and then emerged to grab the coping stone . . . all these people must have approached from the rear and without my seeing them in my driver's mirror . . . and a background noise, an irregular tapping noise . . .

'What?' Patrick said.

'It was a woman,' I said. 'Wearing high heels. Perhaps it was Frances Norton.'

'But you'd seen her go into a house farther along the street!' Carrick exclaimed.

'I only saw her go through the front gate. I didn't stop and made a point of driving right past and going from her sight before I turned round and went back, obviously in an attempt to avoid her knowing she'd been followed. But if she hadn't actually intended to enter the house in the first place and I had been lured there . . . ' I stopped talking, it hurt my head too much.

'Are you absolutely sure it was Frances Norton?'

'I'd followed her earlier when she went to Sainsbury's. She was driving Jason's car and it was definitely a woman who got out of it and went through the garden gate.'

'I appreciate that you're trying to be helpful but it's guesswork,' Carrick said, shutting his notebook. 'And until I find otherwise I really have no choice but to stick to the mugging theory. Despite what Patrick said about your strength or lack of it I'm afraid, Ingrid,' he went on doggedly, 'that, officially, you're still a suspect. I don't for one second think you intended to kill this man but you have to admit that the training MI5 has given you makes you a formidable antagonist.'

I was about to protest that MI5 had never trained me to break people's necks – it's not something you just pick up like watching flower arranging – but changed my mind.

Carrick continued, 'I understand that you're strongly advised to stay in hospital for at least another twenty-four hours. Then I'd like you to come to Manvers Street where we'll talk again.'

'Thank you for the flowers,' I said as he prepared to take his leave.

'They're from Joanna,' he said, and hurried away.

I sighed. 'Sometimes he's impossible. '

'It's how Scots handle emotional involvement,' Patrick said. 'It's either that or they're chopping you into haggis ingredients with their skean dhus.'

'Patrick, I didn't kill that man.'

'I know you didn't. James knows you didn't. You've just buggered up his organised little world again by suggesting what happened to you is somehow connected with the Norton case.'

'But surely he's not going to take me to court just to keep everything nice and tidy.'

'No, of course not. The man's just praying something else will happen – perhaps along the lines of your other attacker being apprehended and confessing to the murder – to sort it all out for him.'

'He never used to be like this.'

'No, but he's very overworked and, don't forget, just lost what would have been his firstborn. James'll be okay though. It's just a bad patch he's going through.' He smiled gently upon me. 'I think a nurse is on her way to chuck me out.'

'Please don't go.'

Patrick rose to his feet and came over to the bed. Leaning over he kissed me. 'You taste of disinfectant.'

'Perhaps someone had scrubbed the road,' I retorted.

Chuckling, he kissed me again and said more loudly, 'I'll come back in the morning. I'm staying with Mum and Dad so I'm only fifteen minutes away. Then I'll get you out of here.'

'Miss Langley ought to rest now,' said the nurse he had seen approaching.

'Don't forget,' Patrick said to me on his way out. 'It takes more than one cuckoo to make a summer.'

'I thought it was a swallow,' said the nurse brightly.

'So it is,' Patrick agreed. 'Stupid of me.'

Left alone, I pondered. 'Cuckoo' was one of our D12 code-words.

A doctor came and shone lights in my eyes, told me that I had a very thick skull and went away again. I dozed and must then have slept quite deeply for when I next awoke I had been moved to the window end of the small six-bed ward and it was dark outside: the orange street lights blurred by rain trickling down the window. I was very hungry but had probably missed the evening meal so had no choice but to concentrate on a private de-briefing.

Patrick would not have commented at this early stage but if Frances Norton had suspected I was watching her as well as endeavouring to dig into her past then, professionally, as far as MI5 was concerned that is, I had failed. D12 operatives should not be detected. I had used my own car, or rather Patrick's, which had also been a mistake, even though I had not parked all that close to the house.

Reading between the lines it appeared that although James had only spoken about the one who had died, both men who had attacked me were common criminals. And if theft, car-jacking or whatever had not been the name of the game then who had hired them? Were Jason and Arabis involved in anything illegal Frances was up to? The next question I had to ask myself was if the whole boiling lot, Max and Sharleen as well, were in some kind of scam together. Had it been Arabis I had heard teetering around somewhere behind me on high heels and not her mother? They both seemed to favour the same kind of footwear. Or had I merely heard another man with steel tips on the soles of his shoes? I thought not, as striking someone on the head with a chunk of concrete was not the act of a professional hit-man.

Perhaps I was just off my tiny thick-skulled head and nothing at all was going on and James Carrick, overworked, grieving, call it what you like, but a top-class detective, was absolutely right in his thinking?

There was, though, the complication of the dead body. Forgetting for a moment about the shadowy third person it was perfectly possible that the two men who had attacked me then had had some kind of quarrel. I am perfectly aware of the undercurrents that feature in the lives of those in criminal gangs; quarrels, revenge punishments for real or imagined misdoings, drugs and alcohol dependency, not to mention the sheer stupidity of some of those involved. One of them could have finished off the other neatly, deliberately leaving the mugging victim to take the blame. If he had panicked it could have been the reason why nothing was stolen. That it had been premeditated was almost too bizarre for words and they could have had no inkling in advance that I was better able to protect myself than the average woman, although a fat lot of good it had done me. I was rusty.

Time passed and some kind of problem beset the elderly woman in the bed opposite that soon evolved into a minor emergency. It seemed selfish with the short-staffed team hurrying hither and thither to attract someone's attention and ask for more painkillers and something to eat. I dozed again for a while but in the end I had to get up and go and find a loo.

When I returned from my quest, shaky and cold as I was clad only in a hospital nightie and socks, a tall, well-built white-coated figure was waiting by my bed. I expected a telling-off but the man said nothing as I approached, standing with his back half towards me, although he had glanced round and seen me coming. There was something about his stance and bearing that seemed strange but I was desperate to get back into a warm bed and it was only at the last second that I paused, heeding shrieking inner warnings.

'Body language,' I said, backing off a little. 'You're not a doctor and you probably don't even work here.'

For answer he drew a knife and came towards me, smiling. I was never to forget that smile.

'Patrick!' I yelled at the top of my voice, praying that the reason for the use of the code-word was what I now hoped it was: that he had changed his mind about going home. 'Patrick! Where the hell are you?'

The neat square of curtains around the bed opposite sort of exploded as most of the people within rushed out. They all slithered to a halt on the shiny floor as the man faced them, the knife blade pointing in their direction. Then he turned and made a rush at me and as I twisted to evade him the socks I was wearing also slithered and I almost fell. Seemingly effortlessly – he had the height and weight of a modest-sized Sumo wrestler – I was gathered up and carried away. A woman screamed.

He was going to take me somewhere quiet, where he would not be interrupted, and there cut my throat.

He was, that is, until he ran into what might have been a train coming in the opposite direction such was the impact. The force of the collision squirted me neatly – I only slid into a couple of chair legs on the short journey – under a fixed bank of seating in a waiting area. I was quite content to stay there while the train, the scent of whose aftershave I recognised, dealt with the situation. Other women screamed and this was followed by the sound of footsteps thumping away down the corridor as someone ran off. Then, everything went comparatively quiet and a face, not just pale now but white with a hint of green, appeared upside down to peer at me from just above floor level.

'You can come out now,' Patrick said.

'You'll have to help me,' I told him.

Moments later hands grasped my ankles and, somewhat jerkily, I was hauled out. I succeeded in preserving my modesty in the nick of time before the nightie went over my head. Patrick then sat down very suddenly and put his head between his knees.

'Oh, I'm so sorry!' a young nurse said, rushing up. 'Is he all right?' she asked me. She was clutching what looked like a baseball bat, noticed she was still holding it and thrust it from her. 'We keep this here in case we get attacked by drunks but I've always been really lousy at sport and when I took a swing at him I hit this man instead,' she went on breathlessly, obviously about to burst into tears. 'Look, I feel really dreadful about – '

'It's okay,' Patrick interrupted, sitting up, rubbing his head gently. He took a few deep breaths and then added, 'We've lost him, that's all.' He gazed into the distressed pretty face before him. 'Don't worry about it, m'dear. I'm fine. When the world's stopped revolving you can bandage me up as well and I can share Ingrid's bed for the rest of the night.'

'What on earth's happening here?' boomed an authorative female voice.

Before anyone else could speak, and there were at least a dozen by-standers by now, Patrick said to the staff nurse, who had come to a halt only reluctantly as though she would have preferred to carry on and grind any troublemaker into the floor, 'A man attacked my wife just now and I tripped and hit my head as I tried to apprehend him. Perhaps you'd be kind enough to call the police. Ask for Detective Chief Inspector James Carrick.'

'Would you know this man again?' Carrick asked.

'Oh, yes,' I told him.

It was the next morning. I had discharged myself from hospital immediately after the incident, at four thirty am, and we had both gone straight to the hotel where I was staying. Despite all the excitement I had gone to sleep as soon as my head had touched the pillow and only woken up when someone had whispered, 'Breakfast,' in my ear. When I had taken a couple of the pills that the hospital had given me and then dispatched eggs, bacon, sausages, tomatoes, fried bread, toast, marmalade and a pot of tea I felt much better. I was still eating when James Carrick arrived: it had been with his blessing that we had decamped, probably because it saved him from having to provide a police guard. Meanwhile a tracker dog and its handler were searching the hospital grounds to try to trace my attacker.

'I know you said the Bristol pair wore scarves over their faces but could it possibly have been the surviving one?'

'No, neither of them was that big,' I replied. 'He was huge, taller than Patrick and broad. The white coat he'd borrowed was far too tight for him. The lights in the ward had been dimmed as it was night time so I can only remember that he had a chubby oval face, blue eyes and fair hair.'

Patrick said, 'I got quite a good look at him. He was at least six foot four inches tall, as you say with blue eyes, thinning wavy fairish hair. Overweight but in a powerful rather than obese way. A very strong man. I would have had to use drastic tactics to really bring him down and was about to when Florence Nightingale hit me over the head with a rounders bat.'

'A rounders bat!' I exclaimed.

'It was a rounders bat,' he insisted. 'It was probably part of the munitions of the female who came along afterwards.'

Carrick, whom I was glad seemed to have taken over the case personally – did he think there was a link with the Norton murder after all? – had already interviewed some of the hospital staff.

'This knife . . . ' he said pensively.

'I didn't see it,' Patrick said. 'He must have shoved it back in his pocket before he grabbed Ingrid.'

'It was larger than the one the man had in Bristol,' I said. 'More like what I would call a working knife.'

'What do you mean by that?' Carrick said.

'I mean it looked as though it wasn't first and foremost a weapon but something that was used every day. Perhaps for woodwork or leatherwork.' I looked at Patrick. 'You know far more about this kind of thing than I do.'

'So it wasn't a throwing knife?' He did not add 'like mine' knowing full well that if James knew that this poetry made by an Italian silversmith was normally in his possession, for purposes of self-defence, the DCI would hoot and skirl himself right off the map.

I shook my head, profoundly wished I hadn't and said,

'No. And the blade was worn, as though it was sharpened a lot. It had a dark-coloured handle.'

'Haft!' Patrick corrected irritably.

'Reddish-brown,' I continued. 'The colour of dried blood.'

A kind of icy shiver juddered down my spine and then performed an about-turn and travelled all the way back up again. I quickly put my teacup back on to the saucer before I spilt the rest of its contents as my hands started to shake too.

'Delayed shock,' James said kindly as Patrick relieved me of the cup and saucer.

'Suppose,' I said, hoping so. 'Suppose it's a hunting knife and used to gut and joint animals. Or he's a slaughterman who prefers to use his own tools. Suppose he's John Norton's killer.'

To their great credit neither loudly pooh-poohed this theory, Patrick just saying after a short silence, 'How did he get on to you then?'

'The red hatchback I saw outside the Norton's place – ' I began.

'We checked that out,' Carrick interrupted.

'Little old ladies have sons,' I said crossly. 'And nephews. And lodgers. And neighbours.'

'Okay, okay, I agree,' he said quickly. 'Sorry.'

'I might have screwed this up completely,' I continued. 'And since the day I saw whoever it was he, or even she – we could be talking about a couple here – have been watching me watch the Nortons.' If so I had better resign from the resurrected D12 before I had even started.

'Just a little too much supposition here,' Patrick commented. 'I hadn't heard the bit about the red hatchback but I suggest we start from there and really check it out before getting in all of a swither and blaming anyone for something that might not even have happened.'

'We?' I said, probably beating James by a short nose to saying exactly the same thing.

Patrick smiled contentedly. 'Now that an operative of D12 has been the victim of what one would normally describe as an unprovoked attack the case comes within the remit of the department. Tim thinks it's a good way to start to work together and is coming down by train tonight.'

Orders were orders and I stayed in bed for the rest of that day. Patrick asked for meals to be brought up and he only went out twice for a little exercise and fresh air; a walk by the river. By late afternoon I had reached the bored stage and got up to have a shower. The bandage on my hand I removed and replaced with one of the dressings I had been given, the cut was quite a long one but not deep enough to have required stitches. The bump on my head felt bigger than it was, the accompanying contusion and bruising colourful but I left the bandage off as it had been rather tight and then combed my hair so as to cover the worst of the damage.

We had promised Carrick that we would stay put until I was well enough to make a full statement. I had an idea Patrick thought it hazarded his parents safety for us to stay with them at the rectory but had reckoned without the authority he now possessed and when he returned shortly after I had got dressed it was to announce that we were indeed to go to Hinton Littlemoor the next morning, after I had given a statement to James.

'Mother's going to have armed men in the onion bed again,' he continued. 'I rang her though, she doesn't mind.'

'Your father doesn't dote on you quite so much as she does,' I pointed out. 'Especially when he's endeavouring to preach the peace of God while men dressed in black reach-me-downs and waving Heckler and Koch sub-machine guns are lurking around the place.'

'They won't be that obvious,' Patrick replied. 'And don't

forget, he was an officer in the wavy navy before he took holy orders.' He gazed at me appraisingly. 'You look almost okay – except for the egg a bantam laid on your head.'

'I shall have the most expensive things on the menu,' I promised him darkly.

'You really feel well enough to go down to dinner?'

'You bet.'

Carrick had managed to keep the full story out of the news-papers and there was only a small paragraph in the *Bath Evening Chronicle* to the effect that a man with a criminal record had been found dead in Bristol alongside his uncon-scious mugging victim, whose name was being withheld for her own protection, and the police were working on the theo-ry that the death was a revenge gangland killing.

So much Patrick and I already knew, of course, but I was nevertheless grateful that more had not been made of it by the media. Right then I did not possess the energy or inclina-tion to pursue the whys and wherefores, only discovering later, when the whole ghastly tale was finally made public, that D12 in the shape of Tim Shandy had strangled the story on Patrick's suggestion.

'I have a little bit of news for you,' Carrick said after he had questioned me again and I had made a formal statement. 'Agnes Meggnessen is dead. She died eighteen months ago. God knows who has her car now but obviously there's some-thing illegal going on.'

'Have you any leads on the surviving mugger?' I asked.

'I'm afraid I can't discuss that with you.'Then he went on, 'But I think I can safely say that you're not in the frame for manslaughter or murder. I've been talking to people, medics, who know about the physics of breaking people's necks and as the deceased was particularly brawny no tricks in the world you could have performed would have achieved what happened to him. As far as his killer's concerned we're talking about someone really strong.'

'The man with the knife?' I suggested.

'Who knows?' was all he said in reply. 'Ingrid . . . '

'Yes?'

'Please be careful. This man is very dangerous.'

I thanked him for his concern and, as all official business had been concluded, left, my own very dangerous man waiting for me in the entrance lobby.

'Oh, yes, the red car,' Patrick said when I relayed the small piece of intelligence to him. 'Did you keep a note of the registration number?'

I replied that I had.

'Do you feel up to coming with me now to show me where you were ambushed so I can have a look round?'

Tim Shandy had arrived very late the previous night, after I had gone to bed, his train having been delayed. After breakfast, which we had had at seven, far too early for someone still feeling decidedly groggy, I had sat down with the pair of them and related events since I had seen them last, which Shandy had tape-recorded, both of them also making notes. This had been a more in-depth account than I had given James Carrick but only for the reason that the police are hardly ever interested in the gut-feelings and intuition of those being interviewed. Patrick and Tim definitely were: my 'cats' whiskers' had paid dividends several times in the past.

And by now I was thoroughly fed up with the sound of my own voice.

'If I'm allowed to go to sleep when not actually required to do anything,' I said in response to Patrick's question. 'Tim's not coming with us then?'

'No, he's back at the hotel getting fully to grips with the story so far.'

'Are you two getting on all right?'

'Fine.'

There were no nuances of tone in this single-word reply, none whatsoever, so I assumed that things were still slightly awkward.

We arrived in Granville Road, which of course looked completely different in daylight. After cruising slowly up and down it a couple of times I identified the garden gate through which Frances Norton had gone and then Patrick turned the car around and we parked in exactly the same spot as I had. This was easy to find as the coping stone on the low garden wall was still missing, presumably retained by SOCO as Exhibit A.

'I'm going to walk back to the house she gave every impression of intending to enter,' Patrick said. 'I'll lock you in as you're still underpar – if anyone approaches you and you don't like the look of them sound the horn.'

My entire surroundings though, clearly a dormitory area, were as quiet as a tomb. I watched Patrick saunter away and knew that behind the casual exterior he was assimilating everything around him with military thoroughness. If there was anything to discover, he would discover it, even details that the police had missed. I was a little surprised though that when he reached the garden gate I had picked out he opened it and went straight in. Precisely four minutes fifteen seconds later – I timed him – he re-emerged and proceded to stroll back. The area surrounding the car, within a radius of about ten yards was then given a much more detailed, almost a fingertip, search. This took quite a while. Finally, after apparently finding nothing, Patrick disappeared into the garden with the missing coping stone where no doubt the same thing took place.

'I haven't really learned a lot here,' he said when he got back behind the wheel, gesturing in the direction of this nearest house. 'The owner, a woman, is in the garden and didn't mind at all when I asked if I could have a look round. I said I was helping the police with their enquiries and we made a bit of a joke of it. She was out playing bridge on the night in question and nothing had been damaged in the truly immaculate garden, not even footprints in the earth on the other side of the hedge here by the wall. I can only assume you were correct in your guess that your two main assailants approached from behind in your blind spots, the third possibly sneaking up from somewhere else while you were busy with the others and concealing themselves behind the car. If that third person was a woman it could have been Frances Norton who by then perhaps had come back into the street. I've been working on the theory that if she had lured you here with malice aforethought there's every chance she went into a house with which she's familiar – it takes a real brass neck to barge into a complete stranger's garden, even at night. For a start they might have any number of guard dogs. No, I reckon whoever lives there could be the man in her life, this Harvey Vindepays, whatever his real name is.'

I said, 'He might just be history.'

'There's a brass plate on the door. Harvey Dupont, Fine Art Export Agency. A bit of a coincidence, wouldn't you say?'

'Oh, well done!'

'I rang the bell all ready with a story of having broken down and left my mobile at home but he was out so I popped in though the kitchen window, which had been left open, the burglar alarm not set. You know, some people are incredibly careless. Every impression points to the guy being wealthy. Or a fence, come to think of it. The place is stuffed with pictures and antiques and there are books on sailing and ships, lots of coffee table books on art, gourmet cooking and wine and – ' this with a big smile, 'native art.'

'You're a genius.'

'And.' He took something from his pocket. It was a carefully rolled up photograph that had been removed from its frame.

'It's the *Painted Lady*!' I exclaimed, the name clearly visible on the bow.

'And I think you'll agree with me that the three people pictured on the deck are Max, John and Frances looking very youthful. At a guess it was taken about twenty years ago and Harvey himself stood on the quay to take the photo.'

'There's someone else though, standing right on the edge of the shot but facing towards the bows with his head turned away. Perhaps he's a member of the crew.'

'A big chap, isn't he? At least six foot four.'

There was a short silence and then I said, 'Are you going to give this to James?'

'Yes, but not *just* yet.'

'Removing this photo and leaving the frame empty might make things happen.'

'Absolutely – more along the lines of a declaration of war really.'

We got our war.

10

'It seems to me,' Tim Shandy said, one hand making what I can only describe as a graceful guillotine movement, 'that it's time I acquainted myself with Max Norton.'

We had finished dinner and were sitting in the hotel lounge drinking coffee, having postponed going to Hinton Littlemoor until the following morning. Patrick was refusing point-blank to allow me to take an active part in the investigation for at least another day, threatening even longer, until my headache had quite gone without the use of painkillers. My plea that the latter would occur far more readily when I was not bored to tears hanging around doing nothing had fallen on deaf ears. My only entertainment then, and I had to admit that my interest was waning rapidly, was to watch these two men – friends and from good backgrounds, well-educated, expensively trained in their slightly different fields – trying in decreasingly polite fashion to find common ground and forge a pattern that would enable them to work together as part of a close-knit team.

And, no, because D12 demanded something different, something other than putting the world to rights down at the pub, it wasn't going to work.

That something different, regrettably, was that whatever made Patrick so good at his job, the something he possessed that would have turned him, with only a slight variance in his mental make-up, into a first-class criminal, was lacking in Shandy. In short, Shandy was too much of a gentleman. Career-wise he functioned as though on the cricket field. I knew he recognised the anarchic trait in Patrick and that it worried him. He still thought that he needed to keep his junior-ranking officer in check and it was this failure to recognise that a certain flair at handling life, not to mention acting ability, not only tended to keep one alive in highly dangerous situations but got the job done.

Nothing could be achieved until Patrick persuaded Shandy that the reverse would have to happen and that Tim himself would have to develop a different mind-set. That would only happen when they both ran out of patience, politeness was swept aside and they faced one another without any kind of veneer. There would be a big bust-up and I was not sure if I could predict the outcome.

'Well, yes,' Patrick said. 'We don't have to refrain from treading on Max's toes just because of Carrick. What have you in mind?'

'Confront him with the photo you made off with.' This had been the cause of a little contention between them. 'Ask who the other character in the picture is. Trace him. Who knows, Ingrid's hunch about a possible connection between the big man, the knife and this crew-member might pay off.'

'Are we trying to track down John Norton's killer though? Or do you think the priority ought to be finding out if Max is still supplying weapons to terrorists? Or what was behind the attack on Ingrid?'

Shandy took a sip of coffee. 'The two latter by all means. All roads might lead to Rome.'

'Or take a look at Carrick's case notes, by fair means or foul and first trace these two hit-men, one of whom is now deceased. It sometimes pays to get to those in charge of organised crime via the thugs they employ. Someone killed him and I'm keen to know why. It might pay to concentrate on that for a couple of days.'

'Despite socking you on the jaw James Carrick still appears to be a friend of yours,' Shandy observed.

'Yes, but he has a job to do.'

'It's hardly ethical though. D12 doesn't usually run counter to the police.'

'To hell with ethics.' The words were softly uttered but lost nothing by this.

'How would you propose to break into his office?' the other enquired a trifle starchily.

'Nothing so drastic is needed. Ingrid can call him out here saying she's remembered something else while I dress up as a window cleaner and do the job.'

'But man, they all know you down at the nick!'

'They haven't seen my manic window cleaner act. He's recently fallen off a ladder so he's just cleaning the insides. Terrible limp – and a squint. Sprays saliva everywhere when he talks. No one comes within a mile of him as he looks as though he might be HIV positive – a bit twitchy as though he's a junkie and due for a fix.'

I bit the tip of my tongue hard to stop myself exploding with laughter. I knew he could do all of these things and bring it off without looking like an act at a Royal Variety Performance.

'Shall I show you?' Patrick said eagerly, halfway to his feet.

'No!' Shandy exclaimed, having glanced around quickly and observed that we were not the only people in the room.

'Tim,' Patrick said gently. 'I confess to trying to wind you up. But not so long ago you blew up a cavern. In Ingrid's words, there was a most humungous bang. I appreciate that a large amount of explosives had been stored in there and they were in a highly dangerous condition and would have risked anyone's life who tried to move them but did you actually examine the ethics of what you were doing before you set the timers? Pondered that the local authority might not actually wish to be left with a thundering great heap of assorted boulders in the middle of a national park? Asked yourself if environmental groups approved of your blowing rare bats sky-high?'

'Bats?' Shandy ejaculated. 'What bloody bats?'

'There you are then,' Patrick said on a sigh. 'Memorising a few details in a police file isn't so heinous a crime, is it?'

'Surely though,' I said, 'the police have to co-operate with MI5 in investigations like this. Why don't you just point that out to James now that our presence is official?'

'Right!' Shandy said, jumping up. 'I shall do it now – or ask whoever's on duty. If I don't get satisfaction I'll ring him at home. It's about time we started getting results.' He strode away.

'Sorry,' I said, actually not at all repentant, having found Patrick gazing at me rather woodenly. 'Did I say the wrong thing?'

'Not at all,' he said ruefully. 'That rounders bat must have done more damage than I thought. Perhaps you'd better sign on again in the morning and take over from me until I've lost my headache.'

'Oh, good,' I said, rubbing my hands together. 'I suggest we raid Harvey Vindepays' place and beat him to a pulp until he confesses.'

'Shall we see what Tim finds out first?' Patrick asked with a guarded smile.

D12's SSO, Senior Surveillance Officer, Nathan Palmer, who as Patrick had once said, 'could hide in your front garden for a week and you wouldn't know it', and his assistant, just known as Jaz and who preferred not to talk about his previous employers, were taking it in turns to watch the Norton household. This was regarded as potentially more fruitful than keeping surveillance on the house lived in by the man calling himself Harvey Dupont and, alas, the budget could not stretch to more personnel in order to watch both. This was because Tim was insisting that the assignment was still, strictly speaking, only semi-official, in a way a rehearsal. There were no more pressing matters they ought to be dealing with, yet. This had the effect of making the job somehow second-grade, which Patrick and I found irritating.

Two days later Jaz was on duty when he saw Max Norton load several large and obviously heavy boxes into his estate car and drive away. Tim Shandy, on standby in the locality, was alerted and tailed him. Eventually the car drew up outside Dupont's residence and Norton went inside.

Required to provide information, James Carrick had released the name of the murdered mugger, one Darren Jones. A known drug-addict living in a squat he had been game for any job, mostly of the illegal variety, in order to feed his habit. No one else in the building owned to knowing anything else about him or, more likely, was not prepared to talk, least of all about Jones's associates or most recent activities. His killer, whom Carrick thought likely to be of the same ilk, might as well have never existed.

Shandy could apply himself to some of the seedier aspects of uncover work with huge enthusiasm and a clear conscience and had spent twenty-four hours in the squat in the guise of a crazed tramp – right over the top but who the hell was I to criticise? – got in a fight after someone tried to steal his meagre possessions and narrowly escaped being knifed. He had learned nothing, either about Jones or anyone else who was now missing and who might be his murderer but, needless to say, had emerged from the experience not remotely rattled.

There had been no point in my looking at mugshots from the point of view of those who had attacked me in Granville Road as they had both been masked but Patrick and I did spend some time at the Manvers Street police station trying to identify the man at the hospital. To no avail.

'It's hard to believe someone like that would have no previous convictions,' Patrick commented as we were driving over to Bristol. It had been agreed that the pair of us would enter Dupont's house and conduct any questioning, both our respective headaches having gone, and hopefully, with thinking processes fully recovered. I was driving and we had borrowed Elspeth's car to lower the risk of being spotted and recognised.

'Now I come to think of it there was something foreign about him,' I said. 'In an odd kind of way he reminded me of James: sort of Nordic. Perhaps it was the bleakness of his blue eyes.'

'James's mother was from Orkney,' Patrick said. 'That's where his Viking wildness and unpredictable moods come from. Eric Blood-axe and all that.' He turned to stare at me. 'God, I'm being slow again, aren't I? This man might be a relation of Agnes Meggnessen after all.'

I said, 'Now that Max Norton has actually removed a question mark about his connection with this Harvey character do you intend to question them both about the other man in the photo?'

'Too right.'

'He might not have noticed that the photo is missing from the frame.'

'That's possible. It was tucked away towards the back of a shelf.' Patrick gestured towards the windscreen. 'Can't you overtake this idiot in front?'

'This is your mother's little shopping runabout,' I reminded him. 'It hasn't the legs. Besides, we're already doing seventy which is something it's never been called upon to do before. And declarations of war on your part are all very well and might make things happen but Harvey could have panicked, upped sticks and gone.'

'It would have been risky though, especially as Carrick's been sniffing around. It suggests guilt if you suddenly do a runner. Which, interestingly, as everyone until now has sat tight, points to the possibility of something going on with huge stakes involved. No, even if my removal of the snapshot was noticed I reckon people are endeavouring to keep their nerve. They aren't new at the game, don't forget. If only Tim had agreed to push for permission to have all their phones tapped.'

Another cause of disagreement. I said, 'So d'you reckon we're talking about drugs, arms, that kind of thing?'

'Could be. Plus stolen works of art, of whatever provenance – stolen anything that's valuable, come to think of it. Easy to hide things in legit stuff packed in a container being shipped abroad. We already know Max is into diamonds, although he assured us he bought them legally. You're not supposed to smuggle them into this country in dried bonces though but I'll leave Customs and Excise to worry about that one.'

'Max has taken a risk – taking stuff over to Bristol in broad daylight.'

'You may depend it's all above board this time – behaving normally and trying to show everyone what a good boy he is.'

'So, strictly speaking, we really ought to turn off the heat for a bit so they relax and then get careless.'

'You can't have it both ways. You were the one who wanted all hell pasted out of them.'

There was no sign of Tim.

'I would have preferred it if he'd stayed,' Patrick commented.

'He's been on call for hours,' I said. 'Perhaps he needed a pee.'

Patrick grunted.

The back of Max Norton's car was still wide open and there was no sign of anyone as we approached the house on foot.

I was wondering where Dupont's own vehicle was parked, the garage doors also being open to reveal an interior stacked with so many boxes and crates there was very little room for anything else, when Patrick said, 'I'm asking myself if it's anything like the house farther along the road whose owner I spoke to the other day where there's a gate at the far end of the garden into a lane. I could see that some people have built garages down there instead of at the front. Even if there's no second garage at this place there might still be access into the lane. I should have thought of that. Tim's been watching the front – what the hell's been going on at the back?'

'Are you thinking the birds might have flown?' I asked.

'Or that we might have been lured here, like happened to you the other day.' He turned to me. 'Perhaps you ought to wait in the car.'

'Balls,' I said.

He feigned polite distaste at my language and we proceeded on our way.

As befitted a premises used, genuinely or not, as the headquarters of a fine art export agency there was an air of elegant grandeur about the front of the house. Closer examination showed this to be mostly pretence, a sham. Clever perhaps, the rendering, stucco and false portico; the latter made of fibreglass, that disguised what had probably originally been an ordinary thirties brick house, the concrete ballustrading on the terrace and steps somehow 'distressed' to make it look like old stone, plants in bright primary colours crammed into too many Grecian-style urns that were made from a kind of plastic which until you touched them were indistinguishable from the real thing. I am not a snob, I use similar ones at home, tens of thousands of people do. It was just that in this setting, and bearing in mind what Patrick had already told me about the interior, the effect was overwhemingly phoney. One half expected there to be a coat-of-arms over the front door.

'This time we don't ring any doorbells,' Patrick muttered. 'Neither do we go in through the kitchen window.'

Regrettably tending to yield to flippant remarks and the giggles when in potentially dangerous situations I was about to remark that all the chimneys appeared to have been taken down but desisted, mindful that his tone had suggested he was bloody-minded enough to kick the front door in.

Then, somewhere to the rear of the house, we heard a car start up.

'Go!' Patrick shouted.

I can run a lot faster than he can now but only because of his leg. For short distances though he moves with surprising speed and he was right behind me as we rounded the side of the house, running on the lawn. But when it comes to making sudden manoeuvres at full tilt he is at a distinct disadvantage, dancing lessons, fencing, playing squash notwithstanding. Therefore when I jinked and dodged the person coming towards us; that well-remembered, stomach-churning huge outline, Patrick practically ended up colliding with him. There was no time for him to get his balance and bring his arms and hands, his real weapons, into play and he had been on the receiving end of a vicious swipe to the side of the head before I had even come to a standstill. Seeing what was then about to happen – I can't remember whether or not I screamed – I leapt upon the man, jumped astride his shoulders, wrenched the head up by the hair, fingers clawing to gouge the eyes, tear, rend, anything.

I was tossed off as someone might swat away an insect. Then, after crashing to the ground I saw, as though I was having some kind of drug-induced hallucination, all the colours of this ghastly garden vivid, rancid, gangrenous, Patrick hurled with enormous force against the trunk of a tree at least a dozen feet away. Then I became the centre of attention.

Somehow I picked myself up and bolted. It seemed that my legs were no longer a part of me, as though I was not running but floating. Inconsequentially I wondered if I was dead. In hell then; to be pursued by *this* for ever.

There was indeed an opening in the fence at the far end of the back garden, which was mostly down to grass, where a gate had been left open. I made for it, hearing footsteps behind me. He was gaining on me. Once through it, I turned sharp right, saw a parked red car, swerved and went in the opposite direction. Almost immediately was next door's gate, also open. I flung myself through the gap, grabbed the gate and crashed it shut. There were large bolts, top and bottom and I shot them across. Then I dashed off again, expecting him either to smash his way through it or climb over the top.

In the middle of a circular lawn I slowed and took a fearful glance over my shoulder.

No one. I stopped.

Then I heard a car door slam and an engine started. The car drove away, tyres squealing.

'Where the hell d'you think you're going?' said a short, fat man, emerging from a greenhouse.

I couldn't speak, just bent over gasping for breath.

'Is someone after you? What's happened?' He had a buzzing sort of voice, like a wasp in a beer glass.

The answer to the second question was murder on two counts – almost.

Max Norton was found lying in his own personal bloodbath in a downstairs room of the house in virtually the same circumstances as had his brother, the difference this time being that he was not quite dead. The house had been ransacked and there was no sign of Vindepays/Harvey. After heroic efforts by doctors and forty units of blood it was announced that Norton would probably live but take a very long time to fully recover, if indeed he ever would. As it was he was in intensive care and unlikely to be fit for police interview for several days, perhaps a week.

All this was in the near future as bracing myself, I had searched for Patrick, discovering initially a completely flattened variegated laurel bush at the base of the tree trunk and then followed a trail of damaged vegetation like that made by an animal that had crawled away to die. Already frantically trying to work out how I was going to adapt the cottage and my life to accommodate someone with a broken back and completely paralysed from the waist down – possessing a writer's imagination sometimes really is hell – I had seen a foot sticking out from beneath the beech boundary hedge. At the time not noticing the twigs tearing at my clothing and scratching my face I had crawled into the bottom of the hedge on all fours.

'Cowardice is sometimes the better part of valour,' had said a voice shakily from beneath dead leaves. 'Please tell me he didn't hurt you again.'

I had located his face, after a little more searching and kissed him. 'Just a bit fragile, that's all. I think you ought to lie quite still until we know how badly hurt you are.'

'I'm all right. I take it he's gone.'

'Yes, he drove off in his car.'

There had been a general upheaval in the detritus, accompanied by oath-laden, albeit muttered, language. Finally we had both staggered out and Patrick had flopped on to the grass.

'I left you to that bastard,' he had whispered, tears glittering on his eyelashes. He really has the most beautiful eyelashes, longer and blacker than mine even when I'm wearing mascara.

'I'm quite sure all the breath was knocked out of you,' I had told him firmly, helping him up and deciding to postpone revealing that the man had been positioning him to break his neck. 'Can you actually remember him throwing you against the tree?'

Patrick had shaken his head. 'No.'

'Well, obviously, you were stunned as well.'

He had shaken his head again, meaning something different.

At least James Carrick could not lay this one at our door. We had horribly and literally caught Max Norton's attacker red-handed. It had not been until Patrick and I had taken a quick look indoors, observed the dreadful state of affairs and called the police that we had noticed the blood on our own clothes, smeared on them by the man's hands. This ensured that everything we had been wearing was placed into sealed bags by the Scenes of Crime team – from Bristol CID as Carrick was not yet involved – and taken away for forensic testing. We ended up clad only in SOCO white plastic suits, not at all comfortable next to the bare skin.

'You know, I'm getting quite turned on by this outfit,' Patrick said for all to hear when we were released, apparently refuting my own reactions. He gave me a raunchy leer. 'Fancy a quick one in the bushes?'

I gave him a bored look back and he guffawed. I was not at all fooled by this play-acting: the man was still haunted by my vulnerability to serious injury or worse as a result of what he regarded as his own cowardice because, dazed and confused, he had tried to bury himself in the dead vegetation under the hedge. He was in considerable pain as well and no doubt his back would be very bruised the next day from his violent contact with the tree. It seemed to me the fact that he could move at all was because his flight had been near the end of its projectory and he had landed mostly in the laurel.

Patrick was also seething mad. With Tim.

This anger had come off the boil, cooled and become cold fury by the time we returned to the rectory and I was profoundly glad that Tim had remained staying at the hotel as he had felt he would be intruding. Postponing the inevitable though might make the situation worse.

'Ah,' said Elspeth, taking one look at her son as we entered the kitchen, having come in by the back door. She went back to preparing the dinner.

Patrick stopped, took a deep breath, went over to her and lightly kissed her cheek, her succinct utterance having been more effective at reproaching his demeanour than a thousand-word essay. 'Do you want me to do something for you?'

'Not if you've had a dreadful day.'

'Is it the kind of thing that can be done before or after I have a shower?' he enquired solemnly.

'I just wondered if you'd cut a small branch off a tree in the garden for me – it's so low people keep walking into it and you know what your father's like with tools.'

'Of course. I'm not a real fan of trees right now. Are you sure you don't want them all down?'

The branch turned out to have a diameter of only a few inches so I let Patrick get on with it. I was just going back indoors when I heard his mobile phone ring. I traced it to the pocket of his jacket which he had thrown over a chair in the kitchen.

'Hello, it's me,' said Tim's voice. 'Where are you?'

'At Hinton Littlemoor,' I told him. I then gave him a résumé of what had happened.

'I assume that the car you heard being driven away as you approached the house was Dupont getting the hell out of there,' he said when I had finished.

'Almost certainly. James put out a call while we were there for him to be apprehended.'

'Do you know what was in the packing cases?'

'No, the police were concentrating on the murder scene and hadn't got round to opening them. The whole place had been ransacked so it's going to take them quite a while and there's no sign of Dupont to confirm what's missing, if anything.'

'What's the latest on Max Norton?'

'I don't know that either – you might just have to ring the hospital.'

After a short pause Tim said, 'I think we ought to have a de-briefing, don't you? This is developing into a complete shambles. Shall I see you at my hotel at seven thirty?'

'No,' I said. 'I suggest you come over here and we meet in the bar of the Ring o' Bells at around six, just after they open. If we talk in private Patrick might just skin you alive and that will be the end of it.' I rang off before he could say any more.

I knew perfectly well that the arrangement would give Patrick and me time to have our showers but as far as he was concerned not too lengthly an opportunity to brood and compose a diatribe that, later, he might wish he had not delivered. It seemed to me that more than enough valuable human resources had been squandered and time wasted by arguments already. I was soon to discover that my ruse was pointless and should have suspected Patrick was up to something when he went off to make a phone call after I had told him of the plan.

As I had hoped the single bar was empty when we arrived – the other having been converted into the restaurant some time previously – but for the old man who appeared to live permanently at one end of it and was rumoured to sleep in the Wellington boots he was never seen without, not even in summer heatwaves.

'How are you doing, Pa?' Patrick greeted him with, adding the more important, 'What are you having?'

'You're a good man,' said Pa, having stated a preference for a half of bitter. 'I reckon we'll see you as rector when your dad retires.' He chuckled. 'Who knows, you might even bury me.'

'Nah,' Patrick said. 'You'll still be sitting right there on that stool in a hundred years time.' He leaned on the bar and spoke in a confidential undertone. 'Seen any strangers hanging around the village lately?'

Pa shook his bald head. 'Can't say as I have. You expecting any?'

But Patrick, with a skinful of painkillers, just smiled, clapped him on the shoulder, bought the drinks and we sat down.

'They're doing a good job then,' I said. 'I assume Tim knows we have a couple of minders.'

'No, actually he doesn't,' was the blandly uttered reply. 'I thought it might complicate matters further. I only wish to God we'd had them with us earlier.' He was not serious, their real brief was protecting the rectory and whoever happened to be inside.

I glanced through the window. 'That's Tim's car just arriving.'

'Shit fan-hitting time.'

'What are you going to do?'

'It depends on his attitude – what he actually says. If necessary, give him the sack. I got clearance – from Daws, who as you know is still over-seeing everything. I told him the absolute truth; that I'm finding it practically impossible to work with someone who still thinks like a tank commander, is a really nice bloke but who goes off for a pee, or whatever, without asking if you'd mind waiting for him so he can provide back-up. I also told Daws that you and I could easily have ended up dead this afternoon at the hands of someone who bears every resemblance to an utterly bananas serial killer.'

'Surely though, Daws should speak to him himself, in private?'

'There's no time for finesse. Besides, Shandy turned up looking like a dog's dinner to pull rank at Carrick's nick so if I have to give him the bum's rush in a public bar it's as good as it gets.'

Silly of me to think he looked so happy merely on account of paracetamol.

Tim entered, came over and sat down heavily. The two men's eyes had met as he crossed the room. There was a silence.

'I already knew, of course – and became convinced after what Ingrid said earlier,' Tim said at last. His expressive hands spread open, palms up. 'I can't keep this up as I'm forcing myself to be someone that I'm not, or perhaps no longer am. Acting the top brass, the man in charge, all bright buttons and gold braid, to try to kid myself that this is the job for me. It isn't. I haven't the flair, the bloody fantastic flair that you possess, Patrick. I thought to myself they don't need me as well just to question a bloke. Forgot all about the maniac with the knife. It was stupid of me, bloody stupid!' he continued, banging a fist on the table. 'If I'd been with you there's every chance that nut-case would now be in police custody instead of somehow one step ahead of everyone and MI5 could concentrate on the real job in hand. But to be brutally honest I came to the conclusion a few minutes ago, driving over here, that I'd rather face a whole roomful of Serbs than carry on. I'm just not cut out for it.'

Patrick got up from the table to fetch him a whisky, a double, returned and placed it before him. Softly, he said, 'What happened to you in Bosnia would have destroyed lesser men. I have to tell you that about an hour ago Richard Daws gave me the authority to let you go – if I thought fit. Before I got chucked against a tree today I probably would have agreed that indeed you aren't the man for the job. But I don't and that's because for several vital moments I hid myself under a hedge while Ingrid was running for her life from this man. I've never met anyone who can toss me around like a puppet. I think the pair of us need to learn a few lessons.'

Tim was shaking his head. 'Thank you, but no. We've always been straight with one another and I meant what I said. If I let you down again I'd probably feel obliged to make like an elephant and wander off to die.'

Patrick smiled sadly. 'And if we *should* happen upon a roomful of Serbs?'

Tim gripped his arm. 'I'm your man!'

11

Patrick was not entirely correct in his prediction that the crates and boxes that Max Norton had taken over to Bristol contained nothing that would interest the police. For while there were no illicit substances, money or arms Bristol CID did discover a large collection of artefacts from Indonesia and other parts of the Far East. There were masks inlaid with gold, other objects decorated with semi-precious stones and, seemingly on its own in an oblong box, a *tau tau*. This was not one of those from the Norton's flat, a fact confirmed by Sharleen Norton, who was immediately questioned. Questioned by James Carrick, that is, who not surprisingly by now had inherited the entire shooting-match. She insisted that the contents of the boxes were Max's own property and that they had been kept in one of the locked garages, a storage area MI5 was subsequently forced to admit it had not quite got round to searching. She went on to say that Harvey Dupont, an old friend of Max's, was arranging the shipping and sale of the items to the States, and no, she didn't know where he was. Max was gradually selling all his collection of cultural artefacts. It took up too much space. No, it wasn't against the law to deal in things like that, as although the Government had been intending to introduce legislation to make handling illegally excavated or stolen artefacts an offence as soon as parliamentary time could be found there was a general election coming up, wasn't there? she rattled on. And even if the law *was* passed it would only cover those items stolen after it came into force. Besides, how could she and Max know that all the *tau tau* in collections in the West almost certainly had been nicked because the Torajans never sold them? She and Max had only ever dealt with what they'd assumed were reputable dealers. So what else do you want to ask or can I go home as I've far more important things to do? she concluded with a triumphant smirk.

Carrick had then produced the silver Georgian coffee pot that had been packed, hidden, beneath the *tau tau*, an object exactly matching the description of one on a list of antiques stolen during a burglary at a manor house near Farrington Gurney some three months previously. Sharleen had angrily denied all knowledge of it and said she was sure Max would have bought the thing fair and square at auction. She had then gone on to accuse the police of having planted it.

All this was bitterly related to us by Carrick himself. 'She was so bloody rude it was only because I'd have had to say cheerio to my job that stopped me from putting her across my knee. But I wouldn't, come to think of it, as she looks like something that died quite a long time ago and has been warmed up again a hell of a sight too quickly. No doubt she reminded Max of some of the other bits and pieces in his collection.'

'That's because most of her face is hidden behind her ears,' I told him.

'But she nevertheless appears to know exactly where they both stand with the law,' Patrick pointed out. 'I'm sure she's lying on several counts. What did she say when you asked her if she could think of any reason for the latest attack on the Norton family?'

'She just said it must be a nutter.'

'One couldn't actually argue with that. But you would think that if they know who it is they'd be only too delighted to shop them.'

I suddenly remembered the photograph taken on the *Painted Lady*. Had Patrick given it to James, or not? Staring hard at the former I said, 'If it's to do with something from the past perhaps it does involve the boat.'

'That photo you gave me yesterday,' Carrick said to him.

'The other person in the shot, the big man whose face you can't see . . . ' He broke off pensively.

'Did you ask Sharleen about him?' I asked.

'Yes, but it was long before she met Max. So she said, and I found myself believing her. She said she'd never seen the picture before. It was taken around twenty years ago, after all. I shall show it to Frances Norton, who just happens to be next on my list.'

'Can I have a go at Sharleen?' Patrick asked.

'Delighted,' James said with a grim smile. 'How's the back?'

'Going to be all colours of the rainbow.'

I said, 'As not one of the Nortons so far has mentioned a possible suspect for the attacks – and surely self-preservation should be a driving factor – and whether it was the big man in the photograph or not, then it's quite likely the person they feared is dead. Therefore we have to find out who the Nortons murdered and if the man with the knife was a friend or relation of the victim.'

After a little pause Patrick said, to James, 'That's one of the reasons Ingrid's in the team.'

Or rather what was left of it. The break-up had been achieved with minimum distress to those concerned but where that left Patrick and me was anyone's guess. At least there would no longer be the distraction of worrying about Tim and Patrick had decided that we would carry on until ordered to do otherwise.

Max Norton was still too weak to be questioned and was to undergo a further major abdominal operation the following day. The police were keeping a watch on airports, railway stations and ferry terminals for the suspect, with or without his car, as well as the missing Dupont so all the law enforcement agencies could do was read forensic reports, conduct house-to-house enquiries and generally pester the relatives of those attacked.

'You!' was Sharleen's greeting when she saw us.

Sweetly, Patrick presented her with his ID card at which she goggled with all the allure of a freshly landed monkfish.

'Is this on the line or another of your stupid tricks?' she demanded to know.

Patrick assured her that we were on the line.

'Look, I didn't even *know* Max when he was mixed up in that arms-running stuff.'

'May we sit down?' Patrick said after we had trailed behind her into the living room.

'Carry on, but it won't do you any good. I'm damned if I'm answering your questions.' She flounced over to the window and lit a cigarette with jerky, agitated movements.

Patrick made himself comfortable in an armchair with every sign of contentment. 'You don't have much of an accent. Are you an American citizen?' he enquired mildly.

'Like hell. I was born in Manchester.' She shrugged angrily. 'All right. I'll tell you. Me and a chum, Des, went out to the States, Denver, about fifteen years ago. He'd set up a small computer company. A real whizz-kid with computers was Des. He told everyone I was his PA. It didn't work out though, him and me, I mean. We soon split up and I'd got to know a bloke who got me a work permit. Don't ask me how: he was a bit of a Mr Fixit. Probably in the Mafia if the truth was known. I worked for him and his family as a sort of Girl Friday – looked after the kids and stuff like that. Then his wife died – she'd been on drugs for ages – and I stayed on. We got married after a bit as he said it made him more respectable in the neighbourhood. What a bloody laugh! The man was into every scam he could get his hands on.'

'When did you meet Max?' Patrick asked.

Sharleen seated herself and blew a plume of smoke at the ceiling. 'A couple of years ago. Romano, the bloke I'd married, had a heart attack and died about twelve years after we got hitched. Right out of the blue it was. He'd left everything

182

to me in his will – nothing at all to his kids. He couldn't stand them. They were grown up by then of course – he was a lot older than me – and cut up very nasty. I had to leave so sold up, the house, everything. Max had a shop, an emporium the silly sod called it, in a mall close by. He bought most of the furniture and stuff off me. It was good to hear a British voice and we sort of became friends.'

Patrick said, 'You came out of this very well financially then.'

I thought she would flare up and tell him to mind his own expletive deleted business but, no doubt in response to the chill he was exuding, she said, 'and a right naive little fool I was too. I gave most of it to him after we got married and he used some of it to buy all that native art junk.' Her gaze went over to the group of *tau tau*. 'I mean, God, they give you the screaming habdabs. Just stand there staring at you as though they're alive. I swear I'll take them straight to the tip if Max snuffs it. D'you know what?'

'What?' Patrick responded obediently.

'I'm sick to death of living in a bloody museum. Those heads I made him chuck away stank to high heaven. It's partly because of me he's selling it all.'

I said, 'You don't seem to have a very good opinion of Max. Why did you marry him?'

'Who's she, really?' Sharleen asked Patrick truculently.

'My heart's desire. Answer the question.'

She scowled at me and said, 'I married him because I was scared of being alone. Romano's sons were making threats. The eldest was a real mobster by then.' She added, reluctantly, 'Max said he had a boat out in Indonesia and a big house back in England. But when he sold the boat he got hardly a brass farthing for it as it needed a lot of work doing to it by then and when we got back here I found out he didn't have anywhere to live at all.'

'You're looking for a property in the million pound

bracket,' Patrick put in smoothly. 'Which would suggest to most people that you're hardly on the bread-line.'

'I don't know what we're going to do now. Not with Max in hospital and likely to be an invalid even if he survives.'

Heart's desire waded in with, 'Inconsiderate of him to get carved up so he won't be able to assume such a big role in your multi-million pound racket, whatever it is, if at all. For someone who's obviously always prided herself on hedging her bets it looks as though your caviar and champagne's on the line again. And if he does die and all your assets are confiscated by the courts . . . ' I gave her a chummy smile.

Patrick pointed a languid forefinger and said, 'You're not a naive little fool and never have been. Ingrid's right: that would be quite a lapse given the rest of what you've said. I think you actually bought in to Max's *other* business, the shop being just a front, with the money you got from your marriage to Romano. Did his wife really die from a drugs overdose or was she helped on her way just a little?'

When Sharleen remained silent Patrick said, 'You're not a very good liar, are you?'

'I'm not lying!' she shouted, stamping her foot.

A small carved wooden figure toppled from the edge of a shelf and thudded face down on to the floor.

'The porky pies god falleth,' Patrick murmured.

'I reckon you're worth millions,' I said. 'Or at least Max is, and the money's all tied up in foreign bank accounts, diamonds, you name it, places where you personally can't get your hands on it. How many of the other Nortons are in it as well? Frances? Jason? Arabis, now she's all on her little own-some?'

Sharleen stubbed out her cigarette, sat back and folded her arms. 'I'm not saying one more word. Bugger off, both of you.'

'And there's this character with the knife,' Patrick continued, frowning as though he'd just had a nasty thought. 'I simply can't believe that you don't have some idea what *he's* about.

Ingrid reckons you lot topped someone and this is revenge big time. Who's next, I wonder? We met him in Harvey Dupont's garden, by the way. That was the second occasion and he always seems to be a little ahead of us. Perhaps when it happens again we'll be ten minutes too late for you.'

She just sat there in silence.

'Why did you refuse to tell Chief Inspector Carrick the name of the crew member of the *Painted Lady*?'

'I told you, it all happened before I met Max.'

I said, 'I don't believe he didn't tell you about it.'

'Seeing he's dead now it hardly matters, does it?' Patrick went on in off-hand fashion.

'That's right.'

'Tell the truth!' he suddenly shouted, making her jump.

'He is dead,' Sharleen spat back at him. 'Max told me something happened to him – some kind of accident.'

'Where?'

'Out in Indonesia. When Max had bought a new boat. The first one caught fire at Shoreham, or somewhere like that.'

'But you were out in Indonesia as well.'

'Only right at the end, when he sold the boat.'

'What was the man's *name*?'

She shook her head stubbornly.

'Was it Meggnessen?'

'No,' she said hoarsely.

'I think it was. What was his first name?' When she still remained silent Patrick continued relentlessly, 'I don't actually have the power to arrest you but we could carry on talking down at the police station if you insist.'

'Look, I'm scared! All right?' the woman babbled. 'Perhaps I'm superstitious too in thinking he might have come back from the dead but he was a horrible bloke and if he finds out I'm telling you all this . . . ' Her hands clutched at her clothing like claws.

'Did you ever meet him?'

'No, but Max said he was horrible. He was stupid and greedy and drank like a fish and when he got drunk was only really happy when he was knifing someone. If Max kept all drink right away from him he was okay, a good worker.' Perhaps hoping to look as though she was being helpful she went on, 'Max also said that was because he came from Iceland – they're all good with boats.'

'What was his name?' Patrick asked again.

There was a fairly long silence during which Patrick waited patiently and then she said, 'I think it was something like George. Only with a J.'

'Jorge?'

'It could have been.'

'Meggnessen?'

'Yes,' she whispered.

'Are you sure he's dead?'

Visibly, Sharleen shuddered. 'Max said so. I don't know the details. You'll have to ask him.'

'Was John Norton involved with all this?'

She shook her head. 'I don't think so. Now go away.'

'But he used to go over to France with Max in the *Painted Lady*.'

'That was ages and ages ago. They used to buy drink and fags and Max sold them to his chums.'

'But you admitted you're aware that at one time Max smuggled weapons into this country for terrorist groups.'

'I try not to think about it.'

'So what's the scam this time? We already know that stolen property was found in the crate with the *tau tau*. '

'That's it. That kind of thing. Nothing else.'

'So where does the stuff come from?'

'God knows. It's nothing to do with me. Max fixes everything.'

'A couple of hired thugs were put onto Ingrid to try to stop her interfering. Whose idea was that?'

She flashed me a glad sort of look. 'Haven't a bloody clue.'

'And one of them ended up with a broken neck. I wonder if our friend with the knife was right behind them. I wonder how he knew. Tell me, do you like Frances Norton?'

'She's a complete bitch,' Sharleen said savagely.

'I'm also wondering if she's master-minding all this and Max now has very little to do with it. And John got in the way. Had he found out and was threatening to blow the whistle?'

She was shaking her head in a robotic way.

I said, 'Or even keeps the knife man on a short leash for most of the time and uses him to make sure everyone involved toes the line. Only he resented it when she called in someone else to deal with me and broke one of the men's neck to teach her a lesson.'

'You're just guessing,' Sharleen said.

'Guesses often hit the mark,' I told her. 'What did Max do to upset her or did he merely want out? Or were you behind it because he wanted a divorce? Was he fed up with marriage to an old harpy?'

The woman was up and out of the chair heading in my direction before I could move but Patrick was a little quicker, stuck out a foot and tripped her neatly. She nose-dived every which way but safely onto the Chinese carpet.

'I'll report you for assault!' she yelled, righting herself.

'I shouldn't shout if I were you,' Patrick told her. 'Frances might hear.'

'I don't care if she does. She's not in charge of anything, she hasn't the brain. She couldn't even get John's funeral right.'

'That's a good point,' I said.

'You don't have to be *quite* so offensive to the people being interviewed,' was the gentle reproof some time later.

'Only harpies spit,' I countered, adding, 'I'm utterly

187

baffled as to why a man like Max would take her on. He's the sort who would go for flashy tarts.'

'Money?' Patrick suggested wryly. He seemed to go off into a world of his own. 'A resurrection,' he murmured. 'I like that. I wonder if Jorge had a twin brother? A surviving twin's as good as a resurrection – or potentially as bad.'

'Dupont's probably in Patagonia by now.'

'We mustn't rule him out, you know. Just because you think you heard a woman's footsteps when you were ambushed in Bristol it doesn't mean he isn't in it right up to his neck. If Frances isn't very bright – and I have to say I'd go along with that verdict on the strength of what you and others have said – she might just do as he tells her. And don't forget he appears to have been involved almost right from the beginning. My guess is that he's in a bolt-hole somewhere. I think we ought to find it. Almost more important is to find the HQ they operate from, which could be one and the same place. James's team found only the usual junk behind just a few packing cases and boxes in Dupont's garage; broken mowers, old bikes, piles of newspapers, that kind of thing. The packing cases were empty but for stuff like bubble-wrap and there were no family papers of any kind, nothing to give any useful information. We must find out if he really is Frances Norton's boyfriend.'

'James'll have his work cut out to get any real information out of her,' I said. 'She might be thick but she's not stupid.

Patrick chuckled. 'Only a woman could say that and get away with it.'

'You know very well what I mean: lack of intelligence can be compensated for by native cunning.'

We were in Barolo's, the Italian restaurant where John Norton had taken me for dinner. There were two reasons for this, the first being that Patrick was famished, neither of us having had time for lunch, the second that we wanted to ask a few discreet questions. Although they were almost fully booked they had been able to fit us in as it was early, having only just opened. I have to say though that Patrick can usually exert sufficient charm to get us in to most places.

'It bothers me,' I admitted. 'This knife-man being on the loose.'

Patrick glanced up from the menu. 'Yes, and I know you were only hoping to provoke that woman into saying something she would rather not have done when you suggested Frances had him locked in her wardrobe. Seriously though, *do* you think they control him in any way?'

'I don't know. I hope not. But he does represent a skeleton in the cupboard from their past. You don't reckon . . . '

'You've had an idea?' Patrick prompted, laying the menu aside. 'I'm not having the squid, in case you were wondering.'

I loathe it when he eats squid. It puts me off my own meal. All those twirly tentacles with suckers on . . . I blew him a kiss and said, 'Norton's killer didn't break in, there was no sign of forced entry. You don't reckon he was expecting him and going to buy him off?'

'That's really intriging. Go on.'

'Well, suppose Jorge really was murdered by the Nortons. On the boat. Perhaps he went on a real blinder and became very dangerous. So they banged him on the head and chucked him over the side. Whoops, our crewman got drunk and was lost at sea. Big dangerous brother, cousin, twin, whatever didn't believe them and swore vengeance. Quite a few years later he succeeded in tracing them here to the UK and John tried to buy him off. Perhaps he didn't offer enough, perhaps the man went there to kill him anyway. It looks as though he wants to kill the lot. Are they getting police protection, by the way?'

The waiter was hovering hopefully.

'The beef with mushrooms in red wine for me,' Patrick said. 'My wife will have the squid, preferably with a double helping of eyeballs if you have them.'

I had not even glanced at the menu but when men are hungry . . . 'No, chicken, please,' I amended, having grabbed it and chosen the first thing my gaze landed upon. 'You're an utter pig,' I hissed when the waiter had departed in the direction of the kitchen.

'Well, Max has an armed guard, in hospital,' Patrick said when he had finished laughing, answering my question. 'I suppose someone ought to be stationed outside the house in Combe Down – especially now we've stood down our own surveillance. I might give James a ring when we're through here and tell him we're working on a theory that they're all in grave danger. Better to be safe than sorry. Oh, in view of what happened, I asked Daws if I could actually carry a firearm instead of having to leave it locked in the cubby box in the car or in the safe at home and he said no. His argument was that this guy's quarrel isn't really with us and we just got in his way.'

'That's hardly fair,' I protested.

'But he's right. Our brief isn't to arrest John Norton's killer – that's down to Carrick – but to find out if Max Norton's still providing weapons for terrorists. Which of course isn't really in D12's brief but we sort of tripped over the job and got ourselves landed with it as a rehearsal. Hence, no guns. There's no authorisation for that until the department is up and running again officially. I'm not even supposed to have a knife.'

I was still mulling over possibilities. 'If John Norton was planning to pay off this man he might have been going to do it with the shrunken head full of diamonds and that was why it was on the shelf in his study.'

'I like that idea too. But why didn't his killer take it anyway?'

'Well, for one thing he might have been super-suspicious and not believed Norton when he told him what was inside it, for another he could have thought it would connect him with the crime – especially if he suspected they were stolen.'

'Max therefore had to be in the know. Unless John had made off with the head without his knowledge – everything points to him not having had a huge amount of ready cash. Or he could have been acting as spokesman for the whole family.'

'The latter's far more likely. I can see Max retrieving it from the murder scene, even stepping over his brother's dead body.'

'But according to an alibi that James thinks is a reliable one he and Sharleen were in Bradford-upon-Avon that night.'

'So they were. I'd forgotten that for a moment. Frances retrieved it then, fearing the police would find it, after a panic phone call to Dupont. She lied about not finding his body until the morning. That rather points to Frances not being in any danger. Or, surely, she wouldn't have remained in the house.'

'The quarrel's perhaps just with the menfolk then. That would figure. I'll still give James a bell though. And who knows? They might not have had any inkling that he'd cut up so rough.' Patrick grimaced. 'Sorry. Too apt a phrase.'

The owner and chef of the restaurant, not a suave Italian by any stretch of the imagination, sat down at our table and then said, 'Keith Bennett. How can I help you? No complaints, I hope?'

'No, wonderful food,' Patrick said sincerely. 'This is partly to congratulate you and also to ask you a couple of questions about one of your customers.' He put his MI5 ID card down on the table.

Bennett peered at it for a moment. 'Ask away. Can't say I've ever come across you lot before. Who do you want to know about?'

'Professor John Norton.'

'The poor chap who was murdered? He was a bit of a lad

was that one. Always with different ladies.' He gave me a quizzical look.

'Yes, me too,' I said. 'Only I'm writing a book and needed his help.'

'Did you ever see him with people who obviously weren't ladyfriends?' Patrick asked.

'Yes, he's been here with all sorts. Colleagues some of them. Medical types. And with a bloke who could have been his brother, a sort of flashier version if you get me. A woman was with them who looked like Dracula's granny. Seriously,' he went on when I burst out laughing. 'Did you ever see that comedy programme on the telly? That family of vampires, monsters and what-not living in a castle. She was like the female with pointy teeth in that.'

'Can you remember when they were last in?' Patrick said.

'A month or so ago, I suppose.'

'Did you ever see him with a really big chap? Blue eyes, fair hair?'

'No, can't say as I did.' Bennett shrugged. 'But I'm not here all the time. A chum runs the place when I have my days off.'

'Strictly in confidence,' Patrick continued, 'we're trying to trace a man by the name of Dupont. We think he's also called himself Vindepays. He lives in Bristol.'

'What does he look like?'

'That's the trouble, we don't really know. In a photo taken around twenty years ago he looks to be of medium height and slight build, with receding dark curly hair. But people can change a hell of a lot over a period of time.'

Bennett shook his head dubiously. 'I remember a completely bald bloke. But he could have been one of the medical bods.' He stared into space. 'Iffy though – bit of a wide boy if you ask me. Yeah, he had an earring come to think of it. You don't reckon . . . I mean it's nothing to do with me but . . . '

'Say away,' he was encouraged.

'All those females Norton was wining and dining. Some

192

wore wedding rings so what did their old men make of it, eh? One of them might just have decided to put an end to it.'

I said, 'Were any of these women known to you? I mean in a local gossip kind of way.'

Bennett leaned forward and when he spoke it was in little more than a whisper. 'Well, I didn't but a couple of the boys knew who one of them was.' He gestured vaguely to where the waiters stationed themselves near the entrance to the kitchen when not actually serving. 'Her name's Gloria somebody or other and she was in the party that included the chap who looked as though he might be his brother. It was her birthday. I'd been asked to provide a cake. She was hot stuff, if you ask me, eyeing up everything in trousers, much to the annoyance of the bloke she was with, understandable I suppose as he was old enough to be her father. A week later she was back in here with Norton, on their own. Must have a thing for older blokes – or more likely they both paid her handsomely.'

'Who was the man she was with the first time?' Patrick wanted to know.

'A character called Joe Thomas – but he's one of those who calls himself something different every day of the week. He's a grubby little git so the woman needs her head examining. He's a mobster from Cardiff. Not far to come is it? – just across the bridge like. This is his patch.' Bennett got to his feet. 'But I didn't tell you. I don't want this place petrol-bombed.'

'Before you go,' Patrick said. 'Was the bald man at the birthday party too?'

'He might have been, but you must appreciate I get hundreds in here every week.' With a quick wave he had gone.

'Surely Thomas can't have killed Norton,' I said.

'No. But we now have a name, the low-life professional criminal connection. I'd put a lot of money on those men who attacked you being his odd-job boys. Good, it means I can give James a promising lead.'

'And?'

'And then I shall ask him where he lives, who fences for him and the addresses where he's been known to stash his loot – all kinds of interesting things connected with the Nortons might be stored here, there and everywhere. Then I shall pay him a call.'

'Patrick – '

'What?'

'James will pay him a call.'

'Yes, but he'll get there first and be quite polite about it as he has no evidence. I don't need evidence – I shall merely go later when Thomas is laughing all over his face and take him and his shitty little empire apart.'

I tried to remember how many men who had lifted a finger against me in the course of our work for MI5 had lived to tell the tale. I could not think of any.

12

'Joe Thomas? A mobster from Cardiff?' James Carrick said wonderingly, affronted. 'This is his patch? Never heard of him. This is bloody-well *my* patch. Someone's sold you a real yarn.'

'But our informant has no axe to grind,' Patrick said disarmingly. 'And the man he was talking about is known to have several aliases.'

'What does he look like?' James asked, still resentful.

'Fiftyish, overweight, around five feet six in height, bloodshot brown eyes, greasy brown hair, quite a few gold teeth,' Patrick replied, having rung Keith Bennett to obtain the extra information.

'That's Benny Cardwell,' Carrick said dismissively. 'He acts and likes to *think* of himself as a mobster. What Joanna would describe as a squillion percent poser. He's not Welsh but thought he could make a killing in Cardiff. He was chucked out of Wales by the real Cardiff bad boys so now lives here in the London Road and is a loan-shark by trade: that and a little light thieving and car stealing for good measure – plus a protection racket, his real source of income, that I intend to nab him for early next month when a cunning ruse of mine comes to fruition.' Having got that off his chest he laughed.

'He might provide Max Norton's muscle,' Patrick explained. 'He was seen with some flash totty at Barolo's with Max, Sharleen and John some months ago. And a bald man who might or might not be Dupont. Any sign of him?'

'Not a whisker.'

'Is Cardwell the kind to employ people living in squats, drug addicts, the lawless homeless?'

'Definitely. He just has two what I'll call permanent staff, a muscle-bound moron who acts as his minder cum chauffeur – no, in case you're wondering, he's not our knifeman, too young – plus a brighter but if anything more dangerous character whom I'm keeping a very close eye on and hoping to soon send down with his boss.'

It was the following morning and having been directed by Sergeant Woods to Carrick's office we had actually come upon him in the main corridor heading that way himself.

'I have a theory that Cardwell was paid to frighten off Ingrid,' Patrick said when we had arrived and the DCI had wearily dropped into his swivel chair.

'That would be in his repertoire,' James said, waving us to a couple of spare seats.

'I also think there's every chance that Dupont's holed up in a premises either owned or rented by Cardwell, the place the Nortons could well hide their wares.'

'Still convinced they're gun-running?'

Patrick smiled in non-committal fashion. 'It's my job to find out. What I would like from you are addresses.'

James pulled a face. 'I was afraid you were going to say that.'

'I appreciate that you're worried we might not be able to make the assault charge stick, plus anything else we come across, and if he then heads for the hills you might lose him on the protection racket scam but – '

'That's only the worst scenario should you draw a blank with everything else,' James interrupted. 'Frankly, I'm over-stretched with more important stuff at the moment and I'd prefer to sit tight on Benny and let MI5 do its own thing. Potentially, what you might nab him for would get him locked up for far longer than anything I have on him. My only condition is the usual one – that you shout when you need people arrested.'

'That's very good of you, James,' said Patrick quietly.

'Yeah, I owe you one.' Unconsciously perhaps, Carrick rubbed his chin.

Patrick chuckled cold-bloodedly. 'You won't get out of it that easily.'

'Okay, we're not going to make a major incident of this,' Patrick said to me a little later. 'If only for Carrick's sake. We adopt the Oirish personas and merely frighten them stupid. But if they offer resistance . . . ' He left the rest unsaid.

We returned to our hotel to change, Patrick into something suitably intimidating; black leather jacket, ditto jeans with a belt that has a metal skull with red glass eyes on the buckle that for some extraordinary reason he thinks adds to the effect but is resoundingly naff, me into my 'tart' rig. Then, my husband having broodingly got into character as one by one he donned the garments, we took a taxi to the London Road. We were, needless to say, being extremely vigilant in checking that we ourselves were not being tailed.

Carrick had given us two addresses; one an upper flat where Cardwell himself was reckoned to live for most of the time, where we were heading for now, the other a house on a council estate in the nearby village of Southdown St Peter, a premises apparently resided in by a varied and shifting population, depending mostly upon who was currently helping the police with their enquiries, where stolen property connected with Cardwell had previously been found. James had gone on to ask, changing his mind slightly, if we planned to hit the latter address that day as, if we found Dupont there he could do with talking to him in connection with the Norton case as well. Patrick had assured him that he had every intention of doing so and would report back accordingly.

I was keeping well in character and also quiet. Patrick was disobeying orders, the short-barrelled Smith and Wesson in the shoulder harness beneath his jacket. I understood this: while conscious that the last thing he wanted was a running street battle in one of the most beautiful cities in Europe

Lieutenant-Colonel Patrick Gillard was not going to die for silly reasons from a petty hoodlum's bullet.

I paid off the taxi and we crossed the pavement to a doorway to one side of a betting shop. The paint was peeling off it, two screw holes and a darker outline revealing where a number 8 had once been attached. Several shops along the road was a passageway that led to the rear of the buildings. We went down it and turned right at the end. There was a fire escape, of sorts. In his leading role, or not, of terrorist but nevertheless dripping with malice Patrick went lightly up the iron staircase, quickly checked by counting along that he was facing the correct door and kicked it in. A loud crash of breaking glass followed as the panes in it shattered, the door having hurtled back to hit the wall inside.

This, I knew, after what had happened to him at Bristol, would be a belt and braces job. True enough, as I was halfway up the stairs – he had asked me to stay out of immediate range – there was a thump from within and then a sound like someone upending a dead cow into an otherwise empty rubbish skip. Seconds later a portly, hairy little man, his mouth wide open in silent but extravagant terror, came bolting out through the door and down the stairs towards me. When he saw that it was only a woman likely to impede his progress he flung back a hand literally to strike me from his path. I ducked, caught the hand, applied a little science to the rest of the arm and he went bouncing merrily downwards reminding me irresistibly of a largish shrunken head. There was a final and utterly satisfying collision with two overflowing and reeking dustbins.

Above, a man exited the flat backwards, apparently airborne, hit the guard rails opposite the door and rapidly subsided. He was then mysteriously drawn inside again as if by a magnet, no other agency being visible and, judging by the audible evidence, joined the cow in the skip.

'Did he trip?' Patrick asked, coming into view, only very

slightly out of breath, his gaze on the untidy state of affairs at the bottom of the stairs.

'With a vengeance,' I told him.

'Poor old Benny. He really shouldn't go rushing about like that.' There followed a derisive hoot of laughter.

Benny was rescued, dusted off as far as this was practically possible and returned at speed to his abode. I followed and shut the door.

The interior of the flat could only be described, even by the most glib estate agent, as being in need of considerable modernisation and improvement. The kitchen in which I immediately found myself had probably last been decorated at the end of World War Two, since when it had never been cleaned. I followed Patrick and the hapless Benny up a narrow, dark passage, the walls covered in anaglypta wallpaper painted brown, noting as we passed an open doorway a bathroom with a gas geyser over a surprisingly large free-standing cast iron bath. In it lay two inert men, just one or two arms and legs overflowing.

Patrick dropped Benny sufficiently forcefully into a fraying armchair for him to bounce a few times and said, 'I want to know everything about the Nortons: John, Frances, Max, Sharleen, Jason, and Arabis. I also want every last detail on a man calling himself Dupont or Vindepays and his whereabouts. After that I shall personally arrange for you to be delivered to the nick where you will sing your heart out to Detective Chief Inspector James Carrick. All that in exchange for retaining your ugly head upon your shoulders.' Patrick bent down and sprang the blade of his knife under Cardwell's nose. 'It will be removed extremely slowly.' He was not bothering with the Irish accent and was merely himself, which was more than sufficient.

I sat down. We might be here for quite a while.

'I don't know nothing about the Nortons,' Benny started to bleat then froze when he felt sharp steel against his skin. 'At least,' he amended, 'nothing about the women. I don't deal with women.'

'I thought it was Frances Norton who muscled in on your boys warning off the person watching the Norton house.'

'They didn't say nothing about that.'

'Your English is bloody terrible. And it couldn't have been "they" could it? – because only one survived to come running back to you.' Patrick grabbed the greasy hair and pulled his head back.

'It was the bloke!' Benny shouted.

'Which bloke?'

'Please . . . '

He was allowed to lower his head.

'Dupont, or whoever he is.'

'The witness reported that she thought it was a woman wearing high heels.'

'No, it was him. He wears shoes with lifts and metal tips to make him look bigger and sound more important. A bald sod. I can't stand 'im.'

'You took his money though.'

'That's business.'

'So Dupont wanted the woman warned off.'

Benny nodded. 'He wanted her put away. But I don't get involved with killings.'

Patrick knelt by his side, the knife a fraction of an inch away from the dirty-looking skin of the man's neck. 'That woman and the witness is my wife. That's her, sitting over there. What you've just said has prevented me from cutting your throat here and now. I can't guarantee I won't change my mind.'

I held my breath for truly, truly, he was not play-acting. And Patrick has killed two men, one because he had been ordered to, the other in self-defence, right before my eyes.

'But some bloody maniac turned up, didn't he?' Benny gasped. 'And broke Darren's neck. Just appeared out of nowhere and done him in. Don't ask me about that 'cos I don't know about it.'

'What did Dupont say about it? You said he was there.'

'I'd got my money so I didn't see him afterwards. Johno said he and Dupont scarpered pronto.Wouldn't you have done with a nut-case like that around?'

'You will tell Carrick all about Johno,' Patrick said, thoughts obviously on the more important matters in hand. 'So you did business with Dupont. Is he the boss man?'

'God knows. He's the one who gives me orders.'

'Where did you arrange to meet him?'

'In the pub on the corner. He rang me on his mobile when he wanted to talk.'

'So you have no means of contacting him?'

Benny shook his unkempt locks. 'No.'

'Did Dupont ever hint that someone was out to get him?'

'Like the Norton brothers, you mean?'

'So you do know about them.'

'I read about it in the papers, didn't I? No, he didn't but he's always like a cat on hot bricks. Nervous, like.'

'Where is Dupont?'

'He'll kill me,' Cardwell whimpered.

'No, because I shall have killed you *first*.'

Benny swallowed nervously and when he spoke his voice was squeaky. 'He's at the place at Southdown St. Peter. At least ... '

'At least what?'

'He was yesterday. I don't have no control over him, do I? He said he was going to move the stuff and ... '

'What?' Patrick barked when the other stopped talking.

'Scarper. But he didn't say where. He wouldn't tell me, would he?' Benny finished pleadingly.

'What stuff?'

'Nicked stuff. They haven't been able to move it because this nutter with the knife might show up again.' He then went extremely pale, regarding Patrick with his small blood-shot eyes in utter horror.

'No, the nutter with the knife's not me. Don't you know what this stuff is?'

Benny shook his head. 'All I know is it's nicked stuff sent abroad in a container hidden in native carvings or junk like that. He asked me if he could stow it in the loft at my brother's place.'

'It seems a damn-fool thing to do though,' said Patrick crisply. 'Hide something really special in a house likely to be raided by the police at any time.'

Seemingly before I had had time to blink he had placed the knife between his teeth, lifted Benny up by his grubby sweat-shirt and slammed him into the nearest wall. Slammed him into the wall three times. I assessed the situation carefully and decided that Patrick still had his temper under control. Just.

'Where is it?' Benny was asked, having been thrown back into the chair.

The man was semi-conscious. He mumbled something.

'I can't hear you,' Patrick said and then paused, listening.

I had heard it too, an upheaval noise in the bathroom.

Patrick swiftly left the room, there was the sound of bone colliding meaningfully with bone and he returned rubbing his knuckles, utter silence in his wake. 'Well?' he enquired, as though there had been no break in the proceedings.

'Dupont's not at the house,' Benny muttered. 'He was but he left. Said it was too risky. He's got a hidey-hole somewhere. It's nothing to do with me.'

'Not one of the places you hide your loot?'

'No. Honest guv,' he wheezed when his interrogator came up close. 'I'd tell you if I knew, the bleedin' shifty little git. He paid me in fifty quid notes and when I looked at them a bit closer yesterday a couple in the middle of the wad were duds.'

'Counterfeit?' Patrick asked sharply. 'Do you still have them?'

'No, I didn't want to get caught with 'em.'

Patrick glanced at me and I shrugged. I might then have gone on to shake my head in an attempt to mitigate any further encouragement to Benny to tell the truth but this was not necessary for all the anger had gone out of him now.He settled for carrying him into the bathroom, reverently placing him, like a votive offering, on top of his henchmen, and strapping the lot down – round and round the bath – with a roll of Duck tape he found in the kitchen. I then rang James on Patrick's mobile.

'Okay, I'll pick up Benny and Co and get some people together and raid the other place,' Carrick said. 'We do it on a regular basis anyway as some of those who doss there are drugs dealers. I'll let you know if we find anything interesting.'

'We're no further on,' Patrick said on a gusty sigh, slipping his mobile phone back into his pocket.

'The counterfeit notes are interesting though,' I said.

'People like Dupont probably have a few of those around most of the time. It figures though, if he had a hideaway he wouldn't tell the likes of Cardwell. He actually gave us quite a good picture of him, didn't he? A jumpy, shifty little git – similar to Keith Bennett's description.'

'Shall we go and have a drink in the pub on the corner?'

'Dupont's hardly likely to be there now.'

'Obviously not. But someone in there might remember him.'

'Okay, we'll give it a try.'

'When Keith Bennett said something about not wanting to be petrol-bombed . . . '

'Yes, I wonder if he is a victim of Benny's protection racket? You know, I really yearn to fill that bath with water and light a large fire beneath it.'

***

The pub, The Golden Fleece, was close by and as it was well after eleven by now we decided to have an early lunch and use the extra time to keep an eye on events. Along with all the regulars and a couple of American tourists we exhibited wide-eyed interest when several police vehicles howled to a standstill in full view from the windows, Patrick keeping a particular watch out for any drinker who might slink stealthily away. No one did.

'It's not as though they're going anywhere,' he said in exasperation, referring to the tub-full, when yet another police car, a Rapid Response Vehicle by the look of it, arrived in a blaze of blue lights and sirens. 'Oh, it's Carrick.'

'He believes in keeping a high crime-fighting profile,' I said. 'He told me it makes visitors feel safer so they stay and spend more money, the city booms commercially and all the people who allocate police funding vote them just about all the money the Super needs.'

'I wish I could work like that,' Patrick said wistfully. He went over and had a quiet chat with the barman and when he returned he was smiling. 'Benny's well known round here but I got the impression the bloke behind the bar was endeavouring to distance this place from people like him. Can't say that I blame him. Benny, with or without his henchmen, does sometimes meet people in here, including a man I'd described to him as bald, nervous-looking and wearing an earring. The barman doesn't know who he is but thinks he might live locally too – but not all the time.' He glanced quickly at the blackboard with a chalked-up bar menu. 'I'm just having a sandwich – mustn't eat big meals when I'm working.'

'It sounds as though the house in Bristol is mostly a front for the genuine export business,' I said when he returned from placing our order.

'Almost certainly. Any ideas? We can't just start knocking on every door in the area.'

'We might have to be patient and wait until Max is well enough to be interviewed.'

'Or until the knife-man finds him first.'

We lapsed into a rather gloomy silence. Then I said, 'Suppose we wait until dark and then I stroll around looking as though I'm picking up men? If he's holed up round here he might creep out when it's dark if he feels like a – '

'No,' Patrick interrupted with an air of finality. 'No. I'm not having you . . . '

'You can be my pimp and be nearby and protect me – it must be someone else's patch.'

'Ingrid . . . '

'It's better than doing nothing.'

'No. It's not. It's a million to one chance he'll appear and you'll probably get so many takers we'll start a war. *Then* what will I tell James?'

He was so put out by the suggestion I was forced to hide my amusement behind a hand.

'There must be an easier way of finding one man,' Patrick muttered.

'He might hear on some kind of local grapevine that Benny's been arrested. Or if he's living reasonably close by he'll have heard the sirens. In which case he'll really do a bunk.'

'Or stick his head in the door here in order to have an excuse to watch what's going on from a bit closer without much risk of being spotted.'

'But surely he doesn't care a toss what happens to Benny.'

'Only if Benny sings, which I'm fairly sure he will. And *he* don't forget, took money from Dupont, who wanted you taken care of for ever, and – ' Patrick momentarily gripped my arm, which was resting on the table, so ferociously that I gasped.

He was not aware that he had inadvertently hurt me, staring at a man who had just entered. It was a short, bald man who scanned the room apprehensively for a few moments, lit a cigarette and then went over and pretended to read a poster advertising a forthcoming jazz night. He kept glancing through the window, at the police vehicles. As he turned I saw that he wore a single earring in his right ear.

'Grab or follow?' Patrick mused aloud but in a whisper, watching more surreptitiously. 'He can't be planning to stay as he hasn't bought a drink.'

A girl brought our sandwiches and I followed Patrick's lead in wolfing one down in case we had to leave quickly without the benefit of refuelling. One of the police vans drove away, followed by an area car. Still the man stood there and we started on another sandwich. Then, a group of young men, bank or office workers judging by their dark suits, noisily erupted through the door and the man we were watching started visibly. He ground out his cigarette beneath a heel, ducked around them and exited.

Outside, it would have been the work of a moment to run up behind him, seize him and frog-march him back to Carrick. But instead, we followed at a safe distance. He walked quickly, hunched into a dirty denim jacket, darting furtive looks left and right. He did not look behind him but if he had all he would have seen was a couple – we were swinging along holding hands – who were probably holiday-makers on their way to the next place of interest.

Dupont, and I was convincing myself it was him, turned almost immediately left and if anything walked more quickly. We paused on the corner and allowed more distance to separate us – this street was far quieter with hardly any pedestrians – and then set off after him. A few yards farther on he crossed the road and carried on walking.

'This isn't right,' Patrick said quietly. 'He's going out of immediate earshot of the main road. Any farther and even if he had heard the sound of sirens in the distance he couldn't possibly have associated it with Benny's place.' He glanced around quickly, routinely checking who, if anyone, was behind us.

As if to remind us, a small red car cruised by. It was a different make to the one used by the knife-man. Patrick noted it too and squeezed my hand, turning to give me a big grin. Then, tersely, he said. 'Don't worry, I'm on multi-vitamin tablets.'

Our quarry stopped in front of one of the small terraced houses, took a bunch of keys from his pocket, selected one, unlocked the door and went in. He left it ajar for one half second too long, Patrick shoulder-charging it wide open. There was a yell of alarm and when I arrived he had the man up against the wall, an uncompromising fist grasping his T-shirt.

'Don't do it, please,' the man sobbed. 'I said I'd pay up and I will. Just as soon as I get my Giro cheque through on Thursday. I know I said that last week but the girlfriend and kid've been ill and I've had to pay out on things for them.' Released as rapidly as he had been captured he nevertheless stayed where he was, flattening himself to the wall.

'There seems to be a mutual case of mistaken identities,' Patrick said. 'My apologies.' He presented his ID card. 'Please tell me who you are.'

The man hardly glanced at the card. 'The name's Mike Graves.'

A child started to wail somewhere in the rear of the house and I became aware that a woman was fearfully peering at what was going on around a door at the end of the hallway. I drew Patrick's attention to her.

'Is that the child's mother?' he asked.

Graves nodded. 'So you're not the heavy Cardwell promised he'd send calling?'

He had not noticed the credentials at all then.

'No,' Patrick said. 'Let's just say that I'm connected with

the police. He's just been arrested with his two henchmen. Do you owe him money?'

'He said I did. I did a job for him once.' This with a sheepish look in the direction of his partner, who had emerged from hiding. 'Never again. He told me he wanted a car pinched back from a bloke who'd pinched it off him but when I came to do the job it turned out it belonged to a girl he knew who'd told him to get stuffed when he asked *her* to do something dodgy. So I turned him down flat when he asked next time and he said he'd paid me a retainer. Balls to that. You say the little bastard's been arrested?'

'You heard the sirens and went to watch what was happening,' Patrick pointed out.

'Yeah, well I was on my way back from the Job Centre and dodged into the pub to see what was going on. I didn't know it was actually Benny though – I couldn't see what the cops were doing. But when you've got involved with people like him you look over your shoulder all the time, don't you?'

'We're looking for a man who calls himself Vindepays or Dupont. You fit the description. Know him?'

'No, I don't,' Graves said slowly. A glimmer of humour broke through. 'Someone else looks like me?'

The woman, a hard-looking but extremely wan blonde said, 'There's Harvey in the hairdressers.' She raised her voice above that of the crying child. 'He looks a bit like you, only posher. And he's gay.'

'In the hairdressers?' Patrick echoed, dumbfounded.

'Yeah, he shacks up with some boyfriend who's a rep for hairdressing stuff, y'know, shampoos and conditioners and things like that. But not all the time – he's got a house over in Bristol and sells antiques.'

'Who told you all this?' Graves demanded to know.

'Shirl. She owns the hairdressers. She said he works there when business is bad. His business.'

Patrick said, 'Do you know if he's there today?'

'No, no idea.'

He asked for, and was given, the name of the hairdressers, its address and telephone number. Then Graves's girlfriend having gone to deal with the baby – they had both apparently suffered from a severe stomach upset – we prepared to leave. Patrick apologised again for his heavy-handed approach and passed over fifty pounds, received by Graves with almost tearful gratitude.

'So much for Frances and Dupont having an affair,' Patrick said when we were back in the street. 'I think you should go in and make an appointment. Ask for him, Harvey.'

'And if he's there?'

'So much the better. We'll tail him all the way home.'

'It doesn't sound as though he's any kind of big boss-man, does it?'

'No, but it could still be a front.'

'Patrick, a man loaded from the proceeds of arms smuggling, or whatever, isn't going to perm old ladies' hair as any kind of front!' I retorted scornfully.

He mimed gibbering terror of me.

The hairdressers was called, believe it or not, *Shirl's Curls* and situated only a short walk away continuing in a northerly direction along the main road. I went in, leaving Patrick 'handy', leaning on a nearby lamp post.

'He's only in weekday afternoons and booked solid until next Tuesday,' said a middle-aged woman, ferociously coiffured, no doubt Shirl herself. She eyed me up and down, decided I was not important enough to justify meddling with the appointment book and then glanced down the salon. I followed her gaze and saw a short, slim, elegant and tanned man whose head was shaven, surely, rather than merely bald, the glitter of gold within the unbuttoned shirt, on wrists and in the lobe of the ear nearest to me.

I made an appointment for the following Wednesday and left, asking on the way out, 'What time do you close?'

'Five thirty.'

'We'll come back at five fifteen,' Patrick decided when I reported this to him. 'Meanwhile, I think we ought to call in at the hospital and see how Max is fairing. I'd like to get to him before Carrick does. Mostly in case he dies.''

13

Max Norton's operation had been postponed for a couple of days, partly because there had been several emergency admissions that had resulted in the operating theatres being at full stretch and also it was thought the extra time would enable him to gather further strength. The medical team looking after him were a little more optimistic than they had been with regard to his chances of making a full recovery but there was still concern as he had an enlarged heart.

I had persuaded Patrick to remove the belt that boasted the skull with red glass eyes but probably unnecessarily for suddenly, talking to the consultant he was very sombre, very charming and very military-looking. Himself, for a few minutes at least, thank everything holy.

'Well, I wouldn't normally agree to him being questioned at this stage,' said the man. 'But I get the distinct impression it would do him good to get some of the questioning over. He keeps asking when the police are going to come and talk to him so perhaps it's preying on his mind. There's still an armed copper here, by the way. You say you're from MI5. Do you mind telling me what your organisation wants with him? I must have his well-being as a priority at the moment, as I'm sure you realise.'

'He was once involved with gun-running for terrorists, the IRA,' Patrick replied. He had left his own hand-gun in the secret cubby-box in the Range Rover in case a wary and sharp-eye armed policeman protecting Norton had insisted on searching him. Which would have been an unnecessary complication. 'Now he's back in the UK, Bath, we need to know whether he's still active or decided to retire on the proceeds. And, as I expect you know, his brother was recently murdered. It would appear that Max Norton was attacked by the same man.'

'Say no more,' said the other. 'But I must insist that you talk to him for no longer than fifteen minutes on this first occasion and leave immediately if the nursing staff request you to do so. As it is I shall have to ask him if he feels well enough.'

The message came back that he was prepared to speak with us.

I think we were both praying, as we entered the small side-ward and approached the bed to which we had been directed, that Norton would not immediately, upon recognising us, start yelling abuse and self-destruct all his drips and other highly personal medical impedimenta. We were therefore completely unprepared for his actual reaction when he saw us; amidst the bandages, a muted snort of contemptuous laughter.

'Look shifty next time,' he said to Patrick, his voice weak but perfectly clear. 'Look shifty when you're trying to be any kind of terrorist – especially the Irish variety of either persuasion. Right, you scared the shit out of us but all along I thought you were *too* scary and too clean and too damned nifty on your feet. They're scum, you know, and they used to come cap in hand to the likes of me with their two days growth of beard, their sweaty shirts with filthy collars and gawp at the works of art I get pleasure from surrounding myself with.'

'The pretence was based on a real man,' Patrick said, seating himself. 'One of the IRA's so-called Chiefs-of-Staff. He's dead now though.'

'You knew him?'

'I worked undercover with him for three months while he planned, among other atrocities, something along the lines of the bombing at Enniskillen. It all went wrong for him because just before he got round to giving the orders to place the charges I called in the cavalry and during the ensuing gunbattle, shot him.' Patrick then formally introduced the pair of us.

'I thought the doc said you were working with the police,' Norton said after a brief thought-filled silence.

'I am, but only because we're now fairly convinced that the attack on you and your brother's murder are inextricably linked. And we don't have much time as you're a sick man and I'm not allowed to really put the screws on you. Yet. Therefore I want you to tell me as concisely as possible about this business venture you have with Harvey Dupont or Vindepays. You can leave out the bits about plundered ethnic art, stolen antiques sourced in this country, diamonds smuggled into the UK inside shrunken heads and any similar grubby illegal enterprises that are really the responsibility of Detective Chief Inspector James Carrick.'

'Dream on, soldier,' Norton said.

'We know where Dupont is working and tonight we'll know where he lives when he's in Bath, the place where he went after you were attacked at his Bristol home. I'm warning you: supplying arms to terrorists is a very serious criminal offence and if you withhold information things can only get worse for you. Oh, by the way, Benny Cardwell and his pair of thugs are in police custody as of this morning.'

Norton stared at the ceiling.

'According to your consultant,' Patrick went on, 'You're keen to get some of the questioning out of the way. Is that because you want this oppo of Jorge's locked up?'

'How did you hear that name?'

'Never mind. Was Jorge the crewman in the photograph I removed from Dupont's house? The picture taken on *Painted Lady*?'

'You said you don't want to know about stolen tribal artefacts,' Norton muttered.

'No, not really. Try this then. Has Dupont called you since

you were in hospital? His place was ransacked. Did the man with the knife – Jorge's brother, is he? – make off with the big prize? Bothering you, is it, that such a moron's walking around with something so valuable?' He leaned forward to whisper, 'Or dangerous?'

Norton looked stubborn while I wondered if his attacker had made several trips to his car with booty before we had come upon him. He certainly had not been carrying anything, obviously on his way back to the house. Another point was that we had just arrived when we heard a car being driven away, surely the fleeing Dupont.

Patrick continued, 'The man's crazy and the police can't provide protection for your wife and your brother's family for ever. You must have some idea where he lives.'

'We'll talk about Jorge and the stuff you don't want to know about,' said Norton. 'On condition that you tell the police what I tell you and then I won't have to go through it all over again or answer any more questions, for a while anyway.'

'That's all right by me and I'm happy to brief Carrick,' Patrick told him, refusing to get annoyed. 'But I can't guarantee what the police will do afterwards.'

'This nutter with the knife . . .' Norton began pensively. 'That's the trouble, I haven't a clue who the hell he is or where he comes from. He didn't say anything, only that he's doing what he's doing for Jorge. He looks just like him though. Jorge was crazy too – when he'd been on the drink. I can usually handle people but when he'd got hold of alcohol he turned into a madman. John and I had to knock him right out with a sedative when he got like that – John went in for ordinary medicine first and we had a good first-aid kit on the boat – it was like darting a bloody rhino. I'd distract the man and John'd bang the hypo into him somewhere, usually his backside.'

'This was on *Painted Lady*?'

'No, that was the boat we had over here years before that I bought from a guy in Shoreham. Jorge crewed for us then too but he wasn't violent in those days. Then there was a fire and the boat was a write-off. It was Jorge's fault – he was living aboard and supposed to be looking after it. Got drunk and fell asleep while he had a fag alight. He almost went up with the boat. The idiot cried afterwards and told me he'd never touch another drop. I must have been mad to believe him but gave him another chance as he was damned good at his job when he was sober.

'After that I went out to Indonesia, with Jorge and Harvey – who'd just broken up from his latest boyfriend and would quite happily have gone to the Moon – hoping to get hold of stuff on Sulawesi as there was a lot of money to be made even in those days. To start with John came out sometimes for a holiday – when he could get away from his studies. He brought Frances with him a couple of times but the bloody woman had always been a real pain in the neck at sea. For ever complaining about the poor facilities, as she called the heads, and sick as a dog in dead flat calms.'

'What was the boat called?' I asked when Norton paused to take a sip of water.

'*Rantepoo*. It's the name of one of the two main towns in Torajaland up in the highlands and made us laugh. We kept her at Pare Pare which is the second largest sea port on the south western peninsula of Sulawesi. The *Rantepoo* was a bigger, much more oceanworthy boat than *Painted Lady* and we used to take her up the coast to near Makale. From there you could get to the best cliff graves, *liang*. The largest grouping of *tau tau*, the wooden figures based on the dead, some of which you might have noticed at the flat, were at the village of Lemo. Quite a lot of them had gone already, to collectors, so it was important to get there fast – before they all went.'

He was speaking matter-of-factly yet with a hint of pride,

like someone who had been in a hurry to buy something before the shop sold out, not steal.

'What sort of prices did you get for them?' Patrick asked.

Norton, whose voice was growing weaker, took another sip of water.

'The originals? Then you could get six, seven, eight hundred pounds each. A thousand for a really good one representing a woman with nice shell jewellery and good clothes. Apparently the Torajans kicked up a fuss when they found them gone – but soon made new ones. These weren't so well done in case they got pinched again but you could still get a few bob for them. They worship the dead, d'you know that? Save up for years to have a proper funeral for old granny and then spend about a week pigging out and getting smashed as rats on *tuak*, palm wine that blows your head off.' He lay back on the pillows, seemingly exhausted and closed his eyes. 'Suppose I don't come out of this, eh?'

'You will,' Patrick said shortly but not sharply. 'How did Jorge die?'

'It wasn't my fault,' Norton said after a pause. 'I didn't know the cliff graves were guarded at night in this particular place as they'd lost some of the *tau tau* the previous month to someone else. There was a wedding in the village nearby, you could smell the *tuak* from about a quarter of a mile away. But there were three men on the cliffs. Jorge had been in a real sweat from the word go, he hated the night raids. His stupid head was stuffed full of old Nordic legends of dark gods who took revenge on those who plundered from tombs – all sorts of rubbish like that. Anyway, we climbed up one of the ladders that are left there all the time. I was carrying the gun – it was to protect us from wild animals more than anything – and suddenly on one of the platforms we were attacked by these clowns armed with wooden staves. I admit I shot at them wildly and thought they'd bolted but when we got back to ground level, having grabbed what we could, we found three bodies by the light of Jorge's torch. We got the hell out of there I can assure you.'

A nurse briskly came up and said to Patrick and me, 'I'm sorry, but you must leave now.'

'Two minutes,' Norton said hoarsely. 'And then no one else will have to bother me for a bit. Where was I?' he continued when she had gone. 'Oh, yes, Jorge. He got very cocky on the boat later that night after we'd put as many nautical miles as possible between us and that bloody place. He'd had several beers – God knows where from, I kept all the booze under lock and key so the bastard must have had a secret store – and was half-plastered. He told me I was a murderer and he wanted ten thousand quid to keep his mouth shut. What was I to do? John wasn't there, he'd cried off by then, and Harvey was asleep below after staying with the boat while we were ashore. I gave Jorge a big smile and a small whisky and said I'd go below and smooth it out with Harvey. I went to my cabin, got the gun back out of the safe, went back and shot him. I was shaking so much I could hardly aim straight and it took six slugs to put him down. I don't think I've ever been so bloody scared. He would have run amok if I'd said no and both Harvey and me would've been dead and the boat probably sunk if I hadn't done it. There, is that enough for you now?'

'And then what did you do?' Patrick queried.

'We threw him over the side, what else? Now clear off. I'm tired.'

'That's not the half of it,' Patrick said when we were walking across the car park. 'Just a little *bon bouche* to get rid of us. We're no nearer to finding out what he's up to now.'

'Four murders though,' I said. 'Just like that. Like throwing rubbish into the dustbin in the same way he threw the remains of that shrunken head into his waste paper basket.'

'He's probably been responsible for the deaths of a lot more people during his illustrious career. His flat appears to be stuffed with objects from all over the world. I propose we tell James the story, if only to save him wasting his time.'

'D'you really think Jorge's oppo has made off with something important? Not just valuable, I mean. You said *dangerous*.'

'I intend to ask James if I can borrow a computer. Get into D12's and MI6's databases and find out if any real hardware has gone missing lately.'

'Munitions?'

'Weapons-grade plutonium?'

The answer to the question was only slightly reassuring, for nothing that represented a major threat to life or national security which could easily be hidden in a container and shipped anywhere, never mind in a private car, was reported as having been stolen, worldwide. Patrick did however come back from some office or other to where I was waiting for him near the front desk at the Manvers Street nick with a list of what he described as 'bits and pieces'.

'Excluding the odd nuclear device then, what do we have?' I asked impatiently. I had related all Max Norton had told us to Bob Ingrams, Carrick's sergeant, James having been out. Not too sure of some of the place name spellings I was hoping the stoical Ingrams would look them all up in an atlas.

Patrick sat down beside me on the bench, his gaze going down the list. 'Oh, anti-personnel mines, Semtex, loads of pump-action shotguns, a cache of confiscated handguns and ammunition destined for destruction, other sundry explosives including a ton of dynamite – ' He chuckled. 'Someone has a sense of humour: an exhibition-only Rapier missile – a live Tomahawk missile – how the hell do the Yanks lose things like that?' Shaking his head he said, 'No. Nothing particularly interesting or valuable.'

'What about germ-warfare? Has any anthrax or smallpox material been stolen from laboratories?'

'There's nothing like that listed here so one must assume that either everything's accounted for or those involved are keeping quiet about it. I would have thought that only the most bananas folk would want to tangle with things like that; Islamic militants and so forth. It doesn't quite fit Harvey and Co.'

'How about the live missile?'

He looked at me, eyes sparkling with laughter. 'You need something to fire it from, like a helicopter. You can't just lob it out of a window.'

'I know that!' I stormed. 'Can't one be sold though?'

'Only to dodgy foreign governments I would have thought. We can't be talking about that surely. Shall we have a cup of tea?'

'What, here?'

'They won't mind, will they? And if James comes in he can buy our sticky buns for us.'

'What are you going to do to him after that clip on the jaw he gave you?'

'I've organised it already.'

My imagination went into terrifying over-drive. 'What, for God's sake?'

Patrick pointed to a poster on a nearby noticeboard. 'Put his name down for a charity bungee-jump off Clifton suspension bridge. I don't think he's too keen on heights.'

'So what do we have?' Patrick said a short while later. 'I've no doubt consignments of weapons have been missed coming into this country by Customs and Excise, ditto drugs, plus, obviously, stolen items of ethnic art, diamonds in shrunken heads – although I've a feeling that was a one-off and Max Norton's personal property as he insisted they were when we first questioned him. Even though we haven't found very much we now know he exports stolen antiques to the States. If we ignore improbables like extortion and smuggling in illegal immigrants is that all there is to it? Am I looking for something that isn't there? Perhaps he really has retired and that's why he's here planning to buy a house. Do we go home and report that there's nothing in it for MI5?'

'What else do criminals make money on?' I said. 'Big time, I mean.'

'And bearing in mind that his regard for human life is just about zero. That's what worries me. The big T-word wakes me up at night. Terrorism. He has connections and form in that direction. To give guns to people is power, isn't it? He was carrying a gun the night they went after the *tau tau* and I'm not at all convinced it was to protect them from wild animals. I would have thought the most dangerous creatures to be found near cliffs in that part of the world would be snakes and spiders and you'd never see those in the dark before they got you.'

I spoke with a mouthful of sticky bun. 'I know. It's that cow Sharleen. She's really a world-class assassin and had all the plastic surgery on her face to hide her real identity. He's imported *her* and going to hire her out for mega-bucks to any faction who wants to knock off top politicians, senior officers of the armed forces or members of the Royal Family.'

'I'm trying to do a job here and you're not being remotely funny,' was the cold response.

Harvey Dupont left the hairdressers ten minutes after the salon closed. He was carrying a loaded supermarket carrier bag that manifestly did contain groceries as a French loaf was sticking out of the top. Strolling in a northerly direction he turned left into a small precinct of shops that had a car park at the rear, got into his silver-coloured car and drove off.

We had prepared for this and it was only necessary for me to sprint a hundred yards to where Patrick was waiting in the Range Rover. The man in my life still wasn't really speaking to me – he gets very annoyed when he deems me to be flippant.

I threw myself in, rattled off the registration number in case he had forgotten it and then said, 'Take it steadily. If he gets held up trying to join the main road we'll be in front of him.'

Predictably, Patrick said nothing, making a play of deeply concentrating on driving, extra grumpy because of having to use our own car, feeding the wheel through his hands just as it tells you in the manuals and generally making me want to smack him.

There were two lanes of vehicles and Patrick stayed in the inner one. We came to traffic lights that I had not noticed and Dupont's car and a dozen others joined the main stream of traffic. It was rush-hour. We crawled along. Then Dupont suddenly turned off and sped down a road with terraced houses on one side and extensive school grounds on the other. A couple of hundred yards farther along he swung into the entrance to the school, turned sharply into a car park close by and stopped.

Patrick pulled up a short distance past the entrance, got out and concentrated deeply on his nearside front tyre. I pulled down the sunshield and adjusted it so that I could watch what was happening behind us in the mirror on its reverse while going through the motions of combing my hair. Nothing happened for what seemed like ages but it was probably only two or three minutes. Then, just as abruptly as he had arrived, Dupont started his car, came roaring down the short length of drive, turned back into the road and set off back the way we had come.

Swearing extravagantly, Patrick got back behind the wheel, reversed at speed into the school entrance, had to reverse a little more and straighten up to allow a large delivery van to turn in and then set off after the other car.

'He knows we're following him,' I said, not expecting to get any response.

'More likely he's expecting the Jorge look-alike to be following him,' Patrick said, going through a set of traffic lights a whisker from red. 'He must know what his car looks like because it was parked in that lane. I think, given the circumstances, I would have changed my own motor.'

We tailed Dupont around a maze of side streets, finally emerging once more on to the London Road and headed back towards Bath. Dupont took the next turning right passed where Benny Cardwell lived, drove fifty yards and then went from sight behind several parked vehicles. When we reached the spot there was no sign of him.

Patrick was swearing again.

'There's an archway along there,' I said. 'Perhaps he went through it.'

'We'll give it a try – otherwise we've really lost him,' Patrick said. He drew level and we peered into what looked like the entrance of a mews.

Dupont's car was parked right down at the far end of what was, in reality, a large yard at the rear of houses that was given over to garages, an old brick building that could have originally been stables, piles of broken pallets and assorted rubbish piled up beside tall, wheeled refuse bins. There were quite a few other cars there, one an abandoned wreck.

'He must be scared stiff if he's going through all this rigmarole every day to drive such a short distance to where he works,' I said. 'That car park behind the precinct can't be more than five hundred yards from here as the crow flies.'

'Perhaps he has a lot to hide as well,' Patrick commented

dryly. 'And *we* haven't found him yet. There must be dozens of flats and bedsits in this terrace.' He allowed the car to trickle to a standstill on the slight slope up to the brick building and applied the handbrake. But for the hum of traffic in the main road it became very quiet.

I refrained, with an effort, from mentioning that we were sticking out like the proverbial sore thumb and was about to ask instead what he intended doing when, in the distance, there was a hoarse scream. Then a crash of breaking glass followed by several other clangs and bangs as might result from someone hurling around anything they could get their hands on in a confined space. All this seemed to be emanating from a ground-floor flat in that part of the building nearest to where Dupont's car was parked. A few seconds later a sash window was flung up and a man leapt the short distance to the ground.

It was Dupont.

Running like a madman he had reached his car by the time the Range Rover had been turned and covered half the distance that separated us. Patrick braked hard when we arrived, actually nudging the other vehicle, the desperate Dupont raking through his pockets probably in a search for his keys. I then noticed the long streak of blood on his left arm.

'Get out of the bloody way!' he howled at us though tears of pure panic.

Another man had climbed out of the window and was heading in our direction. A huge familiar outline.

Patrick alleviated Dupont's immediate problem by jumping out of the car, ran to him, ducked beneath his flailing arms as he tried to defend himself, grasped him by the neck and rendered him extremely unconscious. The resulting limp form was grasped in a fireman's lift and unceremoniously shovelled onto the back seat of the Range Rover.

Time had run out.

'Drive!' Patrick shouted at me. 'Get the pair of you out of here!'

I had already transferred to the driving seat.

Training.

He had his knife and the gun.

No, he didn't have the gun. It was still locked in the cubby-box.

I did as I was told, reversing away the fifty yards or so towards the brick building where I turned and headed for the archway. Halted at the junction with the main road I swore and then caused a prize-winning traffic-jam by performing an about-turn. It took longer than I wanted it to.

I went back.

Under the archway I stopped, yanked up the hinged arm rest between the two front seats, thus exposing more cream-coloured leather. I touched the button that looks like a fixing screw and is sensitive only to Patrick's or my fingerprints and there was a click as the leather-covered panel unlocked. Beneath was a metal plate with a numbered key-pad. I punched in the code, got it wrong in my haste, tried again and the plate opened. Delving into the quite capacious storage-space beneath I grabbed the Smith and Wesson and checked that it was fully loaded. All this had taken only seconds, just seconds when my attention had not been on what was happening.

There was no sign of either of them.

Locking all the doors and closing my window I cautiously drove back. Dupont's car was still where he had left it. I manoeuvred, bouncing over a pile of rubble and scrap wood in an endeavour to see around some of the rubbish bins. I saw only more bins and dark stairways leading to basements.

Frantically gazing around I could see nobody.

Nothing moved.

Changing course I shunted the wrecked car backwards for a few yards, almost into the wall of the building and, through the gap I had made, approached where I had last seen the men from the other direction.

Nobody.

Nothing.

'I'm going bloody mad!' I think I shouted.

I agonised over whether it was time to get Carrick involved.

Then, I saw a movement, no more than a shadow, within the lower room, the window, only a matter of a few feet away from me, still wide open. I looked around quickly and then opened my driver's window far enough to shout through. 'Patrick? Patrick! Are you in there?'

Something shot past my face, actually touching my hair, and clattered noisily against the glass on the passenger side. One glance was enough as it fell down onto the floor. I drove away, flooring the accelerator until the clouds of dust and screaming tyres brought me to my senses.

'Obviously, the red car was not parked anywhere in this area,' James Carrick said. 'Or you would have seen it.'

I watched him place Patrick's knife carefully in a plastic forensic bag. Dupont, fully conscious if a little confused, had been taken away for a quick medical check-up before questioning but I had hardly noticed his going. It occurred to me that there was no need for me to stay in the car and, having stowed away the gun before the police had arrived, I got out into the heat of the late afternoon. The air was hazy, grit between my teeth from the movement of police vehicles, an ambulance and personnel moving around on foot across the baked earth of the yard. Although by my watch it had only taken James and Ingrams eight minutes to reach the scene after my phone call, whereupon they had bravely stormed the flat, they had found nobody. Some of his team were now knocking on doors in the rest of the terrace, others, who had only just arrived, were fanning out to search the flights of dank steps down to basements and the yard itself.

'No,' I said dully in response to his question.

'And he threw this at you from inside the room even though the car window was only open a few inches?'

'He must have done.'

James met my gaze. 'Are you all right?'

Icy fingers were playing my spine like a harp. 'We must look in the rubbish bins.' I set off towards the nearest one and he ran to catch up with me.

'Ingrid, they'll – '

'We must look in the rubbish bins,' I broke in, my own voice booming hollowly in my ears.

Carrick called to those he had just sent off and ordered them to look in the bins first.

Those closest to where we had been standing were over-flowing but I climbed up the side of the first one I came to, bracing my feet on the protruding metal fitments by which they were manipulated and started to pull out the stuff and drop it onto the ground.

'We need gloves!' James exclaimed before hesitating and climbing up alongside me.

'You don't need gloves when you're looking for your husband,' I said inanely.

Carrick transferred to the next one and started to do the same. I saw him retch on the stench of rotting food.

'Sir!' a woman's voice hailed from an opened upstairs window.

'Yes?' Carrick shouted back.

'There's a man's body in this one here!' An arm pointed down to a bin almost directly below her.

'What d'you mean, a body?' Carrick yelled back. 'Can you tell whether or not he's dead from up there?'

Pause. Then, 'No, sir.'

'Well, just watch what you're bloody-well saying!'

I had never seen him really lose his temper before.

I must have run to the bin she had indicated but have no memory of making the short journey, only of arriving and throwing myself up the vertical side, barking a shin as I did so. Then, suddenly imbued with an odd controlled strength, I straddled the rim for a moment and then dropped inside.

The bin was about three quarters full. An old folded-up carpet and cardboard boxes took up a lot of the space but there was household and kitchen rubbish as well and as I landed, slipping on something slimy, there arose a huge cloud of flies. I stood still, looking at what was at my feet.

The body, for surely the woman had been quite correct and he was dead, was lying face down in unspeakable garbage, arms outstretched. The head seemed to be at a strange angle.

I just stood there, turned to stone but started violently when Carrick spoke from a precarious position perched on the rim of the bin for I had not registered that he was there.

'I've called over the paramedics.'

'We don't need them,' I whispered.

It was my cursed writer's imagination playing tricks when I saw a finger twitch. When it happened again I forced myself to crouch down and confirm what commonsense was screaming at me, feeling for a pulse on one sinewy wrist.

I could detect nothing.

When the first paramedic arrived seconds later – I made room for him by climbing up on to a pile of boxes, James steadying me – Patrick jerked as though with shock at the sudden disturbance around him and in the next moment had struggled to his knees and was vomiting terribly and help-lessly. Shrugging off professional help he got to his feet, bracing his arms against the sides of the receptacle as he con-tinued to throw up. Finally, leaning weakly, he allowed his face to be sponged.

'You don't have a pulse,' I told him, for some reason carry-ing on making stupid remarks.

'I never do on Wednesdays,' he said and then fainted.

14

Still feeling heady with relief that a de-briefing was in the offing instead of a post-mortem I was nevertheless expecting that it would be an extremely subdued trio who sat around Elspeth's kitchen table at nine o'clock that evening. The rector and his wife were out, which was just as well, but expected back later.

Patrick, having had both a shower and a bath, had insisted he did not want anything to eat as he felt sick, could still smell rot on himself. Pragmatic, even ruthless when I have to be, I had fetched the green tea and lime massage oil I had been given for Christmas, removed his bathrobe and briskly got to work on a deeply introspective, if now bemused subject. I stopped, reluctantly, before he became sexually aroused – it would have been a fantastic idea but there was no time – and left him to get dressed while I cooked the dinner. James arrived – I had warned the minders he was coming – as I was de-glazing the frying pan with red wine to make a sauce to go with the fillet steak.

'Sorry I'm a bit adrift.' He glanced around quickly. 'How is he?'

'Probably crippled with humiliation, quite a few more bruises but otherwise fine,' I said lightly.

James was not fooled and came over to stir for me while I had another weep.

'He has no other injuries?'

'No,' I gulped. 'James, nothing like this has ever happened to Patrick before.'

'Patrick's a very strong sort of person,' he said gently when I had reached the nose-blowing stage.

'Men aren't strong after they've been chucked in a dustbin,' I retorted mulishly. I did not go on to say that it had taken Patrick a couple of years to fully recover his self-confidence after his Falklands War injuries, mainly because some, ironically the least life-threatening, had been of a genital nature. James though might have been aware of this: I did not know what Patrick had told him.

He handed over care of the sauce. 'Obviously, it's vitally important but do you really think it's a good idea to bother him with questions and talk about the case tonight? I don't mind hanging on until the morning.'

Patrick had come round very quickly and, upon being assisted from the place where he had been so unceremoniously dumped, had refused all further medical attention and asked me to drive us both home, that is to the rectory. He had not said anything about what had happened and I had done likewise, respecting his silence. 'Yes, I do,' I replied. 'He'll only brood about it all night otherwise.'

All fingers and thumbs from nerves I crashed plates about as I heard footsteps coming down the stairs, dreading what might happen, James similarly busying himself by laying the table. When the door opened I glanced up.

Patrick had donned his best dark blue silk shirt and matching cotton trousers. He closed the door.

Carrick sniffed the air and exclaimed in Gaelic. Then he said, 'Man, that's one hell of an aftershave you have there. I've been with Harvey Dupont all evening and it must be catching. I quite fancy you.'

It was exactly the right thing to say to Patrick to make him laugh and he did, uproariously.

Smiling into their amusement I poured them some red wine and took a swig from my own glass of white, the greater part of a bottle of which I had steadily consumed through the evening. I was not sure whether it was helping me or not but we seemed to be over the first hurdle.

I served the meal; newly-harvested runner beans and potatoes from the garden and a green salad with herbs to accompany the steak. Everyone ate with gratifying enthusiasm. Afterwards we had a little cheese and then coffee with some chocolates from an opened box I found when we moved into the living room. I knew that in the circumstances Elspeth would hardly mind the raid.

James sighed and relaxed, stretching his legs. 'Well, I can tell you now that we found, just before I came here, a hell of a lot more stolen property in Dupont's boyfriend's flat and they're both singing their heads off. Blaming Max Norton, mostly. There are tens of thousands of pounds worth of antiques, the proceeds of several robberies over the past year or so from large country houses – so much that I've had to contact the Arts and Antiques Branch to come and sort it all out for us. They're saying that Norton masterminded the robberies from abroad for clients, literally to order. Apparently he has an extensive knowledge of who owns what and an almost photographic memory of the catalogues of collections, private and otherwise. But they weren't allowed to sell anything themselves and Norton was slow in paying them their cut – hence Dupont having to resort to hairdressing when his own, and seemingly legitimate, antiques business was going through a rough patch.' He smiled. 'I honestly don't think your department need concern itself with the case any longer.'

'And the big man?' Patrick asked quietly.

'No sign of him.' A little shrug. 'I thought you might be able to enlighten us.'

This was featherweight stuff indeed.

'I would have killed him,' Patrick said, frowning. 'But only as a last resort.'

'And?' Carrick said.

'I don't know what happened next. I can't explain it. I woke up in the – in the – rubbish.' He took a deep breath, dropped his gaze for a moment and continued tautly, 'Perhaps I passed out, bloody-well fainted like a girl from fright. I mean, I fainted afterwards, didn't I?'

'Did you feel scared, standing there facing him after Ingrid drove away?'

Patrick shook his head, slowly. 'No, just wary – and involved with strategy.'

'It can't have been that then,' James said dismissively. 'You could well be suffering from temporary amnesia and can't remember tangling with him.'

'I tend not to tangle with anyone like that,' was the instant response. 'As I said, I would have killed or disabled him if necessary. With the knife.'

'You would have had to get in close though surely and the man has arms like a gorilla.'

'If I had decided that hands and feet were out I would have *thrown* the knife,' Patrick patiently explained. 'It's a *throwing* knife.'

James turned to me. 'You said the knife was thrown at you from inside the flat through the car window.'

'That's right,' I said, more than aware of Patrick's surprised stare in my direction.

'I'd assumed you'd returned with the police,' he said.

'No, I changed my mind, turned round at the road junction and came straight back,' I told him, deliberately not elaborating.

'Well?'

'James is asking the questions,' I said, adding, 'Sorry, but this is very important.'

Carrick took the cue. 'Ingrid drove almost straight back, having had a bit of bother turning round due to the heavy traffic. She may have been away for as long as three to four minutes. During that time both you and the big man had gone from sight. Ingrid drove around looking for you, actually shifting the wrecked car a few feet to give her better access. There was nobody to be seen – and incidentally the flat-to-flat enquiries we've made so far have yielded nothing useful. No one we've spoken to saw what happened. Ingrid then saw a movement through the open window of the room you say Dupont escaped from. She drove closer and shouted your name through the narrowly opened driver's window. Your knife was thrown through it, just missing her. That's when she retired to a safe distance and called us.'

Patrick shook his head reproachfully at me.

'Only your fingerprints are on the knife,' Carrick resumed. 'All over it in fact, but, patently, you didn't throw it.'

'He wasn't wearing gloves,' Patrick said. Sudden anger took hold of him. 'My throwing knife. Someone got their filthy hands on it and – ' He rose abruptly to his feet and walked to the other end of the room to stare out of the window, hands rammed into trouser pockets.

Carrick looked at me, his concern apparent but I just smiled and shook my head a little.

'Not many people can throw knives like that in this country,' Carrick observed to no one in particular.

'It's Italian,' Patrick said, turning round, his anger having dissipated, as I thought it would. 'And quite heavy for its size as it's made of silver, with, as you probably now know, a retractable stainless steel blade. We can't be talking about a fluke here – whoever threw it knew what they were about.'

'Can you demonstrate?' James asked. 'Just to get it right in my mind so I know what I'm talking about when I end up in the witness box.'

I admired 'when' rather than 'if'.

'No, sorry, not with mother's bread knife. It's got to be the real thing or similar.' He surveyed the other man searchingly and then said in a thick Irish accent, 'Holy Mother! He thinks it's a circus act where you get hold of the bloody thing by the tip of the blade and just miss pretty girls with it. You'd be ten times dead before it had even left your hand.'

'I don't follow,' Carrick said.

'You hope to dodge the bullet and throw before they can fire again.'

There was a short silence broken by James saying, 'Don't you keep your second best knife with the minor arsenal locked away in your car?'

Patrick looked at me and shrugged. 'I should never have called him a Jockenese nit-wit, should I?'

No, it was not a circus act. There was no showmanship, nothing flamboyant, not a hint of flourish, ostentation or pride. Merely an unsettling demonstration of how to disable or kill an enemy with an almost too fast to see, and sideways, flick of the wrist that drove the weapon almost up to the hilt several times into an old tailor's dummy that had been brought down from the spare bedroom to act as a target. He then drew six small circles on it with a red marker pen and centred them, one by one, stating beforehand which one he intended to hit. Intent, grim, I knew in his mind's eye repeatedly killing the man who had now twice humiliated him. Good therapy.

'Thank you,' James said simply, when the dummy had been returned to where it was stored. 'This mystery person then, who can throw a knife like you and who has come right out of the wallpaper, must have overpowered you somehow without you noticing their approach.'

There had been no sarcasm in his tone whatsoever but Patrick grimaced. 'It doesn't add up, does it?'

'That you suffered some kind of brainstorm, made the big man disappear into thin air and then popped indoors where you threw your knife at Ingrid outside before chucking yourself into the bin after she'd gone makes even less sense.'

It was then, when Patrick moved, that I saw the marks on the side of his neck. I went over to him and lightly placed the fingers and thumb of my right hand on the incipient bruises: hardly of any consequence among the many. 'Whoever it is knows how to render people unconscious just like you do too,' I said.

'It could be a coincidence,' Patrick said. 'And caused by

something completely different. Sorry, I simply don't know the answer to any of this. Perhaps James is right and I'll remember – sometime.'

'What you must bear in mind,' Carrick said. 'Is that you saved Harvey Dupont's life.'

For us to carry on with the case gave every appearance of doing so purely for personal reasons; to settle a grudge. No weapons or anything that would remotely interest MI5 were found in Harvey Dupont's boyfriend's flat where the former had headed after things at home in Bristol had become hazardous to say the least. He had immediately admitted to Carrick that he had helped Max Norton dispose of Jorge's body over the side of the boat but no case could be brought against him, especially as such a long time had elapsed since the crime had been committed on the other side of the world. All the DCI could do was concentrate on making a strong case against all three men in connection with the art thefts and the assault on me. Nothing could be proved with regard to the old weapons – mostly so obsolete as to be beyond use – and American currency we had found in the Norton's flat. By Max's own admission the sourcing of the greater part of his ethnic art collection was highly suspect but he had not actually broken any UK laws, a fact well known to him as he was wheeled into theatre the following morning for his operation.

He died two days later after suffering a massive heart attack and other post-operative complications.

Despite having thrown all his resources at finding the Norton brothers' attacker Carrick had drawn a complete blank. Once again, man and car had disappeared. He rang me at home in Devon to tell me he had questioned Frances Norton again and she had emphatically denied involvement with what had happened to me in Bristol or luring me there with intent. She said she had stayed at home after returning from her shopping trip, and had even provided an alibi of sorts as the cleaner had called round for her wages. This local woman, when later asked, said she'thought that had been on the evening in question. Frances did concede that Arabis might have borrowed Jason's car but it was unlikely. Even though the keys to all the vehicles were left on a silver tray in the hall why, as she did not know Harvey, would she go and visit him?

Needless to say Arabis denied having left the house on that occasion, adding that she would never take Jason's car as it was so poorly maintained and likely to break down. I could readily sympathise with this assertion but who was lying?

Jason when interviewed again said that he now had a job, a good one with a local finance company and was planning to rent a small flat of his own when he had saved up the deposit. (James, and it must be admitted, I, had always assumed from his parents' attitude towards him that he had no qualifications whatsoever.) He could not wait to leave home, actually saying that he wished he could put several thousand miles between himself and his mother and sister. He maintained complete ignorance in whatever scams they, their friends and others, were involved in, past or present and had not knowingly lent his car to anyone that night, having gone out for a drink with a friend to a pub that was within walking distance. If someone had borrowed it they had not told him. The family tended to put all their car keys on to a silver tray on the hall table.

'I believe him,' James finished by saying. 'There's not a scrap of evidence to tie him in with any of this.'

'What are the men you have in custody saying about Frances though?' I went on to ask.

'Not a lot. Dupont's boyfriend insists he's never met her, ditto Benny and his hired thugs so we're only talking about Dupont here. As Max had already said she went out on the first boat he had once or twice and also spent a short holiday aboard the second but hated it as she was always sea-sick. She may well have been on board during one of the early arms-smuggling runs Patrick was interested in but not actively it would appear. I don't think I can make anything actually stick and I can't say I want to bother to try. Is Patrick okay, by the way?'

'Well, as you know we came home so he could nurse his bruises but he left almost straight away for London. Tim Shandy's handed in his resignation so the whole project'll probably fold before it gets off the ground again.'

'The re-launch didn't work out too well, did it?'

I told him the truth: it had been a complete disaster.

There was still an armed presence at the rectory at Hinton Littlemoor but Patrick's parents were due to leave shortly for three week's holiday staying with friends on Sark so this protection was being withdrawn for the duration, to be reviewed on their return.

Should I or should I not attend Max Norton's funeral?

James thought it unnecessary but had left it up to me knowing how I felt about the disappointing way all our efforts had come to nothing: there was always the barest chance I might discover something useful. Patrick had voiced this feeling of failure more vividly on our arrival at home before plodding stiffly up to bed. I had not mentioned it to James but despite two showers a day Patrick was still convinced that he smelt of rot and I was beginning to be concerned about his mental state. Perhaps London would give him more positive things to think about.

I would go to the funeral. It would give me more to think about.

The widow was late, altogether worse, I felt, than a bride being a little tardy at her wedding.

When I had attended John Norton's funeral I had, for my own reasons, created a high profile. This time, dressing quietly, I hoped for invisibility but, prior to setting out, had had a nasty feeling that hardly any mourners would be present other than the immediate family and the ruse would fail.

The Nortons and their police minders were standing around in the stiff, edgy manner that people do on such occasions, Frances, who looked positively haggard, with her back to her son and daughter and staring straight ahead. I sat tight in the car. The hearse arrived, parked outside the entrance to the crematorium, people looked at their watches, then down the long drive and nothing happened for several minutes.

Someone tapped lightly on my passenger window and I opened it. James, almost in a rose bed, also keeping a low profile.

'Where is she?' he whispered.

'Isn't she being given police protection too?' I asked.

'No, didn't want it. Said she couldn't possibly be on the big man's hit-list but was going to stay with a friend for a few days anyway as the house is giving her the creeps. She *has* been away – I made sure we checked.'

'Which friend?'

'God knows.'

I forgot to keep my voice down. 'James, the bloody woman's only just come back from the States after living there, judging by the look of her, for at least half a century! *Which* friend?'

But he just grinned at me. 'You really can't stand her, can you?'

Just then the woman under discussion arrived, driving herself in a dark green Jaguar, presumably Max's. She parked and got out. Dressed entirely in black; tight trousers, high black leather boots, a three-quarter length tailored coat and what I can only describe as a Revenge of Zorro hat she was a striking figure. After one sweeping, and scornful, glance around those assembled she strode over to the hearse and a slow procession into the building commenced. Carrick and I brought up the rear and, momentarily, I paused by the Jaguar. Hot metal ticked almost inaudibly as it cooled.

No incident of any kind disturbed the otherwise deadly-dull and dry-eyed proceedings, Max Norton, like his brother, sent off lovelessly into eternity, tidied away and soon to be forgotten.

'You're looking at a very world-weary copper,' James said to me when we were standing by the Range Rover afterwards, none of those present having wished us so much as 'good morning'. 'Sometimes I just feel like chucking it all in.'

'But you've busted a fairly big-time stolen antiques for export gang,' I pointed out. 'And while you haven't yet nabbed John and Max Norton's murderer you know roughly who he is.'

'The odd thing is he appears to have no previous convictions. It really does seem to be a quest for revenge that this man has undertaken. I get the impression that he's brooded about Jorge's death all this time and it's become a real obsession with him and flipped his brain. By the way, did you listen to your radio on the way here?'

'No.'

'The Chief of the Defence Staff, Major-General Sir Michael Hawksbury, has been shot dead. MI5 must be in a real flap.'

I probably gaped at him. 'When did this happen?'

'Very early this morning when he was out for a jog on Hampstead Heath.'

'Didn't he have protection officers?'

'Almost certainly. D'you want to come back to the nick with me and find out more?' He glanced around. 'I think I've wasted my time here.'

'Make a note of the registration number of the Jag,' I said.

He stopped in his tracks and gazed at me. 'Are you serious? Are you saying what I think you're saying? For some reason you hate this woman. Now who has an obsession?'

I said, 'Compressing the carotid arteries in the neck is one method of inducing temporary unconsciousness. Patrick has it off to a fine art. But where the ultimate welfare of those on the receiving end is not of prime concern there is a danger of unpleasant after-effects and even death. In this country it is only taught to special operations military personnel who have reached the highest standards and who aren't naturally ham-fisted. One of the after-effects can be slight amnesia – and we're only talking of a matter of seconds here. I think Patrick had got the better of the big man, without using his knife, when someone came up behind him and rendered him unconscious in that fashion. There wasn't much time, the last thing that person wanted was to linger and risk being seen so they bundled him up into the rubbish bin and got the hell out of there. If the big man had been in any fit state to do anything Patrick would have died right there and then – probably of a broken neck.'

'It would certainly explain quite a few things. So this person carried away the big man?'

'He could have been mobile, after a fashion.'

'And you reckon it's the *woman*? Sharleen Norton?'

'It might have been a marriage of convenience to Max or not a real marriage at all. All the plastic surgery could have been to hide her real identity. Yes, I think she could be a trained killer. When I got hold of her when we paid them a visit it was like holding a thin and fit man. Actually I'm not too convinced she's a woman at all.'

There were sparkles in Carrick's blue eyes that spoke of pure enchantment with the theory. It was however being savagely restrained by professionalism and native caution. *Savagely* restrained.

'It was a trifle breezy earlier and her coat was blown about,' I went on. 'I've only seen her wearing skirts before and the black trousers were pretty tight. Even male ballet dancers have problems with keeping everything – what shall I say? – under firm control.'

'Unless she's really kinky and had borrowed a pair of the late-lamented's socks as well as his car.'

This was uttered from behind us by someone who had obviously approached on the grass under cover of the roar of an over-flying airliner.

'That too,' I agreed, turning slightly to face the speaker.

Despite the seeming humour of the remark Patrick was not remotely humorous, his tone of voice condemning my theory as an irrelevance. I refrained from further comment, waiting for him to explain his presence. Sometimes the fact that you are wed to someone means precisely *zilch*.

'I'm sure you'll get all the info from the horse's mouth,' James said to me, preparing to go, no doubt detecting the tension in the air and thinking Patrick and I were about to have a row.

'You've heard?' Patrick said.

I nodded.

'We'd lost touch but years ago he used to be rather a good friend of mine.'

Both James and I said we were sorry.

Then Patrick said, 'I may as well tell you the rest of the bad news. It's over. Shandy said in his resignation letter that while recognising his own unsuitability for the job he was of the opinion that in view of what had occurred I was over the hill physically and was compensating for it by acting in an over-bearing manner. The whole project's been put on ice while there's further consultation. Whatever that really means. Officially I'm on sick leave – whatever *that* really means.' He attempted a chuckle but failed miserably. 'Binned twice, in fact.'

I put my arms around him, head on his chest, aware of James again sincerely saying how sorry he was and then leaving us, pleading pressure of work. Then, but for the measured beating of Patrick's heart a few inches from my right ear there was a fairly long silence.

'Tim had no right to say that,' I said, standing upright to look at him.

'I spoke with him briefly. He actually seems to have gone a bit strange.'

'Terrible things happened to him in Bosnia.'

'I know. Would you like to go away on holiday?'

'No, I want to see this thing through.'

'That's down to Carrick.'

'I know it sounds stupid but I feel I owe it to John Norton.'

'The job's over, Ingrid. You must understand that. Finished.'

'I'm not doing it because of any job.'

'Please think about it.' He backed off a few paces.

'Wait!' I held out the car keys but he shook his head mutely and walked away.

'Where will you be?' I called.

'I don't know,' Patrick replied without turning round.

I'm afraid I silently damned Tim Shandy to hell.

There was nothing I wanted to do more right now than be snugly at home singing to Vicky, 'There's a worm at the bottom of the garden and his name is Wiggly Woo,' but assumed that kind of pleasure would be Patrick's. I rather hoped so, for there is nothing like the presence of your own very young child to force you to re-align your priorities. Patrick's problem is that he possesses too many loyalties, all of which he tries to give everything. I was rather hoping he would now dump the one labelled MI5.

I had already decided that I would test my theory to

destruction. If indeed Sharleen Norton was behind all the murders, and hey, I might as well throw responsibility for the whole nasty business in her direction while I was at it, then I must be sure of her motives. Wild ideas without basis are just that, wild ideas.

If I held with her story that she had only come on the scene when she had met Max in the States, visiting Indonesia only briefly, which seemed reasonable, and the woman did indeed have the knifeman under some kind of control there was every chance that she had only met him, the murderer, since arriving in Bath. That she had slipped away from the dinner party in Bradford on Avon because of boredom – were all the others blind drunk and did not miss her? – and had come upon John Norton's killer at the house was too neat a coincidence.Or was it? Had the man called there with the murder of Max in mind and, as we had surmised already, mistaken John for his intended target? That would have been easy enough after so many years had elapsed. Frances Norton could well be a heavy sleeper but someone trained to kill learns to sleep with one eye, and both ears, open. Sharleen could well have arrived and caught him in the act. She might have even let him in. Had she seen a way of turning the murder to her own advantage? If she wanted to get rid of Max, who could well have outlived his usefulness to her after getting her back to the UK, no questions asked . . .But no, surely, I told myself, Sharleen was, or had said she was, a British citizen and would have been able to return, no problem. But if my hunch was correct and a change of identity was involved then she, or he, could have been born in the States.

Sharleen could then have decided to rid herself of domestic clutter by allowing the revenger of Jorge to do his worst with Max, to enable her to walk away with all his resources, and also Harvey Dupont as he was probably a nuisance. She had already pointed him in our, or rather my, direction, no doubt saying we were a threat to him. So where was she hiding this man? Was she paying him? I found myself glad that I was staying at a different hotel than the one I had originally.

Pursuing the thoroughly uncomfortable thought that I would have to seek him out in order to prove any of this I ticked off the possibilities on my fingers. Harvey Dupont's house in Bristol was locked and sealed by the police while they catalogued all his antiques in case some were also stolen property, the same went for his boyfriend's home in Bath. Sharleen could hardly be concealing him in her flat at the old vicarage, besides which the house was up for sale and prospective buyers would be viewing the property. Neither Arabis nor Jason could conceivably be hiding him. So where did that leave me bearing in mind that not so much as a glimpse of the man or his car had been seen? The answer was that it left any number of bed-sitters and cheap hotels and the car could well have been disposed of. How do you dispose of a car without drawing too much attention? You take it out into the countryside, set fire to it and either leave it or shove it into a large hole in the ground.

The entire area surrounding Bath and the nearby Mendips are riddled with mines and quarries, mostly defunct, some of which go back to the days of the Romans. Combe Down itself, where the Norton's house was situated, has literally miles of old tunnels beneath it, relics from the days of quarrying Bath limestone.

Someone newly arrived in the locality would not necessarily be aware of these facts: I only knew about the latter through talking to James and Joanna. James though would be well conversant with the places where people dumped cars.

'There was actually a big clear-out at Seven Oaks quarry near Peasedown St John last week,' he said when I rang him at home. 'It's been a favourite place for fly-tipping for several years but the council are finally going to do something about it and turn the place into a nature reserve. I know there were several burned-out cars taken away – all with number plates removed of course ˙ and a check would have been made to see if they fitted the descriptions of stolen vehicles on our lists.It's a good idea. Thank you. I'll put someone on to finding out if any of them could have been the red hatchback and get them to have a look round and about. There are a couple of old quarries in the Wideford Valley area that might be worth investigating.'

After I had hung up, wondering if he had expressed interest out of politemess, I glanced out of the window. It was a fine evening with at least a couple of hours of daylight left. I would drive out to the Wideford Valley. It is always better to make a complete fool of yourself when you are on your own.

15

Three-quarters of an hour later, having stopped to buy the ever indispensible Ordnance Survey map, I realised that this would not be an easy job. Wideford was no spacious and gently winding valley with water meadows like much of the countryside on the banks of the River Avon in the Bath area but a steep-sided combe, almost a gorge, the only access to it an extremely narrow and twisting lane with hardly any passing places that bordered a watercourse called the Black Brook, sometimes crossing it on tiny hump-backed bridges. Stopping to look at the map I saw that the name Wideford actually referred to a ruinous hamlet where there was still a ford – I had just crossed it – the water only a matter of a few inches deep as it slid over smooth rock slabs covered with a slippery green growth.

I stared through the opened side window at a scene that looked as though it had been undisturbed since the Middle Ages. It was an illusion for the whole area, judging by the defunct quarries and workings marked on the map, had at one time been heavily industrialised. Trees and tangled vegetation – branches, briars and wild clematis had scraped against the sides of the car during my journey down from the main road – had all grown since the mines and quarries had closed, literally where their seeds had fallen. Its inaccessibility and the fact that the whole place was full of holes had perhaps saved it, so far, from property developers.

The hamlet, which consisted of little more than a farmhouse that still seemed to be inhabited, a cottage, a tumbledown stone barn and a totally ruined corrugated iron building, the ancient tractor parked inside it appearing to be the only thing holding it up, was on the western side of the stream. It caught the last rays of the setting sun, the light turning decay into gold, rural squalor into something almost magical. I turned round to see that the sun was shining through a rift in the valley sides and it caused me to wonder if this was one of the few days of the year when the buildings, so surrounded by trees, were thus illuminated.

After another look at the map I drove towards the far end of the valley where it opened out into narrow fields through which, disappointingly, the little stream had recently been artificially channelled, the raw earth banks now dead straight and bare of the reeds and rushes that had once lined them. These lay in smelly rotting heaps on the unkempt pastureland at the left hand side of the lane. Behind them was a large bare plot of land that had at one time been enclosed by high chain-link fencing but this only remained standing in one long length and several shorter ones, the rest broken down with weeds growing through. The complex was marked on my map as a quarry and presumably had still been functioning at the time the map had gone to print.

There were a few heaps of broken fly-tipped pallets, rubble and a couple of fridges but no cars or other vehicles. Carefully, I drove through one of the gaps in the fence and then on, turning sharp left through a gap in the rock. A vast space pitted with pools of dark water opened out before me.

Some vandalised huts, a lot of stone piled here and there and not much else.

I went back along the valley the way I had come, pausing to examine a heavily fenced hole in the limestone cliff I had passed earlier, some thirty feet off the road down a path too narrow for the car. There was no hope of entry to the utterly dark interior, a faint smell of drains wafting out, and I walked back grateful in the knowledge that nobody could hide anything there.

After once more crossing the ford I drove slowly, looking from side to side into the jungle of vegetation. Then, surprisingly quickly, I was back at the junction with the main road.

It was obvious that whatever old workings and mines were here were now hidden and inaccessible. I began to wonder if Carrick had made a mistake. Or, if people dumped things they wanted to get rid of in them they dropped them in from the top.

It was almost dusk now but I drove several miles and then turned left down another lane that should take me quite close to the eastern rim of the valley. By this time I was convinced I was wasting my time: this piece of countryside was so remote and off the beaten track that someone like Sharleen Norton would not even know it existed.

I came to a farm. It had a neat and cared-for appearance; glossy dairy cattle in the fields, immaculate hedges, the yard and drive newly hosed clean, bright flowers in the hanging baskets on the farmhouse. Catching a glimpse through a window of a warm-looking kitchen with the gleam of copper and brass I felt a pang of home-sickness. I could be at home right now relaxing with a glass of wine before dinner. It occurred to me that my real responsibility now lay not with a dead pathologist but Patrick.

I actually took my foot off the accelerator. This was just as well for seconds later I was forced to slam on the brakes when an extremely small child on a very small pony rocketed through a gateway right in front of me. The pony braked hard too and both parties came to a halt with some six inches separating them. Feeling extremely shaky I stepped on to the road just as an out of breath young woman emerged from the same opening in the hedge.

'Oh God!' she panted. 'I'll kill him.'

'I could have just killed both of them,' I pointed out angrily.

The rider, with sticking-out ginger plaits, burst into tears.

'Oh Becky, I didn't mean it,' said the woman, giving her a hug. 'Of course I didn't mean it. He's just so naughty sometimes.'

'For heaven's sake get someone to school that animal,' I

told the woman when the combined efforts of the three of us had resulted in pony and rider being returned to a paddock being used as a schooling area. 'And shut gates in future. I have a little girl of my own and you've no idea what a shock that gave me.'

'I really am terribly sorry.' She was gazing at me closely. 'Are you the writer Ingrid Langley? You look just like her.'

Was vanity the reason why I stopped being angry with her?

Realising that I needed the cup of tea I was being offered and also that she might save me hours of wasted time and effort I found myself a couple of minutes later in that gleaming copper and brass kitchen, sitting at the pine table watching the kettle coming to the boil on the light blue Aga while my hostess checked on Becky's progress.

'What strange circumstances to meet one of my favourite authors,' she said when she returned, having introduced herself as Becky's mother, Lizzie Cooper. 'We hardly see a soul along here even though we're only seven miles as the crow flies from Bath. D'you mind if I ask what brings you here?'

'Research,' I said. 'I like to use real locations and these old industrial sites fascinate me. Is there anywhere round here where my criminal character could dispose of a stolen car?'

'Oh *yes*,' Lizzy enthused. 'The Bristol police are always checking because people, or rather yobbos, drive stolen cars across one of our fields, remove the wheels and any other parts they want and then push what's left over the edge into what was Queen's quarry – some say it was called that after Elizabeth the First it's so old. The only way you can get them out is with a crane so most are left right where they are. They can't be seen from anywhere else.'

'But you must be able to get to it from down in the valley somewhere.'

Lizzy shook her head. 'Not now. There was a big rock fall

about twenty years ago. It's all still teetering, so to speak. It's why there's never been anything done to the place, it's just too dangerous. We're losing that particular field at the rate of a couple of feet a year. My husband's put the fence quite a long way back now hoping it'll last for a while.'

'So how do people have access then? – to get rid of cars, I mean.'

'There's a track that runs down the side of the field. It used to go somewhere else. That's gradually disappearing too.'

I then asked if I just carried on driving down the lane to reach it and was told no, I had to turn left by an oak tree a few hundred yards from the farm. The lane finally ended up at a crossroads near Hinton Littlemoor. Lizzie finished by saying, 'You will be careful if you go and look at it, won't you?'

I assured her that I would and then said, 'Have you ever seen things going on – lights at night for example?'

'Only once. About six months ago. We phoned the police but I don't think it was followed up. It probably all happens while we're asleep.'

I had no intention of wandering around looking for a quarry in the gathering twilight.

'There's a parcel here for you, Miss Langley,' the hotel receptionist said when I collected my key. She unlocked a cupboard and withdrew a long slim package well-wrapped in thick brown paper and tied with string. I signed in a book for it.

'Did you see who handed it in?' I asked, having already noted that it had not come by post and wondering if Patrick had bought me a surprise present as a way of saying sorry for being so off-hand.

The girl shook her head, obviously surprised that there was a mystery surrounding it. 'I wasn't on duty this morning, Abby was. You could ask her about it tomorrow.'

When I reached my room I laid it on the bed. It was not very heavy but of quite solid construction and utterly impossible to identify by feeling though the paper. My fingers were busy with the knot when it occurred to me that Patrick would never send me anything without either first phoning to tell me or attaching a card the message upon which would include a code-word. The reason for this was a need for security: I have been sent parcels in the past that contained explosive devices.

There was no card, not the merest clue as to who had sent it.

I rang the rectory wondering if Patrick was there even though his parents were away but heard only the usual answerphone message. I then rang home in Devon and Carrie answered. She told me that Patrick was not there either and there were no telephone messages from him. I dialled his mobile number but it was switched off. There seemed little point in leaving any kind of message with Orange and, short of calling in the Bomb Squad, what the hell could I do?

In the end I very carefully cut through the string in several places and then put the whole thing in the bath having securely sewed one end of a long piece of thread – I carry all kinds of useful bits and pieces with me – into the folded over top edge of the wrapping paper. In theory I should be able to stand right over by the door, or even behind it, pull steadily on the thread and thus unwrap the parcel, its weight causing it to unroll.

The thread kept tearing through the paper. I was getting in a bit of a panic, feeling a thousand and one different kinds of idiot and expecting to hear at any moment someone from the hotel staff knocking on the door investigating the strange hollow bumping noises. Finally, when I was contemplating dropping the whole thing out of the window into the rather unsavoury utility area below, a desperate yank was rewarded by the paper floating free on to the floor. I made myself wait a full two minutes and then walked, on tip-toe, into the bath-room.

Having shed a few grassy bits and pieces a *tau tau* stared stonily up at me.

Or would have stared up at me if the eyes had not been gouged out and replaced by nails that had been left with the heads sticking out about an inch. It had been further modi-fied, another nail hammered up between the legs through the ragged garments, the whole of the clothing heavily stained with blood from which the same stale smell emanated as had from John Norton's study after his murder. I recognised it as the female figure that had stood on the shelf in the upper flat with all the rest.

My stomach heaved but I did not vomit, battling with the crazy notion that Sharleen Norton, or whoever she really was, was somehow, right now, watching me. To throw up would be some kind of defeat.

I left the thing where it was – it could still be booby-trapped – and went back into the bedroom, shutting the bathroom door. She seemed to know my every move but at no time had I been aware of being followed. So be it. I would start carrying Patrick's gun. Plus his second best knife.

Not surprisingly I lay awake for hours that night and when I did finally fall asleep I had a dream, a nightmare in which I collided with the child and her pony. But when I ran to them and saw that both were dead it was not Becky, but Justin, his head bent back at an impossible angle. I awoke, sweating, the scene still vivid in my mind's eye. The memory of the *tau tau* haunted me not, perhaps because it represented not so much a threat as verification, and when I got up at first light, exhausted, to have a shower and saw the figure where I had

251

left it in the bath it just looked pathetic. I felt a strange stab of pity for it.

I had already resolved that, using the map, I would attempt to reach the quarry from the valley floor as tackling crumbling cliffs would be extremely hazardous even with the benefit of ropes and abseilling equipment if I went out and bought them. The plan would entail parking near the ford and walking back because the road was so narrow. I wondered, as I had a quick breakfast the following morning, whether I would bump into whoever James had detailed off to check the area. It would not really matter if I did, I would merely earn myself a lecture. I would get a resounding one anyway, for not telling him straight away about receiving the *tau tau*.

At the top of my mind was a constant thought: why had she shown her hand now? Supreme confidence or quite the opposite? I thought it sensible to choose the first option and act accordingly. Under the circumstances it had seemed banal to very carefully gather up the *tau tau*, examine it closely for explosives and other unfriendly substances and then, having found nothing, put it back in its wrapper in the wardrobe. I did not want it to get about that Ingrid Langley dabbled in the black arts, far happier for her readership to discover that she was going out this dull morning armed to the teeth.

Wideford Valley was gloomy under a dull grey sky, not that I could see much of the sky through the canopy of leaves. I stepped out of the car and the exhaust fumes still hung around me: there was not a breath of wind. I locked up and set off back down the lane, finding myself slightly out of breath for some reason and having to take deep lungfuls of the stuffy, humid air.

A more measured examination on foot of the tangled

vegetation on the side of the road in which I was interested revealed that there were gaps and small clearings, mostly where there were pools of stagnant-looking water. There were no features, natural or otherwise, that pointed to the location of any of the old workings so I was counting my strides, having roughly measured the distance from the ford on the map. Then, reaching where I reckoned the quarry might have been I saw that a couple of large trees some twenty yards in from the road were leaning at an unnatural angle. If they were growing near to the area that had been affected by a rockfall they could have been pushed over slightly. I headed towards them.

As I walked the slight slope became steeper, moss-covered straight-sided boulders everywhere like large teeth actively thrusting their way through the ground between the ferns and coarse grass. I had to force my way through the thick greenery and the going underfoot became very difficult with hidden crevices and a real risk of a broken ankle. A short distance after passing the two leaning trunks I saw that the space beyond, the ground still rising, opened up and was bereft of large trees, covered mostly with scrubby birches and brambles. Beyond this again was the cliff face, hung with ivy in which was caught every kind of rubbish. Beneath the cliff was a mountain of rubbish.

I concealed myself as well as I could in the vegetation and sat down on a boulder. Ten minutes went by and during that time nothing occurred that would lead me to think that I was not alone. No vehicles had gone along the road and it was so quiet I would have heard any. Birds twittered, a crow cawed, and in the distance, probably at least a mile away down the valley, someone was using a chainsaw.

Keeping to the cover of the edge of the trees I skirted the open area until I was much nearer the cliff. The closer I got the more rubbish I could see, including the remains of several burned-out vehicles. It had obviously been used as a dump for years, Lizzie's farmer husband presumably helpless in the face of so many determined fly-tippers and car thieves. I composed a short pithy lecture to deliver to James.

A few small stones rattled down from above and clattered on to something metallic. Then silence, the birds had stopped twittering, just a little cloud of dust lingering.

At the first sound I had flung myself flat into the long grass beneath a small clump of straggly birches, fairly useless cover but it was all there was close by. A small age went by and nothing else moved. Then, a larger stone bounced down and crashed to the ground. Again, silence.

I remembered being taught about distraction tactics.

Crawling, I made for a section of the base of the cliff where there was a substantial curtain of ivy overhanging what appeared to be a small recess behind it. Anyone hiding there would be reasonably safe from missiles dropping from above and also be in a position to watch, as far as the vegetation permitted, the wooded area below. I would be much safer there. A few yards farther on I paused. What would Patrick do now if operating alone?

I could almost hear his voice. Never head for obvious places. That might be right where your enemy has already concealed himself. If in doubt either retreat, or, if you think you might have already been detected and someone has really declared war, fill the position full of lead as a precaution.

Yes, quite. Before I had really sensibly thought it through I had taken the Smith and Wesson from my pocket and, aiming fairly high, fired two shots into the darkness beneath the curtain of ivy. I was moving as I fired the second and dropped down into a small depression in the ground where I could still see the target area.

Things were already happening as I ran. Every pigeon, jackdaw, rook, and crow in this part of Somerset exploded into the air with a rush of wings. Earth and rocks tumbled down the cliff, one of significant size thunking into the roof of a burnt-out car, flattening it considerably. Pebbles continued to patter down from several places but I ignored them, watching the target area for signs of movement.

The ivy moved, stirring in a wave motion away to my right as someone passed behind it. I waited: they would soon reach the end of their cover. If that really was the intention. Or had they been able to sneak back without touching the greenery?

The crack of a high-powered rifle reached me a split second after a neat notch had been cut from the trunk of a tree a couple of feet above my head. I stayed right where I was. Then another shot, unnervingly closer. They were coming from somewhere ahead of me, probably from behind the ivy.

The marksman could not possibly see me when I flattened myself right down in the depression, which was actually the top of a small gully. There was, therefore, an open space behind me. Sort of slithering, I reversed but only for a short distance as every second when I could not keep surveillance was extremely dangerous. Then, when I knew that I presented no target, I stood up and, in the cover of the trees, encircled the open space in a manoeuvre that brought me closer to the cliff. It took about ten seconds and I had been hoping for five more but tripped over a root and fell heavily on to a small boulder, utterly winding myself.

Insects buzzed, my heart thudded and I tried to get my breath back in total silence. Pain stabbed in my chest and I wondered if I had cracked a rib. I had to move though, had to be able to see what was going on. Bent over for at least two reasons I got to my feet and carefully picked my way between the slippery rocks. I wanted to reach a position where in order to be able to fire at me again whoever it was would have to step out into the open.

Behind a hawthorn bush I sank down, crouching. I could hear nothing unusual, no sounds of feet brushing through grass or the faint scrunch of shoes on shattered rock and soil.

I ran across the space between the bush and the burned-out car that the rock had crashed down on to, all the way keeping it between me and the spot from where I estimated the shots had been fired. A handgun is no match for a rifle when it comes to long-distance shooting but at close quarters . . .

I went to ground at the off-side rear end of the car, lying flat. It was a small vehicle of some kind, impossible now to tell which, and, glancing over my right shoulder I could see that the impact had forced something inside it partly out through the opening where the remains of the lower part of the buckled driver's door were still in place. My gaze lingered. What I was looking at was the torso and head of a blackened, charred corpse, the latter lolling down, a cloud of flies busily in attendance. The head seemed to be moving slightly as though still vibrating, a slow nodding. At any moment, it seemed, it would fall off and hit the ground with a revolting thud.

Moments later it exploded in a miasma of bone, teeth, cooked brains and maggots. The stuff splattered all over me. I leapt around to the other side of the car in an effort of get out of immediate range, mostly aware of sections of upper and lower jaw bones still bizarrely together that had landed right by my side.

Another shot banged off the bare metalwork of the wreck, just missing me. I was pinned right down. The shots had come from somewhere above me. Rolling over on to my back partly beneath the charred chassis I scanned the rockface – although my field of vision was severely limited – and when I saw movement near the top in a small tree that leaned crazily over the void, fired. There was a flailing movement and then I saw what looked like a figure scrambling upwards through the roots and ivy. I fired again and it went from sight.

Sirens.

Someone had heard the shots and dialled 999.

'I don't care *what* Patrick's permitted to do,' James Carrick said, hopefully near the end of his lecture. 'As far as I'm concerned you are not allowed to carry this weapon – I'm ignoring the knife – and I'm well within my rights in confiscating it. Please don't tell me that it probably saved your life this morning as you had no business to be there.'

'Hang on a minute! It isn't a prohibited area,' I retorted, stung into self-defence. Not for the first time recently I had had to relinquish all my clothing for forensic examination but at least had been taken back to my hotel for replacements and was not now wearing something that resembled white plastic bin-bags. James's mercy had extended to being given extra time to shower and wash my hair before presenting myself for the inevitable carpeting. I still thought I had cracked a rib: a sharp pain went through my right side every time I moved or breathed.

'But why not just leave it to me?' he went on. 'I said I'd arrange for someone to examine all likely places where a car might be disposed of.'

'Now you're getting petulant,' I told him, adding, 'Hooting and skirling Patrick calls it.'

He frowned, staring into space while, silently, his mouth formed the first three words of my final remark.

'Well, d'you reckon he'd been shot or just roasted to death?' I asked impatiently.

A smile had twitched at Carrick's lips but he ruthlessly disallowed it. 'Ingrid . . . '

'I know, it's too early to tell. James . . . '

He sighed. 'You want the gun back.'

We both relaxed wearily.

I said, 'Patrick'll skin me alive.'

'I do realise that it's officially held by a certificated member of MI5 outwith my control. I'll think about it.'

'No, actually, Patrick was issued with it because we're on so many terrorist hit-lists.'

'D'you reckon you winged whoever it was?'

'No, the angles were impossible.'

'So who was it then?'

'You're not interested in my theories about Sharleen Norton.'

He leaned forward and rested both elbows on his desk, fists under his chin. 'Go on, convince me.'

I gave him my theory. Then I told him about the *tau tau*. I went on to outline what I thought were her motives, ending with, 'And now she's neatened everything off by topping her hit-man. Finito.'

'We don't know it's him yet.'

'I'd put money on it.Did your team find any of the rounds that missed me?'

He nodded soberly.

'It would be really interesting to find out if they match the ones found at the scene of the London murder, wouldn't it?'

'I still think you're barking up the wrong tree and that crime isn't my responsibility, thank God.' He smiled, an idea obviously having just come to him. 'It's yours.'

'James, I have no credentials. I'm not even sure Patrick has now.'

'Why don't you find and ask him?'

This did seem preferable to acting the sitting duck in Bath – and it was still giving me the shivers to realise how closely someone, presumably Sharleen, with or without an accomplice about whom we as yet knew nothing, had been monitoring my every move. So I checked out of the hotel and resolved to give every impression of completely leaving the district while keeping a very close eye on what was happening in my rear mirror.

I was not expecting Patrick to be drinking himself to death in a bar somewhere or in the arms of what the French call *une grande horizontale* but was nevertheless worried. I checked and he still was not at home. There was every chance that he had gone to the rectory after all so I went there first to find there was no sign of life, everywhere locked and bolted. I gained entry via our secret way – there is no alarm system – but it was obvious that he was not in residence, the bed in what had been his boyhood bedroom, where we usually sleep, stripped down to the mattress. There was hardly any food in the fridge, certainly no milk or other necessities.

Sitting in the car, convinced I had not been followed to Hinton Littlemoor, I rang James.

'You and Patrick knocked around a bit on a job when I was once in the States,' I said, coming right to the point. 'Is there anywhere that I don't know about where he might be?'

There was a longish silence on the other end of the line which I broke by saying, 'Come on, I've had a suspicion for quite a while that there's a bolt-hole somewhere he's never told me about purely for security purposes. It's actually quite important that I find him purely from the point of view staying married.'

'Bad as that, eh?'

'It's not like him just to go off and not get in touch when he's not working on something specific and doesn't seem to have the D12 job anyway. We have our own rules and he's breaking them.'

'His reasons must be pretty important, important enough for him to break both my legs if I tell you.'

'No, I think we're just talking about stupid male petty jealousy!' I bellowed down the line.

There was another silence and then he said, 'Okay, as I put my job on the line giving you back the handgun, I suppose I might as well put my life on the line as well. It's not far from where you live. I think he said Terry Meadows helped him put in some cupboards and stuff like that. If you – '

I interrupted with, 'I can remember Terry staying one weekend and arriving with carpentry tools. It was all supposed to be about a barn he was converting. But the whole project just seemed to fizzle out.'

'It could well have done and I was taken somewhere else. The place I went to was just north of Dousland on the Princetown road. I couldn't give you a map reference even if I had a map – we went there in the dark and he was navigating.'

'Oh, I know where it is – I picked them up there one evening because Terry's car wouldn't start. Don't worry. You didn't tell me, I guessed.'

I had been concerned, now I was furious.

'By the way, those rifle rounds we found in the quarry do match the ones that killed Sir Michael Hawksbury. I still don't have any evidence to connect the crimes with Sharleen Norton though. Not enough for a search warrant.'

'You'd probably be wasting your time anyway – she won't be leaving anything incriminating lying around at home.'

'And you may be interested to know that a heavy hammer was found in what had been the boot of the burnt-out car. It may be the murder weapon – that killed John Norton, that is. No forensic evidence on it after the fire of course. Nothing on the charred corpse as yet other than it had been a tall and well-built male.'

We rang off, I wondering when someone from the management of an hotel or bed and breakfast establishment would phone the police to report that one of their guests had failed to return.

16

It looked as though I had found my knife-man, or rather he had been found for me. There was no real reason for continuing to investigate except my own stubbornness and anger in the face of everyone's indifference to my theories about Sharleen Norton. Also, by now the whole thing had become highly personal. I knew she was probably not directly responsible for John Norton's death but if I was right she had murdered the knife man, as good as killed one of the men who had attacked me in Bristol and also Max, not to mention the attempted murder of Harvey Dupont. And me – again.

And Patrick.

Yes, perhaps I was really going after this person because, indirectly or not, she, he, *it*, had tried to kill my husband.

In the absence of Alpha One I started by trying to work out who would have employed a hit-man to take out someone like Major-General Sir Michael Hawksbury. The difficulty lay in the sheer number of terrorist organisations which might have an interest in him following the man's long army career. He had served in just about all the recent and world-wide hotspots, from Northern Ireland to Bosnia. Since leaving active service, subsequently becoming Chief of the Defence Staff, he had advised on many issues including Islamic extremists, a possible war against Iraq and precautions against attacks by Real IRA cells in London. This much I knew off the top of my head.

Any assassin taken on to kill such a man would have to have, of necessity and for practical purposes, an international reputation. Perhaps therefore, if Sharleen Norton was indeed that person and had undergone extensive plastic surgery to create a new identity, it would be fruitful to discover who had fairly recently gone from the sight of MI5, MI6, the FBI, the CIA and other intelligence services. Someone might have incorrectly been declared dead. I was perfectly aware that I would not be the only one engaged on this task.

As we have never been permitted to have an on-line MI5 computer at home for security reasons – and this information could not be sourced from one at Manvers Street police station – I would have to go and find one. It might mean travelling to London. First of all I hit the road for the West Country, intent on checking the 'holiday cottage' first as my real priority was to find Patrick. If indeed the property was his bolt-hole, and the jury was out on exactly what my comments on the subject would be, then it was feasible that now, if the place was sufficiently secure, he had the relevant hardware installed there.

Three hours later I drove past the turning into the rough track twice before I found it, the entrance having become very overgrown since I had last seen it. It was getting dark, the sun setting and in my eyes, another reason for not being able to locate it straight away. I bounced uphill: the track was steep and deeply rutted, an ordinary car would have grounded. I stopped when the track forked, I could not recollect this. There was grass growing in the middle of both ways but the one on the left looked as though it might be slightly more used and there were wisps of hay on the ground and in the hedges that might have come from a farm trailer taking fodder to cattle on the high moor. I took the right hand one.

Almost immediately I came to the farm building I remembered. It could at one time have been a cart-shed and the job of converting it into living accommodation had now been completed. There were no signs of life, no vehicles parked outside, none of the barred windows open even a cranny despite it being a warm evening. I turned off the engine, sat in the car and waited. It looked as though the journey had been for nothing.

In the distance, glancing over my shoulder, I could see

Brentor church on its peak of volcanic rock, very close to where we live on the north-western slopes of Dartmoor. Transferring my attention back again to the building I saw that the lower part – the building was two-storeyed – had no windows at the front but new-looking large double wooden doors that suggested it was used as a garage. There were no apparent exterior locks. I got out of the car and went closer. There were no locks. I set off to walk all the way round but this proved to be impossible as it was set into the side of the hill and the rear butted up against bare granite.

Returning to the front I picked up quite a large stone and knocked on one of the doors. A special sequence of knocks. Nothing happened so I did it again, harder. A minute or so later I was just about to turn away when I heard a sound within, then a kind of sliding, bumping noise. And faintly, music. Patrick's music. Then nothing.

I got really angry then, stepped back and fired a shot up at one of the windows. There was a crash of breaking glass and the Bach organ concerto poured out. Nothing else happened for at least another minute and then there was a click close by and the doors began to swing outwards to the hum of an electric motor.

Memories of recent events had caused me to step sharply to one side at the first signs of movement and I stood motionless, Smith and Wesson at the ready, waiting to see Patrick emerge. For another long minute no one did. Then a hand appeared, holding on tightly to the door nearest to me. I did not look at it at all closely but, feeling rather pleased with myself, shouted, 'Your wife has been captured and tortured to reveal your coded knock sequences. Throw down any weapons you have and come right out. I shall count to three.'

I arrived at home about forty-five minutes later. Lights were on in the buildings on both sides of the courtyard but I went straight into the barn first; barged through the front door, raged through the living room like something demented, ran up the stairs, searched the two bedrooms. Lights were on everywhere.

Someone was in the shower room. I powered into there too and nearly got my head knocked off.

'Bloody hell, woman! Are you trying to give me a major heart attack?' Standing there, wet, soapy and stark naked Patrick lowered his hand.

'I went to that place you once had,' I babbled. 'I thought you were there. I could hear your sort of music. I got really mad when you didn't respond to the coded knocks. But after I'd practically shot the place up all I got was some geek completely smashed out of his skull. He'd fallen down the stairs coming to answer the door.'

'Was he hurt?'

'No, but it was difficult to tell he was so legless. I helped him back upstairs, he asked me to marry him and then I came home.'

Patrick restored himself under the hot spray and carried on rinsing off soap. 'I sold it ages ago to pay for the work we've had done on this place – not long after I took Carrick there.'

'How long have you been at home?'

'About twenty minutes. I got a taxi from the station.'

Our eyes met. We giggled. We fell about laughing. I kissed him.

Which was why I ended up having a shower with all my clothes on.

'It wasn't deception on my part,' Patrick was saying a little later. 'But if you remember, a few years ago things were getting distinctly hot. Literally. Half the cottage was burnt down by those jokers we were on to. I wanted to create a safe haven where we could take everyone at extremely short notice. But James put his finger on the main drawback of the place that I'm ashamed to say I'd missed and that was if anyone succeeded in getting into the garage area downstairs, which was actually quite difficult, they could light a fire and cook everyone on the first floor on account of the bars on the windows. There was an emergency exit of sorts but in a real war . . . '

'So you advertised it in *Geek's Weekly*.'

'Where else?'

Up until now everything had been on this light note, Patrick having apologised for being, as he put it, 'loutish' towards me and for not getting in touch, his mobile phone having somehow gone missing although he had found it now and he had been hellishly busy. Imparting the news that he had been in London for more in-depth talks he had gone on to say that D12's future still hung in the balance and although the vibes were positive he was running out of patience.

To my way of thinking he seemed to have just assumed that I had tired of my quest and returned home. It had been impossible to tell after such a short time with him whether or not his positiveness about things in general was a carefully constructed front.

'What's for dinner?' Patrick asked. 'Or would you like to go out to eat?'

Crunchtime.

I went upstairs and fetched the *tau tau* from my bag and stood it, in exactly the same condition it had been sent to me, in the corner by the fireplace.

'Still hungry?' I asked.

Patrick had been nursing a pre-dinner tot of single malt but now laid it aside to stare at the object.

I took a deep breath and said, 'I've been over to the cottage to say hello to Carrie and the children and she now knows we're in a Red Alert situation. Everything's secured and nobody in the cottage is permitted to leave until we say so, with a review first thing in the morning. If you don't wish to share responsibility for this and like James continue to rubbish my theories about Sharleen Norton then I shall take the family abroad until the pair of you have come to your senses and, or, she is no longer deemed to be a danger to anyone. My intuition, perception and good ideas are the reason I'm in the team and yet when the end-product of this stretches your credulity you're as sceptical as every Joe Bloke. I didn't marry you because you were like every Joe Bloke.'

I swept on with, 'I'm pretty convinced that the knife man is dead, although forensic testing will confirm this. I know this because someone with a rifle that fires rounds that match those that killed Michael Hawksbury took several shots at me in a quarry where I had found several burnt-out cars. There was a large-ish charred corpse in one of them and whoever the marksman was they used the head as target practice and a large chunk of very dead smile almost landed in my lap. I'm sure it was the smile I saw in the hospital. He's dead. She killed him. She sent that *tau tau* to my hotel. Who has some terrorist group hired her to shoot next?'

He was looking at me very hard. 'You're all right though?'

I nodded.

'Sure?' he persisted grimly.

'I might have cracked a rib. That's all.'

He gestured towards the *tau tau*. 'Did you show that to Carrick?'

'No, because he would have confiscated it as evidence and frankly, I thought showing it to you would get a hell of a lot more done about it. I still don't think James is quite firing on all cylinders.'

Patrick was shaking his head. 'James isn't paid to possess a writer's imagination. I'm not convinced that Sharleen Norton is necessarily behind all this. There are other people living in that house with access to the top flat where those figures are kept. We're only talking about a set of door keys here.'

'I don't care what you say – neither Frances nor Arabis fit the frame. And neither does Jason. He might be a demon-driver but underneath is quite a nice lad with the nerves of a rabbit. No, this is all goes back to *Max*. I think just about all of his scams involved stolen antiques of all kinds going from the UK to the States and very little crossed the pond the other way. He might well have smuggled in a shrunken head full of diamonds but Sharleen did let it slip that he'd got very little for the boat. And yet they're looking to spend around a million pounds on a house in Bath. I'm wondering if that money's in dollars somewhere – I mean would they have dared have it wired straight into a bank account with his criminal record? – and it's the sum Max was paid to get Sharleen into this country, possibly by marrying her, plus any fees she's being paid. Only now she wants it all for herself.'

'But you said you thought she was a bloke.'

'There's every chance she's a bloke and the marriage is a front. Or as you yourself said, has a pair of Max's socks stuffed into her knickers.'

Patrick took a pensive sip of his drink. 'I've tried to bury this mentally, haven't I?'

'You're still doing it. What I really need to know – and I'm sorry to be so bloody horrible to you about it – is can you handle the situation?'

Predictably offended – you should never ask a man this kind of question – he shrugged. 'I'll let you know if and when the time comes. First of all we must try to find out if any known assassins went missing in the States, or elsewhere.' He reached for the phone. 'But first I'll get on to the Protection Squad and get some people down here. Then . . . '

'Then?' I queried when he stopped speaking.

Indicating the *tau tau* again he said irritably, 'Ingrid, d'you think you could put that effing thing somewhere else?'

It took me a few minutes for after taking it away I found a claw hammer, and, with difficulty, pulled out the nails and threw them in the bin. Then I removed the stinking, blooded clothing and screwed it up to put it in the woodstove when I returned to the living room. Rolling the figure back in the brown paper I put it in a cupboard.

When I got back Patrick said, 'I've been thinking. After it's all over I'll tell MI5 what they can do with their job. I've been trying to kid myself it wasn't a pig's breakfast from the word go – they're still arguing about definitions, delimitations and who'll be chief bumwiper. I realise now that not being able to get on with anything official made Tim go a bit over the edge although I have to say that now, rather than later, is the right time to find out he tends to buckle under stress. But most of all I'm damned if I'm going to carry on having to arrange for armed men to protect my family every time we hit upon a lunatic.'

'Trouble-shooting does tend to trawl up lunatics,' I pointed out gently.

He had made the phone call. Police from the local TSG would undertake surveillance for the rest of the night, arriving in under an hour, and MI5's own team would arrive early the following day.

'In the morning, after they've got here, you and I will hit the trail,' Patrick announced. 'We'll go and talk to whoever's in charge of investigating Mike Hawksbury's murder, tell them all we know and give them all the relevant insider info we manage to dig out ourselves from MI5's databases. Let them do the work. Then we'll go away on holiday.' He extended a long arm again in the direction of the telephone. 'Right now I'll find out who we have to go and see tomorrow so they'll know we're coming.'

But it rang before he touched it and it was Carrick.

Patrick listened closely for a couple of minutes before thanking him and replacing the handset. 'Developments,' he said, having got up to put a match to the fire. 'He's just had the preliminary report he'd asked for on the PM of the corpse in the car you found. Male, around six feet three in height and between sixty and seventy-five years of age. The pathologist is of the opinion that he had been overweight. Extensive signs of arthritis plus a replacement right hip joint. This fits the description of a man of seventy-two by the name of Hubert Mannering who'd been reported missing by his wife last week. The car's not his and anyway he doesn't drive now because he's in the early stages of senile dementia. According to the wife he sometimes forgets they've moved and goes back to their previous house, which was in Combe Down. Skulls always look as though they're grinning,' Patrick added, almost to himself.

The hand holding the match had been perfectly steady.

'She tried to make it look as though the knife-man was dead?' I said increduously. 'But that car could have stayed in the quarry until kingdom come without anyone finding it! It also means she must have killed the old man days ago and stored the body somewhere.'

'Did you do a recce the previous day?'

'The evening before.'

'Then you were followed.'

'I was *not* followed! I kept checking and no one tailed me.'

'There's only one other explanation – someone's bugged the Range Rover.'

'I checked that too. I always do.'

'What, every time you get in it, even if you've just stopped to buy a newspaper?'

There was no easy answer to that.

'Did you bring the weapons out of the car?'

'No, sorry. I got a bit het up about finding you.'

'I noticed. I'll go and get them – and make sure they're okay over at the cottage.'

'Are you sure you ought to go outside?'

'If you're right we'll probably need them quite soon.'

'To plant a substitute corpse seems to me to be an act of desperation,' I said. 'Everyone knows about modern forensic methods these days surely. Why not just get rid of the right man instead of going to all the bother of killing the wrong one?'

'Whoever it is might still need his services – or just be keeping their hand in.'

I shuddered.

All the lights went out.

'This might be a perfectly normal power cut,' Patrick's voice said in the darkness. I heard him moving carefully around the room and a drawer opening and then a flash-lamp was switched on.

'Shall I phone to check with someone in the village to make sure it's not just us?' I said.

'Good idea.'

There was a bang outside and the burglar alarm in the cottage went off.

'But they're all at home!' I exclaimed above the eldritch howling. Then I realised the truth: Carrie had hit the panic button.

The torch was thrust into my hands and Patrick had gone.

'Wait!' I yelled. 'This might be exactly what they want you to do!'

Then a truly appalling thought hit me.

I ran after him and caught up with him in the kitchen. There was no question of his going out of the front door. 'Patrick wait! Think! It might be *you* who's next on her list!'

'They could have killed me very easily the last time we met,' he said roughly.

'But anyone could have seen them then. They wouldn't have wanted to – '

I broke off because he had opened the kitchen window, disappeared through it and I was arguing with thin air. All I could do was follow.

* * *

There was no drop because the garden rises slightly behind the barn so it was just a question of pushing off from the window ledge and hitting the ground running. This was the emergency that had always been our real dread: that the children would be placed at risk because of the job. There was a plan in place to safeguard them but against this kind of enemy it seemed merely domestic, flimsy and pathetic in the extreme.

The lack of security lighting in the courtyard was actually to our advantage as normally they would have come on automatically and revealed our approach down one side of the barn. The advantage of this route was that we were close to the the tall boundary hedge in the lee of which it was very dark. A hazy moon cast its faint light across the courtyard and I could see that the front door of the cottage was wide open. Inside was in darkness with not even evidence of a torch being flashed around. Where before there had been light and the sounds of children's voices there was only the howl of the siren.Then there was a small movement and Pirate emerged, flat-eared, her stomach to the ground and shot over the bank into the field.

Patrick had been just ahead of me as we rounded the corner of the barn and had paused momentarily before heading for our car which was parked where I had left it, somewhat untidily blocking the drive to the arrival of other vehicles. Then he came to a dead stop as a huge shadowy figure strolled into view, smoking a cigarette, obviously waiting for someone else while keeping an eye on our only means of escape.

Making no more noise than Pirate had, Patrick moved sideways a little more into the deep shade of the hedge. I had already reversed round the corner of the barn wall. I could still see Patrick, or at least, where I thought he was. Seconds later I somehow knew he was no longer there but dared not peep around the building for fear of being seen.

Trying to console myself with the thought that in the darkness cats have the advantage over larger, stronger prey I waited, desperately wanting to dash over to the cottage to know what was happening. But I did not, I could not, it would be madness as I was unarmed. I could not help Patrick either, that was the arrangement in such a situation. If a life had to be sacrificed it would be his. My responsibility, for the children's sake, was to stay alive.

The siren stopped but my ears continued to ring for a minute or so because of the sheer volume of sound it had made. Were the people living locally who had promised to respond to it on their way?

I heard the moment Patrick found the other man in the lee of the car. There was no skuffle, just a heavy falling sound and what might have been a grunt or exhalation. After that the silence continued, if anything now a more profound stillness. It was the last thing I was expecting for this had been instant, no hand-to-hand encounter. I wanted to scream. Or run, just as Pirate had.

Was Patrick still alive?

No, a deep voice with a strong Nordic accent shouted out, 'Are you finished looking now I've done the job for you out here?'

Creeping forward I took the route that Patrick had; along the hedge for a short distance, and then stopped. The blood was beating in my ears, my chest tight: I could hardly breathe. This was like the last time: no one was in sight, just the car. But in the next second someone came from inside the cottage, pushing another person in front of them, Carrie, and stood a few feet from the front door. A slim figure, dressed seemingly all in black and almost invisible, I could just see the whiteness of eyes.

'Where is he then?' Not Sharleen's voice exactly but ...

'Right here at my feet. Are you blind?'

'I've been indoors – in the firelight. I've a little present for you. You can kill her afterwards if you want to.'

I bit my lip hard as the figure walked forward a little, shoving Carrie along. There was the distinct outline of a long distance weapon slung across one shoulder, another, probably a semi-automatic of some kind carried in one hand. I crept a little farther forward.

Someone was standing near the rear of the car, another shape – Patrick's body? – nearby on the ground. Then there was a blurred movement away to the left and the semi-automatic weapon pivoted to follow it in a movement hideously mechanical. The stabbing points of flame and rapid explosions burst into the night and set every dog in the village barking frenziedly. Carrie screamed and tried to run away but was lunged after and grabbed by one arm. She screamed again, with pain and seemed to catch a foot on something. She fell. Then I saw a rapid sliding motion down the side of the car nearest to me before a form disengaged from it, outlined against slightly lighter shrubs in the background. There was a fractional pause and then an arm swung.

Flame was again spurting from the muzzle of the weapon and I threw myself flat as the bullets smashed into the hedge above my head. The sound ceased and I looked up tentatively, expecting to behold mass murder. I could see only one large outline.

I stood up and walked forward. How could I fend him off, unarmed, before help came? Before he got to the children?

'It's all right,' Patrick said.

Amazingly, what I was looking at had split into two, one of them trying not to cry, the other shirtless and bending to kick over the body on the ground and remove the weapons to a safe distance.

I ran to them and we all three hugged and tried not to cry.

'I must go to the children!' Carrie said, breaking free.

We all went, Patrick to find another torch to guide us so that we could make our way easily to the first floor and the built-in cupboard that looks quite small but is actually rather large and has ventilation, a stock of food and water plus a chemical toilet.

Four pairs of rather round eyes surveyed us when we had gained entry by using the concealed locking device.

'There!' Carrie said brightly. 'We said we wouldn't tell you when the next practice was, didn't we?' She relieved Katie of the smallest, Victoria, who is still too young to understand but seemed quite happy that Mum and Dad were back and the game of hide and seek over. Justin was grumpy with tiredness, the two eldest all agog to know what was really going on but aware that, just for now, they should not ask any questions.

The torchbeam imperceptibly shivering, Patrick said to them, 'There is a *real* powercut though, so while I try to deal with it perhaps everyone could sort themselves out and then,' plaintively, 'please find me some supper.'

Everyone laughed of course.

I stayed in the house, found and lit a lot of candles but beforehand, as a matter of urgency, made sure that all the curtains were closed. I heard Patrick move the car to make way for others. The first to arrive were on foot, at the run wearing boots, no doubt those I had been expecting in response to the burglar alarm; Gideon Jenks, a game-keeper friend who lived in the village with his grown-up son Harry. I discovered later that their Land Rover was off the road with a failed water-pump.

Carrie seemed to be managing so after a quick word with her we got the two youngest children, who had already had their tea, off to bed while Matthew put some more logs on the living room fire and Katie engaged in gleeful piracy in the kitchen cupboards searching for supper. Both had been asked not to look out of the windows. I felt it was important for everyone to eat and get warm by the fire so checked on the food situation when I could – against a background of the sound of vehicles drawing up in the courtyard – and discovered that edibles were somewhat thin on the ground. When, with four children in the house, do you ever have anything in the fridge?

I knew I was pushing to the back of my mind what had occurred and could not understand the outcome. For some reason I did not want to be involved with what was going on outside. But it was necessary to raid the barn kitchen for food so I would have venture out. On the way I met Carrie at the bottom of the stairs. She was still very pale and looked worried.

'I should have told you just now. That woman made me turn the alarm off.'

'Not to worry,' I assured her. 'It had done its job.'

'Is she dead?' she whispered.

I nodded.

'She put some kind of explosive in the door locks and forced her way in.'

'We'll replace them with better ones,' I replied, wondering as I spoke about the practicalities of the promise. I patted her arm. 'You all did fantastically well.'

Patrick was standing talking to plain-clothes policemen by a squad car parked in front of an ambulance into which a body was just being placed. Someone had put an anorak around his shoulders, probably Gideon. There was a little difficulty with the loading as there was not much room to manoeuvre and the scene was illuminated only by the headlights of vehicles.

'Selfish of me,' I said to him, hooking an arm through his, adding when he looked down at me, 'Staying indoors I mean.'

'I'll be a while yet.'

'No, you go in, sir,' said one of the detectives. 'I've radioed for instructions and was told that where the security services are concerned the rules are a bit different. Will you consider yourself under house-arrest while all this area is cordoned off to enable SOCO to give it the twice over?'

'Of course,' Patrick said.

'Good. We'll talk to you again in the morning and take statements from everyone concerned.'

'Having to stay at home for a while sounds wonderful,' Patrick said under his breath.

This was magnanimous and unusual and I wondered as he went indoors whether Richard Daws had pulled a few strings. The barn was not out of bounds to us so I emptied the fridge of everything useful there, filling a carrier bag. The light from the torch picked out the knife block on the worktop.

My new Sabatier boning knife was missing.

'They dined on rat and slices of bat by the light of a guttering candle,' Katie paroded.

'It's not bat, it's salami,' Matthew said in superior big brother fashion.

'Can I give mine to Pirate?' she asked. 'It's really yuck.'

'No,' I said. 'That kind of thing's not good for cats.'

Patrick reached over and neatly speared it from her plate with his fork. 'The rat's good too,' he said.

This family really does like cold oven-roasted ratatouille.

It was an adventure for Matthew and Katie; sitting around the table eating by candlelight and while they had been good, and sufficiently hungry, to eat up most of the somewhat outlandish mixture of cold food with salad put before them they fell on what followed – profiteroles I had suddenly remembered were in the freezer. I was expecting Patrick to give them some kind of explanation for the evening's events and he waited until we were all sitting in the living room where the two youngsters were each treated to a small share of the mulled wine heated in an old saucepan on the open fire. It would, Patrick had said quietly in my ear, make them sleep like logs with no nightmares. I was hoping it would have the same effect on us.

'As you've probably realised,' Patrick began, speaking to the children, 'tonight wasn't a practice but something real. It's the reason we had the practices. You already know that I used to have the sort of job that resulted in a lot of dangerous criminals being put in prison. Sometimes they or their friends want to get even. This evening someone tried to get even. They failed. They've gone and I promise you they won't, ever, come back.'

Carrie had been very quiet right through the meal and was now hugging her mug of mulled wine to herself as though she needed its warmth. I had an idea she disapproved of the two older children being told the truth.

Matthew looked extremely uncomfortable, a fact not lost on his uncle.

'Please speak your mind,' Patrick said to him. 'We don't want to keep the main points of this secret from you.'

Matthew and Katie exchanged sideways glances and then Matthew said, 'We don't want secrets kept from you either.'

Patrick smiled upon him. 'What, did you have to wallop Justin because he was as uncooperative as ever?'

'No, I just told him there was a big croc outside and it would get him if he didn't go in the cupboard.' Another sideways glance at his sister. 'We looked out of the window before Auntie came in and said we weren't to. The little one by the cupboard. We were worried about Carrie.'

'I know we were supposed to stay in the cupboard,' Katie whispered. 'But after we'd run up the stairs in the dark like we'd practised and hidden ourselves Matthew and I wanted to see what was going on. We wanted to rescue Carrie. We let ourselves out of the cupboard the way you showed us in case we got stuck in there and looked out of the window wondering if we could escape that way and call the police. It was nearly dark but we saw people outside and then you threw something at that horrible woman. She'd fired the gun at you and when she fell over we jumped up and down and cheered.'

'Quietly,' Matthew said.

'Will you be in the parents' cricket match?' Katie asked Patrick eagerly, bouncing up and down in her seat, mulled wine or no. 'You'd gets loads of goals.'

Her brother looked witheringly at her. 'Goals! You don't get goals in cricket!'

Undiminished, Katie retorted, 'You know what I mean. When they throw the ball at the sticks and they go all over the place. Goals.'

17

The man who had assumed a new identity, his latest of several, and called himself Sharleen Norton had been of mid-European origin and had been associated with several extremist groups, starting in his teens. Before that he had used the alias Frankie Kaminski. The only really reliable information available about him, other than his inherent need to indulge in murder and violence, was in connection with a short term he spent in the Serbian Army before deserting. It appeared that he had spoken several languages fluently, could pass himself off as all and sundry, displayed instant rapport with whichever weapon was given to him and had murdered beggers and the homeless in every manner possible to keep his hand in. Somehow, despite being on the most-wanted lists of several countries, he had entered the United States, possibly via Mexico. There, he had made contact with an Islamic extremist cell that was prepared to pay high fees to anyone with relevant experience interested in assassinating those who could be described as members of the establishments of Western Powers on both sides of the Atlantic. It was not known how he had met Max Norton.

It was only much later that it was discovered there had been a real Sharleen Norton, née Blackwood, and she had been murdered, no doubt by Kaminski. Sharleen had crashed her car and suffered severe facial injuries. Kaminski, who was of similar height and build, had found the perfect identity. Her body was discovered buried beneath a patio of a house where the Nortons had lived before they left for the UK. She had been strangled.

'So all Kaminski needed was to find a bent plastic surgeon, learn to speak at a slightly higher register, stay with a stupid and greedy bloke like Max Norton for as long as it took to reach this country, grab all his ill-gotten gains and, having mopped up all the people cluttering up the place, he was in business.'

The speaker was James Carrick who had arrived the following morning to liaise with Devon and Cornwall police. No one had confirmed anything but I got the impression that the Plymouth boys' fervent wish that, after providing scene-of-crime services and taking statements, they could hand most of the responsibility for the case over to him on the grounds that the whole business had started in Somerset before it had migrated to London, then Dartmoor, might be granted. And, hey, I could almost hear them thinking, wasn't the deceased a prime suspect in the Bath DCI's multi-murder inquiry?

The local DI was unhappy that Patrick had crept up behind an unsuspecting person and felled him with a single blow, causing him actual physical harm. Tossing his shirt to one side to act as a decoy and then throwing a knife at some-one else, killing them, who had been armed with, and firing, a semi-automatic weapon was grudgingly agreed to come under the heading of self-defence. Upon which Carrick had reminded his subordinate that a knife with a seven inch blade had been removed from the pocket of the coat the first man had been wearing, the haft of which was heavily stained with dried blood. And the weapons with which this army officer had successfully defended his entire family against a heavily armed professional killer and his hench-man, he had gone on to point out rather forcibly, were his bare hands and a *kitchen* knife. Shortly afterwards the local law-enforcers had left, a little warm under the collar and threatening that a charge of manslaughter might follow their report to the Crown Prosecution Service.

'Ingrid, I was wondering, – ' James said, 'whether you'd be willing to be my sergeant for a couple of weeks while Bob Ingrams is on leave. I've come to realise that the department is desperately short of intuition, sixth sense and gut-feelings.'

I laughed, thinking it a very graceful apology.

He said, 'Just as I was leaving home to come here I got a call from the nick to the effect that a Mrs Dowling, who runs a B & B in Bear Flat, is missing a large lodger. He's left all his stuff in the room so she doesn't think he's done a runner. Woods got the impression she rather hopes he's gone under a bus. Scared her more than a bit. I've sent in a forensic team. If you remember we have one blond hair that was found at the scene of Professor John Norton's murder and as there's a bit of root on it I'm praying for a DNA match with evidence recovered from the room. And some kind of proof of identity of course.'

After Carrick left, saying that his next task was to search the top flat in the Norton's house, and the local scenes of crime people had departed everything became very quiet. As they were no longer required the MI5 protection unit had been called off and it only remained for Patrick to go outside, don overalls, and get cheek by jowl with his car. I was not too ashamed when he found the bugging device after fifteen minutes or so of screwdriver-wrangling for when he bought the vehicle he went on a course to enable him to take quite a few important bits and pieces apart and put them back together again. The bug was underneath the insides of the air filter.

'I'll post it back to base,' he said when he had come indoors. 'It's one I haven't seen before. Yank. You may depend though that your every move was monitored from the comfort of home. I have an idea it talks to a global positioning gadget that Carrick might just find at the flat.'

The snooping device had been the reason for the rapid departure of the red car from outside the old vicarage: 'Sharleen' must have received a mobile phone call from the knife man shortly after he had arrived and she had told him

281

to clear out fast. 'Sharleen' had been driving Jason's car the night I was attacked. While parked, keeping watch I myself had been under close surveillance. The bugging device must have been planted right at the beginning, perhaps even as early as when Patrick had left the car to wait for me in the garden when I had visited John Norton. Perhaps a deeply suspicious individual, watching from that darkened top flat and aware that some checking might be done on Max, had acted. The inevitable question would have to be urgently addressed: how had access been gained so easily to the engine compartment?

And now she, he, Kaminski was dead, the boning knife buried to the hilt just beneath his left ear.

I gave Carrie a week off, which she agreed to take, after a little argument, and when she returned Patrick and I went away with the eldest two as it was half term and roamed around Scotland. When we returned I closeted myself with the word-processor for ten long days, finished *Dead Trouble* and posted it off to Berkley Morton, my agent. He phoned a few days later to say that he had read most of it, the post mortem scenes had made him feel sick but the novel was a sure hit. It must be said that Berkley is quite a wimp.

The next day I found the *tau tau* in the kitchen cupboard where I had hastily stowed it and took it over to the cottage. Katie had just come in from school.

'You know your shell collection . . . ' I began.

'Oh, the poor thing!' she exclaimed. 'No eyes or clothes. She's not a doll, is she? More like a sort of . . . grassy museum thingy.' The clever, bright gaze came to rest on me. 'Shells for eyes then. Please may I make her some clothes?'

'They wouldn't be like ours,' I told her. 'She's from Indonesia.'

Katie bore it away – it was almost as tall as she was – up to her bedroom and I wondered what would happen. Like most children she is interested in computer games but has lately developed a most unfamily-like fondness for needlework. Nevertheless school, homework, outings, playing with friends, reading, watching a limited amount of television and a few light chores take up a very large chunk of her young life. When I went into her room during the next few days I saw the *tau tau* standing on a chair, the nakedness now covered with one of my scarves for which I had been asked the following day. Katie was not forthcoming about what she planned to do and I did not mention it other than by saying I could find her material but would rather she did not cut up the scarf as it was made of silk and rather special.

On an evening a week or so later, when winter was beginning to embrace Dartmoor and we were over in the cottage because Carrie was out, Patrick had just returned from a career review meeting in London. He was subdued.

'James rang earlier to say he'd done the bungee-jump – having recognised your handwriting – and with the latest news,' I told him. 'The knifeman's name is Otto Meggnessen and he's Jorge's younger brother. The old lady in Chichester was their mother and Otto looked after her for years in their council flat, after she became bed-ridden, until the day she died. He has a fairly low IQ and other than casual work in a meat-packing plant couldn't get a job so they scraped along on social security. There was a social worker involved who's been interviewed and said that Mrs Meggnessen had talked about her other son being lost at sea under what she thought were suspicious circumstances. She'd actually done a little investigating herself before her health gave out.

'After she died Otto seemed just to disappear. He took the car, his few possessions and left.How he traced Max Norton to Bath is anyone's guess but he must have known something about the family from his brother. James has interviewed him but the things that have happened have affected his mind and mentally now he's just like a child. The psychiatrist who's talked to him a lot is adamant he's not pretending. He can't. All Otto will say is that he went to the house to meet John Norton who was going to give him some money. It doesn't seem that threats were involved and James thinks it should have been nothing more than a friendly meeting where John was going to help the brother of a one-time crew member of the boat. But Otto met someone else at the house first, the person who let him in. He refuses to talk about what occurred after that but he must have been present when John Norton was killed as DNA in the single blond hair found at the murder scene exactly matches his own.'

'Kaminski got hold of him,' Patrick said, his voice thick with anger. 'Bent his mind, manipulated him, filled him with hate and no doubt fed him a load of lies. So he could go on a killing spree to get rid of, as Carrick said, some of the clutter in his life but have someone else spill most of the blood. He himself could have inflicted the blows that killed John Norton with that hammer Carrick found in the burned-out car. You can't help but feel sorry for Otto.'

'I wonder if Max knew what Kaminski had done.'

'I doubt he'd risk mentioning it. Presumably, after destroying any bloodstained clothing, he drove back to Bradford on Avon where no one had missed him because, at a guess, they were all plastered.'

'Dupont's place was ransacked though.'

'Otto could have been looking for money, or alcohol, if he was like his brother. We simply don't know what Kaminski had told him – almost programmed him to do. It doesn't come much more wicked than that.'

'Kaminski was a good actor – he fooled us.'

'I prefer not to have to kill my failures,' Patrick said after a short silence.

'That's being extremely harsh with yourself.'

'It's partly why I've decided to chuck it all in.'

'I can't believe you really want to do that,' I protested.

'I'll tell you what happened today. I discovered that D12's up and running as of last week and they're going to promote someone from within to handle trouble-shooting. But it appears they don't want to waste what they refer to as my talents by sending me on another largely administrative posting. Did I want to go back to Staff College only to take a more active role? No, thank you. Would I consider working as an adviser to MI6? No, not really. Had I thought of returning to active service? That would probably still mean another desk job. They need a new ambassador's assistant for the African Republic of Umpopo but it's a front for dangerous undercover work as Marxist guerrillas are trying to take over the place.' Patrick got up to pour himself a tot of whisky. 'What kind of bloody fool do they take me for?'

'And?' I said. 'Or should that be a but?'

'I'm going to resign my commission. I'm sick to death of living like this. It's not me anymore.'

Ye gods.

'I could take private commissions. Open an oggy shop in Tavistock or something like that.' He smiled at me peaceably. 'After all, I do have a high-earner as a wife.'

'This isn't about money,' I said.

'It is if the children are to go to Kelly College.'

'Close your eyes,' said Katie's voice imperiously from somewhere downstairs but fast approaching.

We closed.

'There. You can open them now.'

'Another one?' Patrick said. I had forgotten to mention the project to him.

'No, she's just got some new clothes,' said the young needlewoman.

'But this one's smiling,' said her uncle.

'Her mouth's carved,' Katie pointed out. 'I couldn't have made it any different even if I'd wanted to.'

The new outfit was very simple: a straight cream-coloured cotton robe reached the feet and there was a transverse sash of carefully folded blue material that matched the blue bead irises in the new shell eyes. A pair of blue earrings were now in the holes in the ear lobes.

'Carrie helped me buy some remnants in the material shop,' Katie said. 'As a surprise for you.'

We both told her that the result was absolutely wonderful.

'But it's smiling,' Patrick said again.

'Then we went in the library and looked up Indonesia,' Katie went on happily. 'Did you know this is a *tau tau* and they were put in graves in cliffs? The people made them look like the dead people when they were alive because they thought their ghosts went to live in them. I think this lady was quite young when she died and she misses her children and would like to look after me. Please can she stay in my bedroom?'

'You can have her for always,' I said, host to sudden spooky tingles.

She stood the figure in an armchair and the *tau tau* looked back at us all, smiling.